A Southern Charm Christmas

Seth Sjostrom

Tree Farm Press
TreeFarmPress.com

wolfprintMedia, LLC
Hernando Beach, FL 34607

For information, contact wolfprintMedia, LLC.

Trade Paperback
ISBN-13: 978-1-960501-30-1

1. Peyton James (Fictitious character)-Fiction. 2. Noah Wilde (Fictitious character)-Fiction. 3. Christmas-Fiction. 3. A Southern Charm Christmas-Title.

First wolfprintMedia edition 2025.

wolfprintMedia is a trademark of wolfprint, LLC.

For information regarding bulk purchases, please contact wolfprintMedia, LLC at wolfprint@hotmail.com.

United States of America

A Southern Charm Christmas

Kathi Sjostrom, my wife.

Linda Sjostrom—aka Mom.

The Warner Family—Kevin, Sandra and my dear friend, Megan.

Jennimay Walker for your kindness and gracious spirit.

Penny Tysinger, for keeping my words true to Southport.

Ginger Harper for being an inspiration.

Katie Compton-Boyd and the Old South Tour Company for being amazing storytellers, a genuine Southern Belle and a willing accomplice to the story.

The Royal James and Pat Gaynor for tales of swashbuckling, great drinks and amazing bites.

Editor and grammar artist Elizabeth Thurmond.

My team at wolfprintMedia and Tree Farm Press.

My Hallmark, Christmas Con, Small Town Christmas and Great American Family friends.

All of my North Carolina, Southport, Oak Island, Boiling Spring Lakes, South Brunswick and UNCW friends—you always have a place in my heart.

A Southern Charm Christmas

One

The town of Southport came into view, and it did not disappoint. Tidy streets lined with Spanish moss-draped trees led Noah Wilde and his rented SUV into the heart of the small North Carolina harbor town. To herald the Christmas season, each streetlamp was adorned with lighted wreaths. Every tree was wrapped in lights that would shimmer once the afternoon sun gave way to evening.

With the Southport waterfront in view, Noah turned onto Bay Street. Parking his car alongside a row of homes that stood vigil over the water, he stepped out. For a moment, he was taken by the line of immaculate Southern homes with their majestic white columns and wide, welcoming porches, each draped in evergreen boughs, red bows and white Christmas lights.

It certainly *looked* like Christmas. Noah could see why his editor had sent him on this assignment. The coastal town was overflowing with charm. The colonial waterfront homes he stood in front of and gazed at were each magazine-cover-worthy. Dressed for the season, the homes were a postcard for an Americana Christmas.

Wiping a bead of sweat from his brow, Noah grumbled to himself, "It doesn't *feel* like Christmas."

Grabbing his camera and notepad, Noah walked along the sidewalk, mindlessly running his hand along the fence pickets as he studied the homes.

For a moment, he was lost in the view. His eyes swept the span of the waterfront. Waves from passing boats splashed playfully along the seawall. The barrier islands of Bald Head Island and Oak Island dominated the horizon as sea birds chased a string of fishing boats.

"Can I help you? Or are you just wanderin' around talkin' to yourself?" a woman's voice drawled from behind him, almost causing him to jump.

Collecting himself, Noah turned on a heel and saw a young woman in a flowy sundress fanning herself on one of the stately front porches.

"Oh, hi. Sorry. The view is… breathtaking," Noah said. Straightening himself, he said, "I am Noah Wilde. I'm here to visit with Mrs. James and take a few photos of her house."

"I'm *Ms.* James. So, I guess you're here to see me," the woman said. Folding her fan in a snapping motion, she nodded toward the iron gate. "Come on in. Watch the latch, it can be a bit finicky."

Noah tried to open the gate to no avail. After a moment of fiddling with the salt-and-humidity-distressed hardware, the gate finally popped open, its hinges complaining in a loud screech. Noah scowled and brushed off his hands. "Would have been a better Halloween assignment."

He looked up the brick walkway to the sprawling porch decked out in Christmas decorations that would make a Currier and Ives painting jealous.

"What's the matter? You don't like Christmas or somethin'?" the woman asked.

"I like Christmas. I just prefer it with the thermostat turned down a bit. You know, a chill in the air and the prospect of snowfall," Noah said.

"Hang around. The weather here is nothin' but fickle. Welcome to the South, Mr. Wilde. It'll all change. You'll leave the house in the mornin' all bundled up to fight the chill, and by noon, you're wishing you had on shorts and a t-shirt. It doesn't much matter, the spirit of Christmas is the same. I do recommend dressing in layers, though," the woman said.

"Solid advice," Noah muttered, wishing he had a layer or two of clothing to discard.

"Where are you from, anyway?" the woman asked.

"*Coastal Charm Magazine*," Noah replied.

"No, I mean, where are you *from*?" The woman frowned, her hands slammed to her hips.

"Oh, Connecticut. The magazine is in New York, so I'm a train ride away," Noah said.

The woman studied him with an increased amount of scrutiny. "A train ride away? You take a train to work every day?"

"Only when I have to go to the office. I am usually out on assignment somewhere," Noah said.

"Uhm, hmm. Like being in Southport complaining about our weather," the woman said, her eyes giving Noah a thorough once-over. "What is it you're trying to do here?"

"To capture the coastal charm of Southport at Christmas. I'm a photojournalist for the magazine," Noah said.

"How're you gonna capture all this Christmas charm with a scowl on your face?" the woman asked.

Noah wiped his brow again and squinted in the late afternoon sun while he said, "Hot cocoa or cider usually helps set the mood, but I think I'd melt faster than a snowman right now."

The woman laughed and gave him a welcoming wave. "All right. Come on inside. I'll see what I can do for you."

Suddenly, the woman shook herself and faced Noah directly. "Where are my manners? My name is Peyton. Peyton James."

"Nice to meet you, Ms. James," Noah said.

"You can call me Peyton."

"All right. Peyton it is. Please call me Noah."

"Can I get you something that's *not* hot cider, Noah?" Peyton asked.

"Water, lemonade… or iced tea. Just not the sweet stuff. Anything cold. Thank you," Noah said.

"Honey, around here, our tea ain't nothin' but sweet. But I think I got something to whip up for you. You feel free to roam around and take some of those photos of yours. I'll be right back," Peyton said.

The young woman whisked away down a hallway. Her blue and white star-patterned sundress flowed behind her in a blur.

Noah cocked his head as he tried to wrap his mind around the unusual introduction. Shaking off the notion, he peered around the well-furnished room. There was a casual elegance to the home. The furniture was old and appeared expensive, though welcoming. The seating was neatly situated, facing inward for conversation.

When guests' eyes weren't aimed toward guests in the other sofas and chairs, they were led out to the waterfront. The late afternoon sun played on the water with gold and amber hues against the dark blue confluence where the Cape Fear River and the Intracoastal Waterway met on their way out to the Atlantic Ocean.

Noah snapped a few photos from the interior point of view. The Christmas wreaths hung from each window framed port-hole-like glimpses of the water, a perfect marriage of maritime and festive holiday. He knew instantly that the shot would find its way into the magazine.

Turning his attention back inside, his eyes swept through the Christmas décor. A Christmas village came to life on the coffee table between a pair of sofas. Looking closer, he realized the set was created to mirror the very town they were in. Colonial homes with their columns and porches were set in a line, each with their flocking of evergreen boughs and wreaths highlighted with red bows. In the water, a line of boats strung with Christmas lights paraded by the strand of homes.

A dusting of snow provided the illusion of December that made Noah laugh. "So much for realism," he said to himself.

His head snapped up as a clattering of metal objects rang from the kitchen. "Are you all right in there?" he asked.

"I'm good! Everything's all okay in here! I'll be right out," Peyton called back.

True to her word, she appeared wearing an awkward expression and carrying two mugs thrust out in front of her.

"All right, Noah. It may not be like they serve it up in the North Pole or wherever it is you spend Christmas, but I'm hoping it might work for you," Peyton said.

Accepting a mug she held out for him, Noah studied it. A big, smiling porcelain gingerbread man stared back at him. Eyeing its contents, he tried to peer past a layer of whipped cream that had been dusted with cocoa. Giving the cup a swirl, he tried to identify the concoction.

Peyton smiled a nervous smile as she raised her own mug — a snowman with a bright green scarf tied around its neck. "Frozen hot chocolate. Minus the hot part. It'll cool your insides faster than a January run down a black diamond," she said.

"Black diamond? Do you ski?" Noah asked, looking surprised.

"We *do* have cars here in North Carolina. I have made the occasional trip up to Sugar Mountain or Blowing Rock. I prefer to live where I can put my toes in the sand. Visiting the snow once in a while is just fine for me," Peyton said.

"Now, *those* are some Christmas destinations. Snow on the pines, a crisp cool air that carries the scent of wood fireplaces and roasted chestnuts…" Noah pictured the wintry Blue Ridge Mountain destinations.

"You really like Christmas," Peyton observed.

"I do," Noah nodded.

"Stick around, Mr. Noah. Southport is a magical place to spend Christmas. You'll see," Peyton said.

Noah looked out the window as a trawler made its way back to the harbor. "I've bid a few times to my editor to cover your Fourth of July Festival for the magazine… that seems… more seasonally appropriate."

"Oh, it is a good time, indeed. You've never seen a town so full of American spirit. Our little town grows from a few thousand to tens of thousands for that week. But don't turn your back on our

Christmas just yet. What we lack in snowman building, we make up for with heart," Peyton assured.

Noah chuckled. "I believe it. And I don't mean to knock your holidays. I, uh. I just had plans."

"Oh yeah? So, I gotta know… what snowy paradise were you supposed to spend Christmas in?" Peyton asked.

"I was going to spend the holidays near Gatlinburg in Tennessee. I reserved a cabin over a year ago. With the cold front coming across the country, they are going to have some epic snow over Christmas week," Noah said.

"Sounds lovely. I do really like it up in the Blue Ridge and Smoky Mountains. I get it. There someone waiting up there for you? Never mind. That was rude of me. Not very lady-like. How's your frozen cocoa?" Peyton asked, changing the subject and hiding her face behind a sip of her drink.

"It's different. It's good. It *does* taste like hot cocoa and yet is very refreshing. Almost black diamond worthy, but I'd have to call it a solid blue run to be fair with my review." Noah smiled.

"You have to be here for one of our parties to get the black diamond version. A splash of peppermint liqueur will have you feeling like you're up on one of those slopes. Figured you bein' on the clock and all, we'd keep it on the intermediate side," Peyton said.

Noah laughed, "It is very good. Thank you. Hang a candy cane on the rim and you would really have me believing it's Christmas."

"Candy cane. Good idea, I'll make a note of that for next time. I mean, for my next holiday event," Peyton said, her cheeks glowing a faint hint of rouge. Holding her mug tight to her chest, she asked, "Now what? You walk around and take pictures?"

Noah nodded, "Yes. And… I have a few questions."

Peyton looked at her watch.

"I'm sorry, do you have somewhere to be? I can come back another time," Noah asked.

"I have a standing date. I tell you what. You stay here. Snap as many photos as you want. Make yourself at home. There's another cup of frozen cocoa in the blender, well, almost enough for another cup. Don't bother lockin' up. The house'll be all right 'til I get back," Peyton said. At a heightened pace, she gathered her purse and car keys.

Noah looked confused.

"Come by my shop tomorrow. I might have a book that'll help answer some of those questions of yours," Peyton said.

Noah raised a brow.

"It is in the Old Southport Villages. You can't miss it. It's adorable, if I say so myself. My shop won't be hard to find, I promise," Peyton said.

The energetic woman launched herself out the door and down the steps before Noah could respond. Peering through the window over his gingerbread mug of frozen cocoa, he watched her kick the gate, which seemed to make the latch easier to work. Slipping through the gate, she cast a quick glance back at the house, which made Noah scramble to appear as though he wasn't watching her.

Shaking his head, Noah put his cup down and went to work with his camera.

Two

Noah completed his sweep of interior photos. He did his best to capture the charm of the James House decked out for Christmas. The décor was subtle, yet elegant. Each room had its own classic Christmas hues of traditional reds and greens to icy blues and silvers. There was a warmth to the décor despite its elegant nods and precise placements.

Scrolling through the final shots on his camera's screen, he was satisfied. Making a few notes for wanting to come at a different time to take advantage of morning light in a few of the eastern-facing rooms, he stepped out onto the porch.

He had almost forgotten how warm and muggy it was. The Christmas decorations and the ceiling fan-aided air conditioning inside the house created a successful illusion that it may have indeed been December in North Carolina.

Turning, he took a couple of shots of the front porch as the white lights woven throughout the evergreen wrapped rails and little candles in the windows began to glow. Their soft light still had to fight against the evening sun, which was making its rapid descent past the Oak Island Lighthouse.

As he pivoted back toward the gate, he found a well-dressed woman a decade or two senior of Peyton studying him from the sidewalk. Noah felt awkward and inexplicably guilty as he was leaving the James house unescorted.

"You visiting our Peyton?" the woman asked.

"Just taking some photos. Of the house, I mean." He blushed.

"You must be the man I heard about from the Woman's Club. They said you'd be poking around. Visiting us for a good ole fashioned Southport Christmas," the woman said.

"Yes, ma'am. I suppose I am," Noah nodded.

"Well, if you're done with Peyton..." the woman started.

"She had to leave. On a date. She said to finish taking photos and… not bother locking up?" Noah said, his words coming out one on top of the other.

"Oh, the house'll be fine. With Margaret next door and, well, me, no one will bother it. Not much gets past us porch rockers," the woman said. "Care to come up for an iced tea? Oh, where are my manners? I am Cybil Thomas. My house is on the west side of Peyton's," the woman said.

"My name is Noah. Noah Wilde. It's a pleasure to meet you. I believe we have an appointment tomorrow. And, if I'm honest, I am a bit overheated. I think I'm overdressed for the weather here," Noah said.

"Well, you have to stay hydrated. That's why the iced tea. Come on. You can catch sunset with me," Cybil said and started to walk toward her house without waiting for a response.

Noah looked around before reluctantly following the older woman.

Cybil's home was as lovely as Peyton's, if not even more grand. Despite the same thick columns and expansive front porch, the houses were not copies of each other. They each had their own details that set themselves apart. The James House was tall with traditional squared lines. The Thomas House, as Noah read off the plaque that declared it as such, had a lower roofline with a column of bay windows that rose along one side of the house. Unlike the James House, the property the Thomas House sat on took up an entire block.

"You have a seat right there. That'll give you a wonderful view of the sunset. I'll be right back with a couple glasses of iced tea," Cybil said before disappearing into the house.

Noah stood by the chair his host had pointed out to him. He snapped a few photos from the porch of the colorful sky that had spread over the barrier islands off of Southport's waterfront.

"Lovely, isn't it?" Cybil asked.

"Yes, ma'am," Noah nodded, accepting a tall glass on which condensation immediately began to form. "Thank you for the iced tea."

"You're welcome, dear," Cybil said as she took her seat.

Following Cybil's lead, he sat in one of the rocking chairs and watched the last remnants of the sun slip past the horizon. The light show that followed was even more spectacular than the setting sun itself. Shards of pink and scarlets joined the amber and orange streaks. Noah couldn't pass up taking a few more shots with his camera.

Setting his camera down, he looked at his hostess. She carried herself with a grace and elegance that made him straighten up. His cheeks flushed as he apologized, "I'm sorry. It's just so stunning."

Cybil smiled, "Hard to resist. Something about being on the water at sunset. Makes each day feel like it was a good day."

"My grandfather used to say that. 'No bad days. Just some that are better than others,'" Noah said.

"Sounds like a wise man," Cybil said.

"He was." Noah nodded.

Both sat back and took in deep breaths as the colors continued to rapidly change while shades of indigo joined the color party.

"Southport is a lovely town," Noah said.

"It is." Cybil nodded. "It grows and changes with the time, but somehow, it has managed to stay itself as well."

"Have you been here long?" Noah asked.

Cybil laughed, "All my life! They say there are three types of people in Southport. Those that never leave. Those that leave and find their way back. And those that are just plain lost."

"You must really love it here," Noah said.

"I do. I'm at the age I'm starting to miss a few of my fellow porch rockers, though. I used to look down the row, especially at this time of night, and see all my friends waving back. Some on their own porches, some sharing sunset on the porch next door. That whole change thing I mentioned is about to be tested here, along the waterfront," Cybil said.

"Oh?" Noah frowned over his glass of iced tea.

"Sadly, some of my friends have, well, moved on. Called on for their time to join the Heavenly choir. Investors swoop in and snatch up homes to turn into rentals or those that do move in tend to try to make Southport more like where they were from instead of embracing the charm of their new home the way they found it," Cybil said.

"Must be tough to watch the place you love change so much," Noah said.

"It is. It's the life changes that make it tough as well. Take poor Peyton over there. She's been through the wringer the past few years," Cybil said. "First, it was her momma, God rest her soul. It was nearly three years ago to the day that she was lost to us in a car accident. Then, this past year, her daddy had a stroke — a powerful one, too. Poor girl."

"I'm sorry to hear that," Noah said.

"You wouldn't know it just talking to her. But I know it eats her up inside," Cybil said. "Pretty sure her father is the only family she has left. Well, outside of us porch rockers, but we ain't blood family. We're just Southport family," Cybil said.

"It sounds like you really look out for each other," Noah said.

"We do." Cybil nodded. Casting a wary glance at Noah, she asked, "Is it not like that where you're from?"

Noah laughed. "Just outside of New York City? Not in the same way, no. Life moves so fast, people don't really have much time for each other. They just keep their heads down and strive to survive."

"They don't *take* the time for each other. We're on the same clock, here and there. It just matters what you choose to do with it," Cybil said.

"These porch conversations are insightful," Noah said with a raise of his iced tea glass.

"Aren't they?" Cybil grinned.

A noise from inside the house stole their attention.

Noah looked over at Cybil to see if they should check.

Cybil's eyed furrowed. "Now, Ellie! I done told you to keep it down when we have guests. It's not polite!"

"Ellie?" Noah asked.

"My husband's grandmother. She's a sweet soul, but she gets a bit rambunctious from time to time," Cybil said.

Noah started to do the math in his head.

"Oh, she passed a while ago," Cybil said. And then with a raise of her voice said, "She just decided she wasn't done meddlin' in things just yet."

Noah smiled politely.

"Y'all don't have ghosts where you're from?" Cybil asked.

"Uhm, not that I've met. No," Noah said.

"Ellie's harmless, but at least she keeps me company," Cybil said.

Noah lifted his nearly empty iced tea in the air and announced, "Well, thank you for the iced tea. It was lovely. But I should get going."

"I scared you away with the whole Ellie thing, didn't I? Ellie's my cat, but she has the same attitude as Grandma Ellie. Named her as such. So, I have a little fun with it," Cybil said.

Noah laughed. "No, ma'am. You didn't scare me off. I just had a long day in the car and want to catch sunrise in the morning."

"Nothing wrong with scheduling your day around sunrise and sunset. Too many people sleep past one or the other," Cybil said.

"Yes, ma'am," Noah said as he rose from his rocking chair.

"You sure are polite to be a New Yorker," Cybil said, taking his glass from him.

"I wasn't always from there. It's just where the job is," Noah said.

"Well, story for another day," Cybil said. "It was a pleasure to meet you, Mr. Wilde."

"Noah. It was a pleasure to meet you, Mrs. Thomas," Noah said. "Good night."

"Good night, Noah," Cybil said as she watched the young man walk down her steps and slip past her gate.

Three

Noah was up early to take in the sunrise. He moved his
camera around in a slow, steady sweep from Fort Fisher at the
southern tip of Pleasure Island across ferry-access-only Bald Head
Island and then to Oak Island Lighthouse at the edge of Caswell
Beach.

Sea birds chased early boat traffic as captains navigated the
waters of the Intracoastal Waterway and the Cape Fear River en route
to the Atlantic. The colors of dawn looked as though they were
painted across the sky. Deep, dark blue dominated the top of the
photos before giving way to a palette of lighter blues, streaks of
oranges and reds that ran along the waterways and barrier islands.

One thing Noah particularly appreciated in the early morning
was the lower humidity and markedly cooler air. Wearing a jacket to

fend off the morning breeze, he felt at least a season closer to Christmas.

Relocating his photographer's eye to downtown, he focused in on the tall, blue water tower that dominated the skyline. A line of blue stars preceded the bold letters that spelled out "Southport". The morning sun gleamed off the tall tower with wispy clouds carrying the array of sunrise colors into the background.

Noah captured the trees that lined the streets, their glisten of still ablaze Christmas lights helping to herald the new day. Snapping off his camera, Noah decided the new day also heralded a need for coffee.

Pulling up the shops that Peyton had mentioned to him on his phone map, Noah smiled as the coffee shop was listed as "open" on his app.

Making his way across town, Noah pulled into a wide gravel parking lot. A sign held up with wooden posts welcomed visitors to the Olde Southport Village Shoppes. An American flag waved proudly in the morning breeze. The rest of the plaza looked like it would have been at home in the North Pole.

Evergreen boughs wound with garland and lights flanked the signposts. A brick walkway snaked through the village, and fake snow piled against the edges carried the illusion of a wintry landscape.

Noah found the shops themselves particularly charming. Each of the dozen or so businesses was contained in its own small building. Looking like a village from the late 1800s, it transported visitors from a modern harbor town to an era of quaint penny candy shops and apothecaries, right down to hosting a rustic General Store.

Linked by elevated wooden walkways, each building was unique. The General Store was straight out of a spaghetti western. Its weathered-gray exterior and hand-painted signage fit the part, while a pair of benches on either side of the door welcomed guests to relax and enjoy their treats while they visited.

One building looked more like an old schoolhouse, while another was reminiscent of a tiny church. To Noah, it reminded him of a Christmas village his grandmother used to place around the Christmas tree. In addition to the General Store, there was a bakery, a gift shop, a toy store, and several clothing boutiques. The coffee shop, with its whirring burr grinder, stole his attention.

A wreath hung from an open screen door. Classic Christmas music competed with the busy sounds of coffee making and the soft, sleepy voices of the shop's customers. A remarkably bright-eyed woman smiled from behind the counter.

"Good morning… and Merry Christmas!" The barista beamed.

Noah smiled back. "Good morning."

"What can I get for you?"

"How about an eggnog latte?" Noah asked.

"One of *those*…" the barista said as she selected a cup from the rack.

"One of those?" Noah asked, one eyebrow raised.

"People either like eggnog or they don't," the barista said as she filled up a stainless-steel pitcher with eggnog.

"I see," Noah said.

"You a pumpkin spicer?" the barista asked as she tamped grounds into the filter basket and wrenched it into the machine.

"No. But, I'm not a hater, either. I do like a little nutmeg on the nog, though," he admitted.

"So noted," the barista said. "What brings you to town?"

Noah cocked his head.

"Southport is not very big, especially out of tourist season," the barista explained.

"I'm covering Southport at Christmas time for *Coastal Charm Magazine*," Noah said.

The barista's eyes widened. "I love that magazine! There's always a copy on my coffee table at home. The homes are so beautiful!"

"The Hatteras and Cape Cod covers were mine," Noah beamed with pride.

"Beautiful work, I remember those!" the barista said as she handed Noah his coffee. "Where will Southport at Christmas fall? Isn't the December issue already out?"

"It is. It will be a Christmas Day digital edition. If it does well, it could be next year's cover…" Noah's voice trailed off.

The barista shot Noah a wary glance. "But…"

"Usually Christmas covers… well, have snow in them," Noah said.

"Right, that makes sense," the barista said. Holding her hand across the bar, she said, "I'm Krista."

"Krista the barista?" It was Noah's turn to cock his head.

"Yeah, that's why I go by coffee shop owner. It's a little longer to get out but a bit less Dr. Seuss."

Noah laughed. "Well, Krista, the coffee shop owner, it was a pleasure to meet you."

"Likewise," Krista said. Starting to greet the next customer, she paused, "Oh, Peyton should be at her shop in about twenty."

Noah looked questioningly at Krista.

Krista grinned with a shrug as she said, "Small town, even smaller village."

Noah nodded and retreated to the wooden porch to sip his coffee. Setting the cup on a rail, he picked up his camera and snapped several shots of the village as the morning sun worked to crest the shop rooftops.

For a moment, he was *in* a Christmas village. The boardwalk railings were wrapped in the same evergreens woven with twinkling lights that welcomed guests into the village. Red bows were tied in the centers between the posts which themselves were spiraled in candy cane stripes. Wreaths hung from each door. In the center of the village, atop a circle of what at least looked like white snow, was a gleaming red sleigh. A throne, Noah presumed for Santa himself, sat next to the sleigh.

Nodding, he took a few more photos in between sips of eggnog latte. He felt like he was beginning to capture the spirit of Christmas in Southport.

Swirling the last sip of coffee, he squinted. The sun found its way over the trees and village rooftops. It didn't take long for it to heat up the square, melting the momentary vibe that Noah was enjoying.

Wriggling out of his jacket, he draped it through the strap of his camera bag.

Leaning against the rail, he pictured children running through the decorated courtyard. He knew that not every part of the country was set up for white Christmases and some locales had to celebrate with lit palm trees in place of fragrant pine trees. But for him, it just didn't *feel* like Christmas. A part of him wanted to be in his car or on a plane heading somewhere with a wintry forecast.

Noah's thoughts were broken up by the sounds of footsteps and alarm. He turned to see arms wrapped around two large boxes, the top one threatening to give way.

Letting his camera dangle from his shoulder on its strap, Noah grabbed the top box as it listed and began to topple.

"Here, let me get that," he said. With the box in his hands, the owner's face came into view.

"Good morning, Ms. James," Noah smiled.

Peyton offered a sheepish smile in return, "Thank you, Mr. Wilde. You just saved two dozen hand blown Christmas ornaments."

"I'm glad I could be of service this morning," Noah said as he followed Peyton to her shop.

A banner read "Peyton's Place Gift Shop". Her building was a tidy cottage painted in a light hue of Carolina blue. It looked perfect among the other village shops as much as it would have been at home on a beach boardwalk.

Using the colors of her shop as a cue, Noah noticed Peyton used silver and blue ribbons in place of the traditional red for her wreath. Shells and starfish replaced the baubles. Just as the James House was decorated along the Southport waterfront, the shop was both elegant and welcoming.

"Well, here's my home away from home!" Peyton said as she sat her box down and opened the front door.

Allowing Noah inside, Peyton slid her box across the threshold.

Noah peered around the shop. While Christmas dominated the displays with traditional and nautical inspired ornaments, the gift shop was filled with candles, artwork and books. Most items leaned Southport, coastal or North Carolina themed.

"Well, what do you think?" Peyton asked.

Noah saw a genuine gleam of pride in Peyton's eyes. "It's nice. I wasn't sure what to think. It reminds me of your house."

"My *family* house. Unless you've been stalking me," Peyton said.

Noah looked at her, his face airing his confusion.

"I live about four blocks north of the James House," Peyton said. "For me, that house is still my grandparents' and then ultimately my parents' house. It feels good to visit. But that's *Dad's* house."

"I see. That makes sense," Noah said, his voice trailing softly. Sensing the conversation was trending into a sensitive area, he asked, "How long have you had the shop?"

"This is my third year. It has been a wonderful experience. I get to meet so many people who travel through, especially during the summer months. The rest of the year, I get to serve the community. And, my fellow villagers are amazing!" Peyton said.

"You and the other shops put the whole Christmas wonderland together out there?" Noah asked.

"The owner helps, a lot. On the weekends, he has even arranged to bring a horse-drawn carriage in. Not that the courtyard is that big, but it's a fun event," Peyton said. "And for people like *you*…"

Walking over to the window, Peyton leaned against the pane and pointed. "Watch."

Noah leaned his head close to hers as he peered out into the courtyard. For a moment their eyes met before Peyton's eyes led his back out the window. Hitting a button on her phone, a series of tall candy canes placed along the brick walkways began emitting a flurry of snowflakes.

"It's snowing!" Noah said.

"See. It is the perfect place to celebrate Christmas. You won't be building a snowman with that, but at the end of a cooler night, you might be able to toss around a snowball or two," Peyton said.

Noah pulled away from the window. "What a wonderful experience to share with the community."

"Oh, we do s'mores by the fire, stories in the courtyard for the kids, caroling, and, of course, we welcome the big man himself on Saturdays. He also spends a few hours here Sundays after church," Peyton said. Her voice took on an almost childlike exuberance.

"It sounds amazing. I'll have to make the villages part of my story," Noah said.

"Be sure that you do. These aren't just replica buildings, you know. The owner brought them in from all over Brunswick County. They're actual historic buildings that the owner has refurbished and brought back to life. They get to live on here, in the Southport Village Shoppes," Peyton said.

"What a great idea. It really is charming," Noah said. "Where I grew up, near Mystic, there's a similar setup of shops along a winding creek with old colonial buildings, or at least replicas. It's on a different scale, but it kind of transports you to a different time. It's really quaint. If you have to shop, it might as well be an experience."

"That's kind of the idea," Peyton said. "But what makes the village really special is the people. All of us shop owners are like a big family."

"That's nice. I'm sure that is part of the charm. Buildings are one thing, it is the heart behind them that shines through," Noah said.

"Look." Peyton pointed out the window again.

Once more, Noah leaned in close. Rocking chairs and benches were being filled up by guests enjoying their coffees and breakfasts in the morning sun.

"Exactly," Noah said. Suddenly, his eyes brightened. "You think they'd mind being in a photo? The people coming together helps the photo tell the story."

"We can ask. I'd ask Mabel. She's kind of the leader of the group. She runs the book club at the library. And the Southport Woman's Club. And chairs Southport Winterfest," Peyton said.

"Sounds like an important contact," Noah said.

"You have no idea." Peyton laughed.

Peyton led Noah across the courtyard and to the opposite elevated boardwalk.

"Ladies, I would like you to meet Noah Wilde. He is doing a story on how amazing Southport is at Christmas for *Coastal Charm Magazine*, despite the unseasonably warm weather," Peyton announced.

Noah blushed. "Good morning. Your town is lovely. I really get a sense of Christmas spirit here."

The ladies gave Noah a solid once-over.

"Welcome to Southport, Mr. Wilde. I hope you find our town as charming as we do," one of the women spoke up.

"Noah, this is Mabel Gentry. She is as knowledgeable about Southport as anyone," Peyton said.

"It's a pleasure." Noah nodded. "Nice to meet all of you. I've been taking pictures of all things Christmas. The village certainly tells a great story. But, seeing you all out here, spending your morning together, I realized, it isn't the buildings, but the people that tell the *real* story."

"He was wondering if it would be all right if he snapped a photo or two?" Peyton asked.

Mabel looked serious for a moment, her eyes squinted in the morning sun. Finally, she said in a very serious voice, "Only if you catch me from this angle. It's my good side."

"Yes, ma'am," Noah promised. "Just, don't mind me. Go back to enjoying your morning and I promise, you will all look as lovely in the photo as you do sitting here right now."

The ladies giggled and blushed.

"You've got a charmer there, Peyton," Mabel smiled.

Peyton's eyes went wide. "Oh, he's not mine. He's just passing through. I… I have a book about Southport I wanted him to read. So, he came by to collect."

"Mmm, hmm." Mabel flattened her lips and shot Peyton a wary glance. Turning to Noah, she said, "If you want to really learn about Southport, come meet me at the Fort Johnston Museum."

"Mabel is also a town historian," Peyton said.

"I'll be sure to visit," Noah said.

Noah and Peyton excused themselves to find the right angle for the photo. The ladies' outburst of murmurs and giggles made it clear that they were enamored with the young visitor.

Peyton giggled as Noah worked his camera. She said, "I believe you have made quite the impression with the ladies of Southport, Mr. Wilde."

"Just fans of the magazine," Noah said.

"Eyes on the first eligible bachelor to swing into town in a while, more like," Peyton teased. "Not suggesting you are available. No offense to your girlfriend or whatever."

Noah grunted as he put his camera down. His eyes caught the woman next to Mabel waving her arms at him from across the courtyard.

"Oh, Mr. Wilde!" the woman called. "If you're free for supper, I make a mean low country boil!"

"See!" Peyton whispered as she elbowed Noah in the ribs.

"Peyton, you should come, too. She's available, you know, Mr. Wilde," the woman called.

Noah turned to Peyton, his lips spread into a grin. "I think they may have other motives in their interest."

Peyton pursed her lips and her eyes narrowed. "The downside of a small town. If you're single, it becomes everyone's mission to try to sell you like the catch of the day."

Noah frowned. "I thought you had a date last night."

A serious expression melted over Peyton's face, "It's complicated."

She spun toward her store, clearly wanting to change the subject, and said, "Let's get you that book."

Four

"I have to say, I'm a little surprised," Peyton said as she led Noah back into her shop. "The ladies must really be impressed by you. They aren't usually that friendly to a Yankee right out of the box."

"I don't know if I would call myself a Yankee. I'm more of a nomad," Noah said. "I've lived all over. I think that's why I like my job. I get to see so many different places in their best light. I get to witness how they embrace the seasons."

"Like Christmas in the South during a heatwave," Peyton drawled as she smiled.

Noah nodded. "I suppose so."

"In all my years in Southport, I've had Christmases that topped eighty degrees and I've had the occasional cold and even more rare, snowy Christmas. To be fair, it's usually somewhere in between," Peyton said. "It's the reason for the season. It's the people… family…"

Noah noticed Peyton's voice drifted off as she said family. "Cybil told me about your mother, I'm sorry."

Peyton nodded, "Yeah. I miss her every day. I'm glad I get to see Daddy. She lives on in his eyes. He loved her so much."

"I'm sorry I missed out on knowing her myself. The town seems to have really loved her. She must have been pretty special," Noah said. Watching Peyton turn toward the window, he added, "I'm willing to bet she lives on in you, too."

Peyton turned and cocked her head. Through slightly squinty eyes, she stared at him and said, "You would make a fine Southern gentleman, Mr. Noah Wilde."

"I, uh, I'll take that as a compliment?" Noah said in a questioning tone.

"Not too many stronger compliments in the south," Peyton said. Realizing the moment between the two had become awkward, she said, "Let me find that book for you."

Rummaging through her shelves, she tilted a book back to reveal its cover and pulled it free from the row.

"You won't find Southport's deepest and darkest secrets in here — you'll need someone like Mabel for that. But this will give you a really good idea of the town's backstory." Peyton handed Noah the book. "On that note, I do recommend you visit the museum when you get a chance, too."

"Thank you." Noah pulled out his wallet to pay for the book.

"That one's on the house. Just see if you can't get a shot of the village in that magazine of yours," Peyton said.

Noah hesitated to put his wallet away. "I can't promise what the editors will select…"

"I have faith that you'll do your best. That's good enough for me," Peyton said.

Flustered, Noah whirled around. Plucking a tiny plastic tree with little ornaments dangling from its boughs, he thrust it forward. "Okay. But I'd like to buy this tree. I need to put some Christmas in my hotel room."

Peyton laughed, eyeing his selection. "You want a Christmas tree with… cartoon character ornaments?"

"Well, I'm open to suggestions." Noah let out an impish smile. Giving the tree he hastily selected a glance, he realized he had no idea how the tree was decorated before snatching it up from the display.

"I tell you what. Why don't we get you a bare tree and you can select the ornaments that you want on it? You'll have a higher chance of them all making it from here to your hotel room in one piece and you can select ornaments that better reflect your vision of Christmas," Peyton said.

"That—" Noah pointed in agreement—"Is a better idea."

Setting the tree he hastily snatched up back onto the table, he followed Peyton to a shelf full of ornaments.

"You want traditional, nautical…" Peyton asked as her finger ran across the sets. "Nope. Let me guess, traditional."

Noah nodded.

Grabbing a box of red and silver balls, Peyton placed it in Noah's hand. Surveying the display, she gently lifted an ornament by its silver string. A little red truck hauling a Christmas tree spun in the air. Seeing Noah's eyes light up, she added it to the box of balls.

"Look around and see if there is anything else that catches your eye. I'll grab you a tree in a box. When you're done, set that stuff on the counter, I'll put it in a bag for you to carry it all," Peyton said.

Noah complied as Peyton met him at the counter with a boxed tree. Ringing up the sale, Peyton looked thoughtful. "Every tree needs a personal touch. Something unique for the year…"

Reaching across the counter, Peyton plucked an ornament from a display and handed it to Noah.

Inspecting the item Peyton selected for him, Noah smiled seeing the depiction of a town, its blue water tower making it easy to identify. "It's Southport," he said.

"It's Southport at Christmas time," Peyton added.

"It's snowing…" Noah eyed the ornament with an air of suspicion.

"It's a snow globe. Of course it's snowing. I thought it might help you with your vision. That's what you do when nature throws a warm and sunny Christmas season at you. You don't let it cloud your mind. It's still a season about warm hearts and holiday magic," Peyton said.

"I think you might be the next head of Southport Winterfest," Noah said.

Peyton leaned over the counter and surveilled the store, "Don't let Mabel hear that!"

Noah laughed. "I didn't mean to offend her."

"No, they've been trying to get me to take Winterfest over. I have my hands full with the store and the village events. And the house…" Peyton said.

Once more, Peyton's tone changed at the end of her sentence.

Noah smiled. "Mum's the word. I promise. You are an excellent ambassador of the town and the holiday, that's all."

"Thanks. I got that from my mom," Peyton said.

Noah nodded. Glancing at his watch, he said, "Thank you for the ornament and the book. I'm due to take photos at Cybil's house."

"You'll love it. Very traditional décor. And Cybil is a sweetheart," Peyton said.

"I met her leaving your house yesterday. Somehow, she sequestered me for sunset," Noah said.

Peyton laughed. "She's a siren, that one. Buckle up. You might be there for sunset again tonight."

Noah frowned. "It's not even noon yet."

"I know," Peyton said. Suddenly, her tone shifted, "You know what? How about I give you a reason for a polite exit? We're doing S'mores with Santa tonight and…"

"You want me to play Santa? I'm not sure that's better than sunset on a sweet old lady's porch," Noah said.

Peyton laughed. "No, but that *is* a good idea. The girls and I get so busy with looking after the treats, we could really use someone to read a story to the kids."

"Oh." Noah straightened up. "I can do that. What are we reading, Dickens?"

"They're mostly first and second graders. I was thinking more like Rudolph or Frosty," Peyton said.

"I can do that." Noah nodded.

"And sing…" Peyton pressed.

"*What?*" Noah took a step back.

"They both have songs," Peyton argued.

"Sunset it is…" Noah started to turn toward the door.

"Fine. You don't have to sing, at least not alone," Peyton said, shooting Noah a hopeful look across the counter.

"Deal," Noah said.

"I'll see you at five o'clock, sharp." Peyton smiled.

Five

The Thomas House looked even more like a Christmas village house when Noah pulled up to the curb. Cybil Thomas greeted him from the porch as she placed the last in a row of gleaming brass hurricane lanterns adorned with red bows hanging above the porch rail.

Cybil smiled at Noah. "Just sprucing things up a bit."

"It was already lovely, but the extra touches are really nice," Noah said. His eyes moved from the grand waterfront home to the home's owner. Cybil was dressed to the nines in an elegant sparkling dress and pearl earrings that dangled from her freshly done hair. The widow certainly seemed excited for the company.

"Come in, come in. Can I get you a cup of coffee or tea?" Cybil asked.

"A glass of water would be great," Noah said as he subconsciously took a swipe at his forehead. The brief cool morning was quickly giving way to another warm and humid Carolina day.

Noah studied the home. The wreaths that hung from each window were joined by strands of evergreen garland intertwined with white lights and finished with red bows around the door frame to match the rails that ran the length of the wide wrap-around front porch.

"It's like walking into a Christmas movie," Noah said as he eyed a shot of the entry.

"Holidays aren't just days on the calendar around here. They are heart and soul. They are the stitches that bring the community back together as time tries to fray the edges and pull them apart," Cybil said, handing Noah a glass of water.

"Heart and soul do not seem to be lacking in this town," Noah said, taking a sip and setting his glass down to work his camera with both hands.

"Some people come here to visit because it looks like a postcard town. But for us who live here, it is a way of life. Like a boat in the harbor, we get to drift slowly along, but the anchor of traditions keeps us from drifting too far. Those traditions keep

Southport true to itself," Cybil said. "There's a salty side to it, too. Even the prettiest brass lantern picks up a patina now and again."

Noah smiled to himself. He enjoyed the way the sweet woman spoke.

"Tell me about the Thomas house. Has it always been in your family?" Noah asked.

Cybil smiled. "This house and Peyton's are two of the last homes to remain in the same lineage. Most of the others have changed hands at least once or twice over the years. Historical home designations help keep a lot of them architecturally true to their original form, thank goodness."

"I'm glad that's the case," Noah said as he snapped a photo that was able to capture multiple porches down the waterfront in one shot that celebrated the architecture Cybil was mentioning.

Swinging the lens to capture the view of the waterfront from Cybil's porch, Noah watched as a man in a gleaming Land Rover pulled to a stop alongside Peyton's house. He watched as the man rolled down the window and took photos of the house with his phone and scribbled a hasty note on a pad of paper before pulling away from the house and roaring off.

"This house holds so many memories. My siblings and cousins would spend every holiday here. It was the hub for our family. It was also a hub for the community. The house would host grand galas. I remember sneaking out of bed to peer down from the stairs where my bedroom was to sneak peeks at the holiday events my parents hosted. The ladies in their dresses would find their way to the porch to gossip amongst themselves in the cool night air while the gentlemen would swap stories and politics in the parlor with ice rattling in their drinks," Cybil said. Her voice was lost in the spectacle of her memory.

"But Christmas… oh, Christmas. Coming down those stairs right there with my brother and sister, we could barely contain ourselves. My mother would have already been bustling in the kitchen preparing sweet rolls. Father would sit on the end of the sofa, his legs crossed as he watched us descend and dance in front of the tree. This house has so many memories," Cybil said.

"It sounds amazing. I only hope I can capture some of that magic in these photos," Noah said.

Cybil smiled. "Be sure you do. One thing about homes like these is their memories are meant to be shared."

"Well, if my story can make the cut, the shot of your front porch would make a wonderful cover," Noah said.

The sound of a rumbling engine pausing alongside the house caught Noah's attention. Leaning toward the window, he watched as a man exited a well-used pickup truck.

Cybil took notice as well and peered out the window.

"Trouble," Cybil muttered under her breath.

"What?" Noah asked as he watched the man set a tool bag down on the sidewalk and begin fiddling with the latch on Peyton's gate.

Cybil shook her head. "Nothing Peyton can't handle. Just some of the salt air crust and patina I was talking about."

Pulling away from the window, Cybil said, "This house. All the houses along the waterfront and the historical set pieces scattered around Southport — they aren't just memories for a family, which I hold dear. They are heritage. They mark the birth of a nation. The men and women who fought for the very land we stand on today, changed the world. Forever."

Noah looked thoughtful. "A different perspective from just capturing décor and architecture. I can almost imagine men poring over battle maps. Ladies keeping vigil over the harbor as they waited for their sons and husbands to return. Even better, the grand galas during times of peace."

Cybil smiled. "That is the magic of these historic homes. The view is pretty. The memories are priceless."

"Every conversation with you is enjoyable and insightful," Noah said.

"There's more where that came from. I can pull Mabel and the ladies over for a sunset party," Cybil said.

"While I appreciate the offer and sunset from your porch is tempting, I told Peyton that I would help her and the other shop owners at their S'mores with Santa event," Noah said.

"Another time then," Cybil said.

Noah nodded. "Absolutely. Thank you again for allowing me to take photos and sharing the history of the Thomas House."

"Good evening, Noah," Cybil said.

"Good evening, Mrs. Thomas."

Six

The Southport Village Shoppes S'mores with Santa event was bustling. Noah had to circle the gravel parking lot twice to find a parking space. A stream of mothers and fathers made their way along the brick walkways, holding hands with excited children.

A little wisp of smoke from a wood fire in the center of the courtyard snaked its way into the air. The aroma reminded Noah of mountain retreats, with whiffs of wood-burning fireplaces greeting his nose. There was an odd comfort to the scent.

With the early evening still plenty warm, the fire pit in the village was certainly not intended to ward off a chill. Instead, it was a cooking medium for eager children to roast marshmallows on long sticks provided by the shop owners of the village.

On the amoebic shape of fake snow, the sleigh was used to hold donations for a foster care toy drive. Dads would hoist their little ones up to allow them to personally drop their gift into the sleigh.

To their delight, they were greeted by a jolly Santa Claus who handed them a candy cane and directed them to the s'mores table, followed by a hearty "Ho-ho-ho."

Some shops stayed open late and welcomed the guests of the event. Peyton waved at Noah as he walked down the path. Taking a quick photo, he made his way over to Peyton.

"I see you made your escape from Cybil's clutches," Peyton said.

"It was a pleasant day, though there was the threat of inviting more of her porch-rocking friends to join us for sunset," Noah said.

Peyton beamed. "I warned you about Cybil's charm. She lives to be a beguiling hostess."

"I give you credit. Cybil is good at getting what she wants," Krista said as she set a fresh carafe of cocoa on the table next to the s'mores supplies.

"Hello, Krista," Noah greeted the coffee shop owner.

"Peyton said we had a special guest to do the reading tonight. I should have guessed it was our resident stranger," Krista said.

"I didn't know there was a donation drive. I would have brought something," Noah said.

"Your voice and reading skills are your gifts tonight," Peyton said.

"I can pick something from your shop," Noah pressed.

Peyton shrugged, "I won't say no to a toy for the foster charity. I can open up the shop after the story."

"What do I need to do?" Noah asked.

"Eat a s'more. Have cocoa. Take a few pictures, if you like. Attending is consent as Krista usually posts a photo or two on social media," Peyton said. "Warm up that voice, you'll be on in fifteen."

"What story are you regaling us with tonight?" Krista asked as she hung a candy cane on the rim of a cocoa cup for the next family working their way through.

"I'm going to stick with the classics and read Rudolph," Noah said.

Peyton nudged Krista, nearly making her spill the next cup of cocoa she was preparing. "Told 'ya."

"You already find me predictable," Noah groaned.

"No, you like tradition. There's nothing wrong with that, we're big on tradition around here," Peyton said.

Families had completely circled the fire with marshmallows ranging from barely beige to coal black for their graham cracker and chocolate treats. Noah snapped a few photos until he saw Peyton give him a nod.

Walking over to a basket of books, Noah found his story and was led to a tall stool near the fire pit.

"Everyone, I would like to introduce you to tonight's reader. Noah Wilde is visiting Southport from *Coastal Charm Magazine*. His job is to experience and share a Southport Christmas. I thought, what better way to help share how we do Christmas than invite him to S'mores with Santa? Mr. Wilde is going to read one of my favorite Christmas stories that I think you all will find plenty familiar, but good just the same," Peyton said as she presented Noah to the crowd.

The families clapped as Noah nervously cleared his throat and slipped his finger into the first page of the storybook.

"Thank you. I have only been in Southport a couple of days and I'm already appreciating the charm and heart of this town during the Christmas holiday season," Noah said. With a deep breath, he scanned the crowd, smiling at the anticipation on the faces of the little ones.

"Once upon a time, in a place we all know and love, there was a little reindeer…" Noah read.

As the story came to a close, the children cheered.

Peyton walked up to Noah and addressed the crowd. "Let's all give another round of applause for Mr. Wilde!"

When the crescendo of applause finally started to peter out, Peyton told the parents and children, "Santa is over by his sleigh. He is eager to hear what every one of you would like for Christmas!"

"Yay!" the children around the firepit erupted, their parents barely able to contain them from rushing over to the man sitting on the intricately carved throne.

As the group wrangled into a reasonable shape of a line, Peyton bumped into Noah's shoulder and said, "Nice job. You held each one of the kids' attention. Not everyone can do that."

"It felt touch and go from where I was sitting," Noah said.

"Nah, you had them well engaged," Peyton said.

"How about the donation?" Noah asked.

Peyton looked thoughtful for a moment and said, "How about this? I will donate this basket of Christmas books on your behalf."

Noah studied her for a moment and said, "I don't mind…"

"I know. I want to do that for you. I mean, you did give up your sunset to come and do this for me… I mean, the kids. To come read to them," Peyton said, a slight hue of rose on her cheeks.

"Fair enough," Noah said. "Hey, do you mind if I stop by the James House tomorrow morning? I want to take a few photos with morning light."

"Yeah, sure. Have at it," Peyton said. "I can run by before the shop opens and let you in."

"Thanks," Noah said.

From the corner of his eye, he saw Krista pick up the large carafe, accidentally knocking over a stack of cups. He and Peyton lunged at the same time to help, narrowly missing crashing their heads together. They looked up, finding their eyes locked together.

"Thanks," Peyton said in a whisper.

Picking up the cups nearest to him, he had Peyton add her stack to his.

"You know what, why don't I stay and help? You can make sure the line for Santa doesn't get unruly," Noah said.

"You don't have to stick around," Peyton said.

"It's okay. I'd just be going back to the hotel," Noah said.

"All right. That means you can be here for the big finale," Peyton said.

Noah smiled. "See, I wouldn't want to miss that."

"Oh, it looks like Santa needs another box of candy canes," Peyton said.

"Go on, I've got this," Noah said, securing his stack of cups.

He watched her for a moment as she interacted with the crowd en route to deliver a box of peppermint treats for Santa to give out to the children that shared their Christmas wishes.

The campfire was allowed to smolder as the cocoa and s'more ingredients were put away. When the last child had visited Santa, the candy cane snow machines came to life, to the screaming delight of the children.

Noah took several pictures of the fun scene. Despite the evening air being very mild, for a moment, it seemed like it could be snowing in the village.

A thwack against his back stole his attention. Turning slowly around, he dodged just in time to see a snowball whizzing past his head.

Across the courtyard was a grinning Peyton.

"See, I told you there was enough for a snowball!" she said.

Noah nodded for a moment. Quickly dropping to his knee, he scraped together enough snow, which reminded him more of ice chips from a slushy to assemble a ball and sent it sailing toward Peyton.

Peyton tried to dance away, but Noah's projectile found its target, glancing off her hip. Letting out a giggle, she began to make another when a powerful beam of headlights cut across the courtyard. They looked up and noticed the families had left. Santa and Krista waved signaling they were on their way out.

A man hopped out of a pickup truck that parked facing the village courtyard, so its headlights cast stabbing beams into the scene.

Peyton let out a sigh.

"You okay?" Noah asked, finding his muscles tense up.

"I'm fine. He's harmless. He has attachment issues, but his bark is way worse than his bite," Peyton said. "Thanks again for coming."

"I'll… I'll see you tomorrow?" Noah asked.

Peyton nodded. Her voice was unusually terse, she said, "See you tomorrow."

Noah walked along the brick path toward the parking lot. Wincing as he tried to look past the bright lights of the pickup truck, he studied the man leaning against it. Receiving a scowling glare, Noah walked past and toward his rental car. As he did, he recognized the man with the truck as the one who had stopped and messed with Peyton's gate earlier that afternoon.

"Whatcha doin' out here, Ty?" Peyton called.

"Just came by to give you this. Mama's famous Christmas Pirate Rum Cake. It was always your favorite," the man said.

"You tell that sweet lady to come visit me proper like. Not like her son who bushwhacks me in a parking lot after a long day," Peyton said. "I've always told her she could sell her rum cake by the truckload out of my store. Just as long as *she's* the one deliverin' it."

"Aw, come on. Don't be that way," the man groaned. "Let me buy you dinner."

"In no way is that a good idea, Ty," Peyton said.

"Come on, it's Christmas! It can be your present to me," the man pressed.

"I *am* fresh out of coal…" Peyton said, a sarcastic playfulness in her voice.

Not wanting to eavesdrop, Noah started his rental car and began to drive away. In his rearview mirror, he could see the man and Peyton still negotiating in the parking lot.

While he didn't like leaving her there, he could tell Peyton was not alarmed and in full control. Whoever the man with the truck was, there was clearly a history between the two. A history that was none of Noah's business.

Seven

Noah pulled up to the James House to see a vehicle he recognized parked in front.

The gleaming Land Rover that took photos of the house and tore away the previous afternoon was parked alongside the antebellum waterfront home.

Hopping out of his rental car, Noah inspected the vehicle as he walked by. The personalized license plate read "Homez".

Noah flipped the latch on the gate, expecting to fight it, only to have it swing open with ease. Even the groan of the worn hinges was gone.

"Hmph!" he grunted as started up the stone path to the porch.

The front door to the James House opened with Peyton's voice carrying out to the street. "You can't do this!"

A man in a well-pressed suit turned and looked over his shoulder toward Peyton and said in an unnervingly calm voice, "I already have, Ms. James."

The man faced back around, coming eye to eye with Noah. Smiling a cocky grin, the man slid a pair of sunglasses on his nose.

Noah's eyes followed him down the walk and as the man climbed into his expensive SUV. Starting the engine with a roar, the man accelerated briskly away from the house.

Spinning back toward the porch steps, with a bit of trepidation, he expected to see Peyton at the door. Instead, the door was closed and the porch was empty.

With a shrug, Noah marched up the steps and knocked on the door.

He could hear Peyton shuffling inside. The sound of a drawer slamming was followed by mumbling through a cracked voice. "Noah!" He could hear Peyton clearing her throat. "Noah, come on in!"

Noah slowly opened the door and took a cautious step inside. Peyton appeared around the corner. Frustration was clearly painted across her face.

"Is everything okay?" he asked.

"It's nothing. Just the modern challenges that come with trying to keep up a historic waterfront home," Peyton said, a ring of disgust in her voice.

Noah raised a brow but sensed he shouldn't press. He couldn't resist noting, "I see the gate latch is fixed."

Peyton paused for a moment and found herself raising a brow. "It is, isn't it? That wasn't you?" Her face fell and she shook her head, "Ty."

"Ty?" Noah asked.

"Part of my past. One of the few downsides of a small town. Break-ups don't allow for a lot of breathing room," Peyton said.

"The gentleman from the parking lot…" Noah said.

"That was Ty. What he lacks for in polish, he makes up for in earnest," Peyton said.

"I didn't want to pry," Noah said.

"I noticed you vanished real quick like," Peyton said.

"You seemed like you had whatever was going on under control," Noah said.

"I did. I do. I was going to hook you for an excuse to not have dinner with Ty. Fortunately, I got a call from a friend who needed setting up her Christmas tree," Peyton said.

Peyton looked away for a moment and took a deep breath.

"I'll, uh, I'll just get to work," Noah said, giving his camera a little shake.

"I'm sorry. There's just so much goin' on. You need anything from me? I think I'd better head back to the shop," Peyton said.

"Sure." Noah nodded. "I'll be okay here."

Peyton moved to open a drawer. Snatching an envelope, she stuffed it in her purse and shuffled off.

Noah watched her cross the foyer and slip out the door without another glance or word. He took a deep breath. Her strong and steady, effervescent persona was noticeably absent. Noah wondered which of her mysterious visitors was troubling her, if not both.

With a shrug, he knew there was nothing he could do to help her but finish his task and be one less thing for her to worry about.

Checking his notes for photos he wanted to retake in the morning light, he pulled out his camera and set to work.

Noah crossed off the last scribble in his notebook. Adding a few more photos he thought might share the elegant yet welcoming vibe of the home in its full Christmas glory, he packed up and readied to leave. Pausing at the door, he scrunched his nose. He wasn't directly told to leave it unlocked this time.

Hesitating with one foot on the porch, he didn't know what to do.

"Good morning, Noah!" a voice called from the porch next door.

Noah looked over to see Cybil waving at him.

"Good morning, Cybil," Noah said. With a frown, he asked, "I'm done here, I wasn't sure if I should… just…. leave?"

"It'll be fine. I'm around all day. But you can stop in and check with Peyton at the shop," Cybil suggested.

"That's a good idea," Noah said. Closing the door behind him, he walked to the far end of the porch and leaned against the rail. "Hey, Cybil. Do you know the man who was here when I pulled up?"

"Stuffy man in a tailored suit? Dashed away in that European vehicle of his like he owns the street? Yeah, I know of him," Cybil said, a scowl creasing her forehead.

"Would it be out of place to ask what he was doing here? Peyton seemed pretty upset when he left," Noah said.

"The man is a shark. He comes sniffing around, trying to buy homes along the waterfront. He smells blood in the water at the James House. I thought Peyton could handle him, but I gotta say, something seems off lately," Cybil said.

Noah nodded. He started to walk away but spun back to the rail. "And the man in the pickup truck? I'm sorry, it's none of my business."

Cybil deftly ignored his retraction. "That'd be Ty. He's a story for Peyton to tell. Even us porch rockers know our limits."

Noah chuckled. "Thank you, Cybil."

As he started to leave, Cybil called out, "But don't let that stop you!"

Noah spun on his heel. He frowned. "Stop me?"

Cybil just grinned.

Eight

Noah spent the rest of the morning walking through downtown Southport, taking photos. While the shots he took of the coastal town were gorgeous, few inspired him as sparking the magic of Christmas.

Climbing into his rented SUV, he glanced at his watch. He felt uncomfortable leaving Peyton's house unlocked without her tacit instructions, especially with the man in the suit and that Ty fellow hanging around. He didn't know what their interests in the James House were, but his gut screamed at him to be wary.

Pulling into the Southport Village Shoppes, Noah walked up the wooden steps to Peyton's Place Gift Shop. Through the screen door, he could hear Peyton was having a heated conversation. She paced by the screen door with her phone clenched to her ear. She seemed clearly frustrated, but her responses were ambiguous, not allowing Noah to know whether it was the mystery man, the man with the pickup truck or another problem.

Hesitating to open the door, Noah tried to step in quietly, but the metallic complaint of the steel spring warned Peyton of his presence.

Setting the phone down on her check stand, Peyton took a deep breath before turning around to face Noah. Forcing a smile, she asked, "And how is *your* day?"

"Okay…" The hesitation in Noah's voice was obvious.

"Sorry. It seems like drama is all around me right now. I'd say I live my life fairly drama free, but I don't think you would believe me after the past twenty-four hours," Peyton said.

"Is there anything I can do to help?" Noah asked.

"No, but thank you," Peyton said. Her eyes squinted. "Seriously, how was *your* morning?"

"Photos at your house were great," Noah said. His eyes widened. "That's why I'm here. I wasn't sure if I was supposed to lock up or not."

"I probably should have told you to lock the front door. It probably doesn't matter," Peyton said. She studied Noah for a moment. "You seem a bit off yourself."

"I'm just a bit concerned about you," Noah said, a question in his voice.

"That's sweet. I'm fine," Peyton said. Studying Noah, she pressed, "There's something else."

"It's nothing. I did a little walking tour of downtown. I took some great photos, but, despite the décor, they look like it might as well be August," Noah said.

"It's the vibe. You're missing the vibe. You need a field trip. You can't just capture Christmas in Southport through your camera lens. You need to *experience* it," Peyton said. "And to be honest, I could use a distraction myself."

Hooking her arm in Noah's, she yanked him toward the door. "Come on. I'm driving."

Passing by the boutique next door, Peyton called, "Hey, Sissy! I'm heading out for a bit. Can you keep an eye on the shop?"

"You got it, Peyton! Marie is here in an hour. I'll send her over to mind your store. It's pretty quiet today anyway!" a voice called back from inside the shop.

Peyton looked at Noah. Her expression was a mix of seriousness and mischief. "Let's go!"

Whatever she had in mind, it wiped away the dour mood that had enshrouded her. That made Noah a willing participant in following her to her car.

The drive was a short one as Peyton stopped at a location Noah had already used as a photograph spot. The Christmas House was a colonial home turned year-round Christmas store. Inside and out, the shop was decorated in holiday fare from top to bottom and filled with so many Christmas wares, shoppers could barely fit through the aisles.

On the outside, candy cane shutters adorned each window. Garland with red balls was permanently fixed to each peak. A gazebo strung with lights was built onto the wrap-around porch where shoppers could sit and enjoy a cup of cocoa or cider.

The inside of the shop was where the magic happened. Every Christmas decoration ever thought of was available in the store. Christmas books, candles, stockings and puzzles filled the shelves and hung from the walls.

"This is… Christmasy," Noah said as his eyes swept over the almost overwhelming displays.

Pulling Noah by the hand, Peyton led him to a what appeared to be an indoor forest of Christmas trees. Each had its own theme. They waltzed past a candy cane tree, a crab trap tree and a flamingo tree.

Peyton grinned. "These must really tax your traditional sensibilities."

"I don't deny anyone else's vision of Christmas décor. I just prefer decorations that bring me back to my childhood. I think that's why I like the reds and greens," Noah said.

"No bears playing in the snow?" Peyton asked as she stopped by a tree that was filled with bear ornaments. Bears riding sleds, ice skating and building bear snowmen hung from the boughs.

"Is that a snowman or snowbear?" Noah asked.

"Good question," Peyton said, giving Noah a nudge.

The photojournalist panned around the store that was filled with customers doing their best to take it all in themselves. While he didn't have his big camera, he took several shots with his phone.

"This place is definitely… Christmas," Noah said.

"It is a Southport institution. Well, at least for the past couple of decades. The place is always packed year-round," Peyton said. "Come on. There's more."

Hooking her arm in his, Peyton led Noah to a back room that emanated Christmas carols being played on a classic record player. Two tables were set up with piles of evergreen boughs. The aroma of the room was like walking through a pine forest.

Peyton took in a deep breath and yanked on Noah's arm. "Isn't it great?"

"It smells amazing. It smells like Christmas," Noah said.

"Have you ever made a wreath?" Peyton asked.

"Maybe a paper one in elementary school," Noah said.

"Well, if you have time, these ladies are the best and they'll teach you," Peyton said. "But that's not what we're here for."

Looking around the room, Peyton found a woman restocking items for the wreath-making. "Hi, Sue. Those look great!"

"Are the ones you and the girls made for the Village holding up in this heat?" Sue asked.

"They are. The cooler nights are helping, I think, and the overhangs of the porches help keep direct sunlight off," Peyton said. "Is Henry around? I was hoping he'd be up for a Christmas mission."

Sue set her items down on the table and looked at Peyton and then at Noah. A smile cracked the corner of her lips as she eyed

Peyton's companion, "Hello. I'm Sue Benton. My husband and I stock a lot of the trees, boughs and berries this time of year."

"It's a pleasure to meet you. I'm Noah Wilde. I'm with *Coastal Charm Magazine* doing an article on Southport at Christmas."

"Nice to meet you. Southport is a magical place. I could do with a few degrees cooler this time of year all the same," Sue said.

"That's what I've been saying." Noah grinned at finally finding a confidant.

"Noah's from the *north*," Peyton said, a playfully condescending tone in her voice.

"Well, we won't hold that against you unless you give us good reason," Sue said. Turning, she waved over her shoulder. "Come on. Let's find Henry."

Sue led Peyton and Noah through the backroom of the Christmas House and out to an alley behind the historic building. A man pulled the last of several wrapped evergreen trees from the bed of the truck and stacked it with others in a neat row protected by the shade of the building.

"Henry, Peyton was hoping you were heading back to the farm. This young man is doing an article on Southport at Christmas," Sue said.

"There's no better spot than your farm, Henry. I was hoping you'd be up for a hunt?" Peyton asked.

Henry grinned as he eyed Noah. "A hunt, eh? You good with a rifle?"

Noah looked surprised as he glanced at Peyton and back at the farmer. He said, "I've done some skeet shooting. I did okay, I guess."

"That'll do. You pilin' in or you gonna follow?" Henry asked as he closed the gate of his classic pickup truck.

"We'll follow you out there, Henry. Thank you," Peyton said.

Noah still looked confused.

"Don't worry, hon. Henry's just messin' with you. Mostly," Sue said with a smile.

As the farmer duo slid into their old pickup truck, Peyton and Noah made their way to her car.

Following the old truck with "Benton Tree Farm" barely visible in the faded paint, they left downtown Southport and headed north of town.

Turning off the highway, they snaked their way along a bouncy dirt road. Noah looked out the window at the Carolina pines.

Their foot-long needles stuck out on the branches like a cheerleader's pom-poms.

Peyton rolled down the windows as a light breeze had picked up. The pine trees seemed to whisper a song as their needles clattered together in the wind.

Clearing the pine wood forest, they entered a fenced drive with a big wooden sign nearly as faded as the old pickup they followed. "Benton Tree Farm circa 1977".

The truck pulled to a stop between a red barn and a house. Each was adorned with long strands of evergreen boughs and a massive wreath hung beneath the eaves of the barn.

Henry hopped out and shoved a pair of gloves into his jacket pocket.

"Y'all ready to hunt? Let me get our gear," Henry said, wandering off into the barn.

"Y'all have fun! I'll have iced tea and cool cider ready for you when you get back," Sue said as she hobbled toward the house.

"Thank you, Sue!" Peyton called.

"Bag some of them critters for me!" Sue called back.

Noah scanned the tree farm wondering what he had gotten himself into. "I'm… I'm not much of a hunter…"

Peyton laughed with a hand on his shoulder. "You'll be fine. I promise."

Henry marched out of the barn with an arsenal of tools, among them a long, double-barrel shotgun. "I reckon this'll do us."

"You a twelve-gauge or a twenty?" Henry asked.

"A what?" Noah frowned.

"Aw, it don't matter. Either'll get the job done," Henry said as he placed his hunting tools in the back of a large ATV. "Hop in, this is our ride out to the hunting grounds."

Noah began to perspire beyond the afternoon heat, unsure of what he had unwittingly signed up for. Taking his seat in the rear of the ATV, he held on as the vehicle lurched into gear.

The trip led them past rows of Christmas trees. Beyond the cultivated evergreens, Henry took them into a forest of scrub oak.

"We get good huntin' right on the edge of Green Swamp," Henry called out over his head.

"Swamp? As in alligator type swamp?" Noah asked.

"Sure, we got 'em. Cottonmouth moccasins too. If you ain't lookin' for them, they're sure lookin' for you," Henry said as he drove along a crude trail.

It wasn't long before the ATV slid to a stop.

Henry hopped out with the agility and zeal of a teenager.

Following Peyton out her side of the ATV, Noah stretched after the bumpy ride and studied the terrain. White sand and tall pines had given way to almost marshy soil and scraggly oak trees. Swaths of Spanish moss hung from the trees.

Henry gazed up into the trees, "Yep, good huntin' up here this year."

Noah's eyes followed the farmer's and he asked, "What exactly are we hunting for?"

Peyton jumped in with a smile, "You'll know it when you see it. Just, uh, I recommend you stick by me and let Henry do his thing."

Noah gave a nervous nod as Peyton wrapped her hands around his arm.

"If it's all right with y'all, I'll take the shotgun. You two'll do fine with the poles," Henry said.

Peyton and Noah selected long, extendable poles, each with a hook on the end.

Noah studied his tool and shook his head.

"I told you." Peyton grinned. "You need to experience the magic of Christmas in Southport. You can't get this from your camera lens."

"No. No, I suppose I couldn't," Noah mumbled, still examining his hook having no idea what sort of creature he was supposed to be poking his stick at.

"Come on, you two. We're wastin' daylight!" Henry called and began ambling further into the woods.

Noah's head dropped down to his feet. "Is it safe out here?"

"Safe-ish. Just walk the same path Henry does," Peyton said as she led him further into the swampy forest.

The trail that Henry took kept them on dry ground, which Noah was grateful for, as he had only packed one pair of shoes on his trip.

Whatever they were after, Henry's eyes were glued to the forest canopy. Peyton's search moved from the ground in front of them to the tops of the trees.

"Stop!" Peyton froze, her voice in a hoarse whisper. "I think I see one."

Noah's wide eyes scanned the trees, unable to see what Peyton was seeing.

"Come here," Peyton continued to whisper and pulled Noah closer. As she pointed with one hand, she tugged on Noah's arm with her other.

Noah strained to find the critter they were after when to his surprise, Peyton's lips met his.

His cheeks flushed as he tried to stammer a reply before his muscles relaxed and he succumbed to the kiss.

Peyton pulled back as she looked into Noah's eyes. She whispered, "Do you see it now?"

Confused, Noah attempted to comply by inching his lips closer to hers. Instead, he was cut off by Peyton's finger pressing against his lips.

Letting out a giggle, she pushed up his chin so that his eyes looked directly above her. "Mistletoe, silly. That is what we're after out here."

Amidst the leaves and lichen coated scrub oak branches was a dark green ball of foliage.

Noah's cheeks glowed. "I see."

"Well, what do you think?" Peyton asked.

"I think I'm glad I took your advice and stuck near you instead of Henry," Noah said.

Peyton giggled again. "I warned you."

"So… what do we do now?" Noah said. He quickly added, "With the mistletoe."

"We take our poles, raise them up. Get as close to the branch that you can and…" Peyton said as she stretched her pole up to the branch and gave it a yank.

The clump of mistletoe fell through the air to Noah, who caught it like a football.

"Nice catch. Now your turn," Peyton said. Her eyes led his to another clump a few trees further down the trail.

As they moved into position under the second clump of mistletoe, Noah squared up with Peyton. "Is it tradition to kiss under each one?"

"You are big on traditions…" Peyton grinned. "You don't have to… but you can."

Leaning in, their lips close enough they could feel each other's breath, they jumped back as a shotgun blast rattled the forest, sending a group of mourning doves scattering into the air.

"Ha, ha!" Henry's voice rang through the forest. "That's the way we used to do it!"

Peyton laughed and scrunched her nose. "He's not kidding. That was the traditional Southern method. It's not the best for the trees and can damage the mistletoe, but it *is* kinda fun."

"Come on, you two. Looks like only the Yankee is missin' his haul, plus I gotta bring one back for Sue," Henry said as he bounded down the trail with his lump of mistletoe in hand.

Noah looked at Peyton, who had repositioned herself under the mistletoe. Now with an audience, Noah felt the moment had passed. Swallowing hard, he took his eyes off of Peyton and eyed the mistletoe up in the tree.

"Aren't you forgetting somethin', son?" Henry barked. "This stuff ain't for eatin'. It's for kissin'. It's how I wrangled my Sue!"

Peyton cocked her head, a hint of rose in her cheeks. "I guess you'd better…"

Before the words could leave her mouth, Noah's lips were pressed against hers. For a brief moment, the world had disappeared. Henry the farmer wasn't staring at them from the trail. Noah's assignment didn't weigh on his mind. Whatever challenges were taxing Peyton had vanished.

As the world came back into view, they parted.

"Well, that was a pretty good one," Henry said from the trail.

Noah closed his eyes and nodded. As he opened them, Peyton smiled back at him with a wink.

"All right, let's get this mistletoe," Noah said. Extending his pole, he held it in the air. Letting it slide along the branch, he yanked down as the hook aligned with the clump of foliage. Catching the mistletoe in one hand, he looked at Peyton. "Thank you. You were right. Some things have to be experienced. This was amazing."

Peyton squinted, "You talking about the kiss or foraging for mistletoe?"

"Yes." Noah grinned.

Nine

The ride back to Southport was heart-pounding for Noah. He had no idea whether the moments on the hunt for mistletoe were merely nods to tradition or something more. Their suddenly awkward conversations only added to the anxiety and the mystery.

Noah would glance over at Peyton and her eyes would suddenly become fixated on the road ahead of her. Shaking his head to himself, he discarded any misplaced notions, since he was only in town for a little short of two weeks.

He liked Peyton. She was smart. She was fun. She was playful. She also lived nearly a thousand miles away. And she clearly already had a full dance card, if a complicated one.

Clearing his throat, he said, "Thank you for setting up the trip to the farm and the hunt for mistletoe. It was quite the experience."

"You are welcome. I hope it helped put you into the Southern Christmas spirit," Peyton said.

"It did," Noah said, as he nodded. Under his breath, he repeated, "It did."

"We aren't done, if you're up for it. Nothing as exciting as tromping through the Green Swamp searching for mistletoe, but I could use a little more fresh air," Peyton said.

"Sounds good to me," Noah agreed.

Parking her car alongside her family's house, they got out.

Taking a deep breath of the sea air, Peyton held her arm out.

Noah readily accepted the invitation to link his arm in hers. Crossing the street, they strolled along the waterfront. To their right was the water. To their left, the row of waterfront homes that sent Noah on the mission to Southport in the first place.

From their vantage, the homes, including the James House, lit up in their holiday splendor were magnificent. To Noah, if you placed them along a frozen lake or a snowed-in downtown scene, they looked like the Christmas village you would put under your tree and build a train set around.

A light coastal breeze kicked up, giving the evening a much more seasonal feel. To Noah, it seemed more like Halloween weather, but it was a whole season closer to what it had been.

"So, you spent your life in that spectacular house," Noah said, glancing up at the James House.

"That was home," Peyton said, her voice cheery. Letting out a big sigh, she said, "It was a *great* childhood. At first, that was Grandpa and Grandma's house. We would be there for every holiday, and as I hope you're starting to gather, Southport likes its holidays. We moved in not long after they passed. Daddy said tryin' to manage two households was too much."

"Where did you live before you moved there?" Noah asked.

"We had a lake house in Boiling Spring Lakes, just a bit up the road. It was close to the schools I went to and where Daddy worked," Peyton said.

"A lake house to Southport's waterfront… which was better?" Noah asked.

"Both had their pluses. Livin' on the lake was great. Once you chased the snakes and alligators away, the water was rather refreshing. It was quieter out there. A *lot* quieter. But that also felt a bit disconnected. Bein' here, you are in the center of things. The community is tighter. Privacy is at a premium, but the heart and soul of this town… you could feel it in your chest livin' here," Peyton said.

"It sounds nice. Where I live, now, at least, it's definitely not quiet. But it lacks the heart and soul that shines through you when you talk about Southport. There's work, and a lot of it. But I've lived on my street for two years. I still don't know most of my neighbors. I think I know more of yours now than I do my own," Noah said.

Peyton laughed. "There is a trade-off, believe you me."

"I bet." Noah nodded. He stopped their stroll and just listened. He just watched. "I definitely don't get this."

"What?" Peyton asked.

"Unless I'm heading to the airport at 4 am, it's never this still. Never this quiet," Noah said.

"I *need* those moments," Peyton said.

Subconsciously, the pair squared up along the walking path. The water gently lapped against the sea wall as the breeze continued to wisp cooler toward them. The moon flickered as clouds moved by.

Their breathing fell into sync. Their eyes found one another's.

Noah leaned in ever so slightly.

Peyton's mouth opened in a slight breath.

Noah felt his heart pound as he was drawn in toward her lips, which Peyton subconsciously licked against the dry evening air.

As if pulled in by an imaginary sprig of mistletoe, their lips hovered dangerously close to one another.

Before they could meet, Peyton's phone buzzed. Her eyes shot open wide. A glance at her phone made her wince.

Stammering, Peyton said, "I'm sorry. I have somewhere I need to be. Ugh, I am so late."

Placing her hand on Noah's chest, she repeated as she looked into his eyes, "I'm sorry."

Spinning before he could reply, Peyton raced across the street toward her car.

Panning over her shoulder, she called, "See you tomorrow?"

Noah nodded.

Peyton gave a quick nod. Starting her car, she roared away from the sidewalk, leaving Noah in a glow of brake lights.

Bewildered, his eyes moved from the wake of Peyton's exit to the water and the steady flash of the Oak Island Lighthouse.

Groaning, he realized his car was at the Village Shoppes. With a shrug, he started his long walk and decided he would stop for a bite somewhere between the James House and his car. The walk would allow him to get a deeper feel for the streets of Southport lit up for Christmas.

Ten

Noah's day began following a freighter as it navigated from the Cape Fear River to the Southport Channel toward the open water of the Atlantic Ocean through his camera's lens.

The massive size of the ships running just offshore of Southport's coastline fascinated Noah. At least one of the photos, with the morning sun just cresting the horizon, would make an interesting addition, at least in the image file B-rolls. Noah appreciated that the freighter had Christmas lights running the length of the ship and a tall Christmas tree affixed to the pilothouse.

A heron drifted by his shot toward Bonnet's Creek. As he steadied his camera for a shot, his phone rang. Ignoring the phone long enough to take several photos of the bird standing tall in the marsh grass, Noah answered.

"Noah…" a familiar voice called through the phone.

In truth, he had been anticipating the call from his editor at *Coastal Charm Magazine*.

"Good morning, Jennimay," Noah replied.

"I see you've taken some beautiful photos. Thank you for uploading them," Jennimay said.

"It's just the start. There are more on the way," Noah promised.

There was a pause on the other end of the line. "Here's the thing," his editor's voice finally continued. "They are good. Some of them are *very* good. I can see garland. I can see evergreens. I see a lovely coastal town. What I am not getting is a vibe. It isn't singing 'Jingle Bells' to me, Noah!"

Noah sighed. "It isn't exactly sleigh ride weather here, Jennimay. There *is* a lot of heart and Christmas spirit in this town. Capturing it has just been more challenging than I expected."

"Your two picks for cover houses are intriguing. They do scream *Coastal Charm Magazine* cover, I just am not sure they are… Christmasy enough," Jennimay said.

"Christmasy… is that a word?" Noah asked.

"Don't edit the editor. I've seen you make up words more times than I can count," Jennimay said.

"Yeah, you let a few go, too," Noah said.

"I liked them enough to give them a pass. I thought they would register with the readers. That's not the point. I need a little more ho-ho-ho or I might need to yank this assignment. Don't worry, we can use the content you've provided for a filler article near the back, but I was hoping for a cover story here, Noah," Jennimay said.

"So was I. I mean, it's a beach town in the South. I can't change the weather," Noah said.

"Find a way. I'm counting on you, Noah," Jennimay said.

"I'll see what I can do," Noah said. He thought of his experience hunting mistletoe with Peyton. If only he had a way to capture that experience.

"You've got twenty-four hours to show me there is still cover potential in Southport," Jennimay said.

"I'm on it," Noah said, his voice almost a grumble as he hung up the phone.

Noah stepped back out onto the hotel room patio, only to be blasted by the morning heat.

"More ho-ho-ho, huh?" He sighed.

Noah pulled alongside the house behind a familiar vehicle. He knew it didn't make sense, but the sight of the old pickup truck made his stomach flip-flop.

Grabbing his gear, he stepped out of his rental car. He needed to find a way to convey Christmas through his photographs. He knew there was promise in the waterfront houses, especially the James and Thomas houses.

Waiting by the sidewalk, he fiddled with his camera as he assessed the scene at the James House.

He could hear Peyton's voice rise, as she was clearly unhappy with what conversation she was having. To Noah's surprise or disappointment, it wasn't Ty on the other end of her frustration. Her ex-boyfriend leaned against a porch post with his arms crossed, waiting for her.

Finally, Peyton's screen door flew open and she stepped out onto the porch. She seemed in no mood for her visitor. She glared at Ty before pacing around the porch with her phone in her hand.

"I fixed the latch. On the gate," Ty said. "And the squeaky hinge!"

"I noticed," Peyton said. Her voice was quick and flat.

"I told you I would," Ty drawled as he chewed on a toothpick.

"A year ago," Peyton snapped.

Ty stepped away from the post he was leaning on and strode toward Peyton. "What's time between…"

"Friends," Peyton cut him off, her voice sharp. Eyeing Noah wandering by the front gate, she asked Ty, "Is that what you came here for? An attaboy? Well, attaboy, Ty!"

"The boat parade, Peyton. I came by to ask you to join me on the Christmas boat parade. I need a first mate. That's you," Ty said, his voice almost pleading.

"That *was* me. Now, I have a house to manage. I have the waterfront row viewing party to host. I have Dad to take care of. *And* I don't want to be your first mate. I want to visit with my friends as the other boats go by," Peyton snapped.

"Come on, Peyton. Anyone in the Woman's Club can manage the viewing party for you," Ty said. "You can wave to them from the boat."

"A member of the James family has always been here to host the viewing party," Peyton said. "This year, that is me."

"Does that even matter anymore?" Ty said, instantly regretting his words.

Peyton glared at Ty and could only utter a growl in her frustration.

"Peyton, I'm sorry…" Ty pleaded as he took a couple of steps toward Peyton.

Peyton froze him in place with a glare and a hand extended in front of her.

"You're always sorry. Here's the truth, I don't *want* to be your first mate. There is a reason we aren't together anymore, Ty. There is a reason we won't ever work out. I'm sorry," Peyton said, her voice icy and even. "Goodbye, Ty. Don't let the gate with the shiny new latch hit you on the way out."

Ty studied Peyton for a moment. Realizing he wasn't going to get anywhere with her, he spun and stomped down the steps.

Seeing Noah, Peyton abruptly changed her tone. "Good morning, Noah."

Ty brushed by the photojournalist with his shoulder while giving him a sly head nod as though he didn't just completely bomb with his ex-girlfriend.

"Good morning. You must be Ty." Noah stretched his hand out.

Ty froze in place and studied him for a moment before snorting and walking by without giving the offer of a handshake any credence.

Noah had to admit that he was confused, as he was certain his evening walk was ended by Peyton being late for her date with Ty.

As Ty reached the gate he fixed the day prior, he gave a half turn as he watched Noah ascend the steps.

"What time are you picking me up for Winterfest tonight, Noah?" Peyton asked in a voice loud enough for Ty and the ladies on the three nearest porches to hear.

"I'm sorry to interrupt. Is everything okay?" Noah asked.

Peyton's eyes briefly diverted to Ty as he climbed into his truck and roared away from the house.

Letting out a sigh, she said, "Yes. Maybe. Not about Ty. He is the least of my worries. And no, none of that had anything to do with you."

"I can come back later…" Noah said, tossing a thumb over his shoulder as a sign he should leave.

"Don't be silly. You're here. I need to do some planning for the boat parade viewing party, which you *really* need to attend. It is an amazing sight and should definitely be in your article. And not just because I told Ty I couldn't go and you were going to be my date at Winterfest," Peyton said.

Noah squinted slightly, "Date? What's this about Winterfest?"

"The official launch is tonight. It's a must see. A must experience..." Peyton said, a smile pursing her lips. "Date... I mean it's a day and time and we go together?"

"Okay... It's a date... I mean, I look forward to it," Noah said, his cheeks flushing.

Peyton studied him for a moment and said, "Noah Wilde, I'm glad you're here. I'm glad you are telling Southport's Christmas story."

Noah nodded meekly, his editor's words echoing through his head.

Eleven

From the vantage of the James House front porch, the entire town of Southport seemed to be descending on the waterfront. The South Brunswick High School band played Christmas carols as they marched toward the towering, unlit tree in the town's favorite meeting spot, Whittler's Bench.

Families strolled through the streets, some getting front row seats, others making a beeline for tables handing out cocoa, cider and cookies.

Noah watched from the corner porch post as he waited for Peyton to join him. The evening was just cool enough to don a light jacket. Noah hoped that would reflect that it was indeed not summertime in his photos.

Snapping a few shots of the families gathering, he knew the money photos would be in the glow of the evening lights.

Hearing the front door open and light footsteps across the porch, Noah set his camera down. Turning, he found Peyton in a shimmering red dress with a white faux fur shawl. Her hair was held up on one side with a real holly clip.

In the glow of the porch's Christmas lights, Peyton looked ethereal as she strode toward him. Pausing, she cocked her head and asked with a raised brow, "What?"

"You… you look beautiful," Noah said, not expecting the words to make him blush.

Peyton's cheeks joined his with a hint of rouge.

"I, uh, I made real hot cocoa tonight. Unless you wanted to shimmy through the line down there for a freebie," Peyton said.

"No," Noah said, his voice soft as he peeled his eyes away from Peyton to glance at the still-growing crowd. "I like the view from up here."

Joining him at the far rail, closest to the action around the town tree, Peyton handed Noah a Christmas mug.

Holding it up to the light, Noah inspected it. A little old red farm truck was hauling a Christmas tree. Approving, he grinned. "I *do* have an affinity for Christmas tree farms."

"I kinda do, too," Peyton said. Her Southern-primed thermostat found the evening cool with just her shawl wrapped around her, leaving her arms bare. Leaning in, she pressed up against Noah.

The mayor of Southport stood in front of a podium which had been placed on a flat-bed trailer affixed stage and addressed the crowd. "How about the South Brunswick band, huh? *That* gets you in the Christmas spirit. I want to welcome you all to Winterfest. This is such a magical time of year and it is an honor to celebrate it with all of you. As always, the days leading up to Christmas will be chock full of fun events to gather, to share some Christmas spirit and to help those who could use a little extra cheer. We have Ms. Mabel Gentry to thank for that. She and her amazing group of volunteers work countless hours to make each holiday season more memorable than the last. And with that, I give you Mabel!"

The mayor clapped along with the crowd as he stepped aside for Mabel to take the spot in front of the podium. As she started to speak, the microphone was over the top of her head. The mayor reached over and lowered it, releasing a bit of feedback through the speakers and making the audience cringe.

"It seems like that is a yearly tradition… the adjusting of the mic," Mabel said enticing laughs from the crowd. "As Mayor Clemmons said, we are so excited to see you all out in the crowd. We are grateful that the band could serenade us. We'll soon have the choir help us sing some songs together and of course, the Southport Beautification Committee for hosting us with cocoa, cider and cookies. With that, let's sing some songs and we'll light that tree!"

Stepping away from the podium, Mabel turned to the music director and, with a nod, the high school choir's voices rose into the night air. For a moment, the crowd was still and quiet as the choir owned the moment. As the song hit its first chorus, the dignitaries on the stage joined in, followed by the crowd.

"I hate to pull away and grab my camera, but this is a great shot," Noah whispered.

Peyton laughed. "That is *experiencing* the moment, not just capturing it."

As Noah set his cocoa down and began to pick up his camera, he noticed a shiver from Peyton. Taking his jacket off, he held it out, "May I?"

Peyton blushed. "Well, thank you, kind sir."

Draping his jacket over Peyton's shoulders, he grabbed his camera with one hand and slung his other arm around Peyton, ensuring the jacket covered her as best it could.

"Impractical being so unprepared for the weather, really. A silly price to pay for tryin' to look pretty," Peyton said.

"Well, for what it's worth, you nailed it," Noah said.

"Got a jacket for *me*?" a voice called from the porch next door. Cybil's hand reached over the rail to wave to her neighbors.

"I can find you one," Noah said.

"Just kidding, dear. We all have Christmas quilts over our laps. We ain't no spring chickens at this," Cybil said. Getting up from her seat, she walked over to her rail. "You know what, you two should be in a picture. You look so lovely!"

Reaching for her friend's camera, Cybil took a photo of Noah and Peyton leaning against the rail. The Christmas lights strung around the porch gave them a warm glow.

"There's your cover shot, Noah!" Cybil giggled.

"Thank you, Cybil. Good evening, ladies," Noah called to a chorus of hellos and hand waving.

He could feel Peyton chuckling in his grasp.

"This really is a sweet town," Noah said.

"You've *no* idea," Peyton said. With a nudge, she added, "Get your camera ready. It's about that time."

"I'll enjoy the moment. Get my shots after," Noah said, setting his camera down.

Peyton wriggled her way into his chest so that he could wrap both arms around her.

As the choir led the crowd through the final chorus of "O Christmas Tree", the mayor walked back up to the podium.

Clapping his hands, he waved for a man in a wheelchair to join him. The man, dressed in full military uniform, rows of ribbons and medals dangling, wheeled his way to the podium. The crowd cheered.

"Everyone, give it up for Colonel Walt Williams, our most honored tree-lighter this year," the mayor said.

With Colonel Williams in place in front of a tall candy cane wrapped post with a big, bright red button at the ready, the crowd counted down from three. Noah could hear the chorus from the ladies next door and Peyton's soft voice joining them.

As the crowd hit "one" in unison, the colonel slapped the button and the park was ablaze in light from the tall tree. The veteran's face glowed in the Christmas lights. Noah couldn't help but dive for his camera and capture the colonel's smile as he looked up at the tree. Even from the James House porch, you could almost see the reflection of the lights and the joy in the colonel's eyes.

"In a season of wonderful moments, that might be my favorite yet," Noah breathed.

"It's pretty special," Peyton said with a nod. Turning, she faced Noah, her hands on his chest. A grin creased her lips. "That, and I gotta try harder to climb your favorites list."

"Oh, you're up there," Noah said, looking into her eyes.

As his head bowed and Peyton pushed up on her toes, their eyes and lips seemed drawn toward one another. As they were about to meet, a voice rang through the night.

"We're about to head up and visit the Storefront Showcase. You two care to join us?" Cybil asked.

Noah and Peyton's heads pivoted to the porch next door.

"Thank you, Cybil. That would be lovely," Peyton said.

Reluctantly pulling apart, they made their way down the porch steps and out onto the sidewalk.

Meeting Cybil and a string of ladies close to her age at the gate, the bubbly woman handed Peyton a fuzzy hand muff that matched her shawl.

"To keep the chill away," Cybil smiled and gave a wink to Peyton.

Noah held the gate open for the ladies to stream through, and several offered little giggles in between Merry Christmases.

As Peyton and Noah fell in line, the gaggle of women shared how lovely they thought the event was. Peyton cocked her head toward Noah as she slid her hands into the muff.

"What is it?" Noah whispered.

Peyton drew her hand out to reveal a small flask.

Cybil nudged Peyton's shoulder. "A little Schnapps to ward off the chill, my dear."

Opening her own flask, Cybil sent a fiery blast of peppermint down her throat. With a wink, she said, "Good for kissin', too."

The ladies within earshot giggled.

Peyton and Noah shot glances at each other.

Following the procession of ladies, along with a good portion of the town, they strolled along Howe Street before making a sharp hook onto Moore Street.

Each shop's windows were set in different themed Christmas displays, each more spectacular than the last. It reminded Noah of walking past Macy's in Manhattan's Herald Square at Christmas.

Scenes depicting the North Pole, Mrs. Claus baking cookies, reindeer playing with their toys and even a nativity scene graced the windows of the downtown shops.

As they moved across the street to complete their loop, they passed Bull Frog Corner. The long stretch of windows allowed for a more intricate scene. The first vignette was an author writing with a quill pen in a flickering light. The second was the author asleep on his writing desk, quill pen still in hand. The third vignette was a vibrant, colorful scene of Santa kneeling by a child who had fallen asleep on a sofa in front of the Christmas tree. The mechanical Santa slid a stuffed bear into the sleeping child's arms.

The rest of the scene did its best to recount the rest of 'Twas the Night Before Christmas, including a mouse opening a wrapped present from Santa, a wedge of cheese.

The tour ended at The Christmas House, which held themselves exempt from the town's voting for best Christmas display as they would always hold an unfair advantage.

Wrapping up their walk, Cybil's growing group paused outside the Christmas House picket fence.

Turning to Peyton and Noah, Sybil said, "We are off to dinner at the Frying Pan if you care to join us."

"Thank you, Cybil. Your company on the tour was fantastic. I think I would like to show Noah the tree and the town a little after the crowd has slipped away," Peyton said.

Cybil smiled as she placed a hand on Peyton's. "Very well. You two enjoy your time together. Goodnight, Noah."

"Goodnight, Cybil. Ladies…" Noah nodded.

Finding a quieter corridor to follow, Peyton led Noah back toward the waterfront.

"This was nice, thank you," he said.

Her arm in his, Peyton meandered down the sidewalk until the town Christmas tree came into view. From that vantage, the row of colonial homes and the town tree could be seen reflected off the water.

"Oh, wow," Noah breathed.

"Take a picture," Peyton nudged.

Turning to face her, he said, "I'd rather experience the moment."

Leaning in, Noah's lips met Peyton's as she pushed up on her toes.

"Me too," Peyton whispered.

Twelve

Noah arrived along the waterfront intent on taking photos of additional homes. As he parked his rental car, another vehicle drove up behind him.

A smiling, bubbly Peyton popped out from behind the driver's seat and called out, "You up for a day trip?"

"Sure," Noah said with a wary shrug.

Sliding into her passenger seat, he asked, "Where are we going?"

"A little Christmas tradition you certainly can't get from your mountain towns," Peyton said as she wheeled her car away onto the road.

Navigating through downtown Southport and dense traffic leading to an intersection, Peyton headed south again.

Soon, they found themselves crossing the Intracoastal Waterway on the G. V. Barbee Sr. Bridge.

"Welcome to Oak Island," Peyton said. "This is where you could find me most summers, if I could wriggle past the tourists, at least."

As Peyton followed the road onto the island, she allowed the flow to take them east. Continuing her guided tour, she pointed in the opposite direction. "Normally, you'd see me heading that way toward Long Beach. True to its name, it is a gorgeous long stretch of beach. You can be in the thick of it near Ocean Crest Pier or find a spot pretty much all to yourself," she said.

"What about this way?" Noah asked.

"It's a smaller, quieter beach. It's a magnificent spot to find sea turtle nests, which I highly recommend you come visit for that season. It is something truly special. *Today*, we are after something a little different," Peyton said as she pulled into the Caswell Beach parking lot immediately across from the one-hundred-and-fifty-three-foot-tall Oak Island Lighthouse.

"To think I used to stare at this lighthouse from my bedroom window every night," Peyton said, her voice a bit dreamy.

"It's a good view from either direction," Noah said.

Putting the car in park, Peyton hopped out. She pulled out a couple of buckets and handed one to Noah.

Before he could even inquire as he studied the bucket with curiosity, Peyton called, "Come on!" and waved excitedly as she kicked her shoes off and ran along the sand, her hair blowing in the breeze.

The sight took Noah's breath away. All he could do was smile and run after her.

As they closed in on the waves lapping against the sand, Peyton slowed down, her eyes intently scanning the beach. Pointing, she said, "See this line of shells the waves are pushing in? Look along there."

"We're looking for shells?" Noah asked, still confused as to what his task was.

"For this!" Peyton's eyes grew wide as she held a coin-shape up into the air.

Noah stepped closer and inspected Peyton's discovery. "That's a sand dollar!"

"This is what we are after," Peyton said, shaking the sand dollar in the air before gently placing it in her bucket.

"All right, game on," Noah said, his eyes scanning the sand.

"Ooh, a competition. Good idea. First one to an even two dozen wins a prize," Peyton said.

"I like prizes," Noah said as he brushed the sand with his hand, uncovering his first find. "Got one!"

"Make sure it doesn't have any cilia," Peyton said.

"Have what?" Noah asked.

"Velvety little hairs, especially on the bottom. That means the poor little guy… or gal is still alive but got tossed up in the surf," Peyton asked.

"This one is smooth. It feels pretty much like a shell but a bit more fragile," Noah said.

"All right. You have a keeper. Oop, here's one!" Peyton said as she reached down toward the sand.

Soon, they were scouring the beach, their eyes firmly fixed on the sand. Occasionally, they would hear the sound of a sand dollar being placed in the competition's bucket and they would pick up their search.

As Noah reached for one, a hand darted in at the same time. His hand ended up over Peyton's. Looking up, they smiled at one other.

"You win that one. Next one's mine, but don't be cheating in this direction," Noah teased.

Suddenly, he cocked his head and knelt on the sand, "What do we have here?"

Noah picked up the object he had found.

"A starfish! That's a great find," Peyton said.

Noah studied the poor creature. As he did, he thought he felt movement.

Looking over his shoulder, Peyton said, "Place your hand to the water."

Doing as instructed, Noah dipped his hand into the oncoming wave as it slid up the beach. As soon as the starfish hit the water, it twitched.

"Well, there, little guy. I think you still have some fight in you. Here you go." Noah put his hand completely into the water and allowed the starfish to get its bearings.

"You saved a life today. My hero," Peyton sang.

"Well, that was fun," Noah said.

"If you see any that are bleach white, they are keepers along with the sand dollars, but otherwise help them find their way home like that one," Peyton said.

After a while of searching, they paused to count their shells.

"I have two dozen!" Noah announced.

"I have… twenty-three and a half," Peyton said as she held up a fragile sand dollar that didn't make the trip into the bucket.

"Here's one. Now you have two dozen," Noah said, placing the sand dollar into Peyton's pile.

"Thank you, good gentleman." Peyton curtsied.

Noah smiled and with a slight sideways nod of his head said, "I still win."

Peyton nodded. "You won. This time, Noah Wilde."

"And about that prize…" Noah said.

Peyton grinned and said, "Later. We still have work to do."

"It hardly feels like work being here on the beach," Noah said.

"I know, right?" Peyton took a deep breath of sea air and looked at the crashing waves. "I love it. I could spend all day, every day here."

They both stood for a moment appreciating the view as a flock of little sandpipers ran by, racing the surf.

"You're going to tell me that a freezing, snowy mountain is better than this?" Peyton asked.

Noah seemed to search for an answer in the oncoming waves. "Not better. More traditional maybe, but not better."

"There you go with traditional again." Peyton nudged him with her hip and smiled. "It's okay. I like traditional too."

Finding a stick, Peyton handed Noah her bucket. "Here, a little photo op for you."

Just outside the reaching fingers of the surf, Peyton began to draw in the sand. She started by etching a Christmas tree. She completed her sand art by sketching spiraling strings of garland and a five-pointed star on top.

Next, she drew a gingerbread man and woman, their round arms touching as though they were holding hands. Finally, she sketched a pair of candy canes in the sand, turned in opposite directions so that they made the shape of a heart.

Noah smiled at her creations and took photos. Looking at his camera's screen, he nodded, "These look great. Definitely a nod toward a Carolina Christmas."

Panning, he frowned and shook his head.

"What is it?" Peyton asked.

"No snowman. I mean, is a Christmas photo shoot complete without a snowman?" Noah asked.

Peyton held a finger in the air and, chewing her lip, she said, "I might regret this, but I think I can do you one better."

Noah looked on with interest.

All at once, Peyton flopped on her back. Spreading her arms and legs wide, she swept them back and forth for several swipes. Laying there for a second, she tilted her head and gasped, "Help me up… carefully. Don't mess up my artwork."

Reaching as far as he could stretch, Noah grabbed Peyton's hands and helped her to her feet. Using Noah's hands as leverage, she leapt away from her creation, landing several safe feet away.

"You made a snow angel," Noah said, eyeing it through his lens.

"In the sand. So, a sand angel, technically. For you," Peyton said as she fluffed the sand out of her hair and patted off her clothes.

"One of the nicest, most sacrificial gifts anyone has ever given me," Noah said.

Peyton scowled, interpreting sarcasm.

"I'm serious. I love it!" Noah said.

Peyton nodded and picked her bucket off the sand. Handing Noah his, she said, "We're ready for the next phase of this operation. Wait here."

Noah watched as Peyton made fresh tracks through the sand back to her car to return with her arms wrapped around a storage container.

From the container, a safe distance from the rising tide, Peyton spread a blanket out on the sand. Kneeling on the edge of the blanket, she poured a few capfuls of bleach and a bottle of water into each bucket.

"Gently swirl it around," Peyton said.

"Is this how they make them so white?" Noah asked.

"Yes, if the sun didn't do it first. But these little guys tend to stink if you don't clean them and that would spoil the posthumous next phase of their lives," Peyton said.

"I see," Noah said, gently swirling his bucket.

Peyton dug a hole in the sand and poured the diluted solution out. With a towel, she began drying her sand dollars and placing them carefully back in her bucket before helping Noah with his.

With their cleaned and dried treasures, they sat back on the blanket. After rummaging once more in the plastic container, Peyton produced two pieces of balsa wood cut in the shape of donuts. Handing Noah a bottle of crafting glue, she said, "Start at the top, barely overlap with the next and fill up the circle with sand dollars."

Doing as he was told, Noah began arranging sand dollars onto the wood frame. His tongue stuck out of the corner of his mouth as he concentrated, and by the time he looked up, Peyton had completed her sand dollar wreath complete with a red bow tied to the bottom.

"Uhm, would you help me with that? I'm not so good with bows," Noah said.

"Sure." Peyton inched closer and helped Noah tie his bow. "Here you go."

Holding his wreath out in front of him framing the Atlantic Ocean, Noah admired his handiwork.

"One last finishing touch," Peyton said, digging into her container. Taking out a pair of starfish, she said, "I didn't figure we'd find any today, so I brought some just in case."

At the top of each wreath, they attached a starfish star.

Leaning back, they let their creations cure and dry as they watched the tide roll in.

"My mom and I used to do this every year. It would be our 'Christmas project day'," Peyton said, shaking her head sadly. "I miss her so much."

"I'm sorry," Noah said.

"She had a good life. I just wish she was still here," Peyton said. "This is the first year without her that I made those wreaths. I didn't have the heart to do it without her. All this talk of tradition with you around reminded me of how important traditions can be."

Noah leaned in close to Peyton. As Peyton turned her head, she saw the lighthouse flash for the first time that evening. Her eyes grew wide and she pulled her head back. "Oh, my gosh! It's almost time. Come on, we have to go!"

Gathering up their items and stowing them carefully back into the plastic bin, they hurried to her car.

Jumping in and starting it, she said, "You might want your camera handy for this."

Driving into Fort Caswell at the eastern tip of the island, they were greeted by the Light of the World Festival, an annual Christmas celebration of holiday lights displayed by the Christian retreat that occupied the eastern end of the island. At the road's end, they faced Southport directly across the confluence of the Intracoastal Waterway and the Atlantic Ocean.

The town Christmas tree began to shimmer in its multicolor lights as night fell. Soon, the houses along the waterfront row began to glow with their porch displays ablaze.

"Magnificent," Noah said, his voice nearly a whisper.

They both enjoyed the view for a moment until Peyton saw a string of cars making the loop behind them on their way to enjoy the Light of the World festival themselves.

Snapping her car into gear, she shot Noah a glance and asked, "Got time for one more stop?"

Thirteen

Peyton pulled to a stop alongside a small cottage several blocks from the water. "I just have to run in and grab something."

Dashing out of the car, Peyton ran to the front door and jabbed the lock with her key.

A simple wreath hung from the door. While tidy, the house and yard looked almost unlived in. Given that Peyton had rights and access to the magnificent family home by the water, he wondered why she stayed in the modest cottage instead.

The front door flung open and Peyton careened around the front of her car, sliding into the driver's seat. Stuffing an envelope between the seat and the center console, she smiled. "Ready? I want you to meet someone."

They hadn't driven far before Peyton pulled into a parking space.

A glance at the sign at the entrance of the lot told Noah they were at a nursing home.

Glancing at her watch, Peyton said, "If you see me running off at about this time, this is where I'm going."

Grabbing the envelope, Peyton opened the back of her car to grab one of the wreaths they had made on the beach. A quick glance told Noah that she had specifically selected the one that he had made.

"Come on!" Peyton said, looking anxious to get inside.

As she pushed through the front doors, a woman at the front desk waved at Peyton. "You're running late again."

"I know. Just give me a few minutes," Peyton said.

The woman nodded, "Just don't be tellin' no one how nice I am to you."

"It's okay, Gladys, they'd never believe me anyway," Peyton teased.

Gladys laughed. "Girl, that wit of yours is goin' to get you in a heap o' trouble one of these days!"

Peyton rushed down the hallway. As Noah moved to follow, Gladys reached across the desk with her hand like a crossing gate.

"Whoa, whoa, whoa! Where do you think you're going?" Gladys barked.

"I'm, uh…" Noah pointed toward Peyton.

"He's with me, Gladys," Peyton called, standing in front of a door near the end of the hall.

Gladys scowled, "Girl, that's gonna cost you double!"

Peyton grinned, "You know I'm good for it."

"I know you are!" Gladys said. With a wave, she said, "Go on, fella. Just mind yourself."

"Yes, ma'am," Noah said, ducking his head as he hastened down the hall.

"She rules the roost," Noah whispered as he caught up with Peyton.

"Aw, her bark is worse than her bite," Peyton said. Turning the handle, she slowly pushed the door open and called into the room, "Daddy…"

After a moment's silence, Peyton pushed the door all the way open. Again, she called out, "Daddy!"

"What… huh, yes. I'm here!" an exhausted sounding voice replied.

Peyton waved for Noah to follow.

Rushing to the ottoman, Peyton sat in front of a man who was nestled into what looked like a very comfortable lounge chair. Peyton placed her hand on the man's and settled them on the armrest together.

"How're you doin' today, Daddy?" Peyton asked.

"Oh, as well as expected," the man said. Peering around Peyton, the man looked at the television. "Well, darn. I missed it again."

Peyton swiveled in her seat to see the town of Bedford Falls celebrating with George Bailey.

"It's okay, Daddy. We can rewind it. Where do you remember leaving off?" Peyton asked.

Peyton's father frowned and said, "About the time poor ol' George hid Zuzu's petals in his pocket."

"Okay, I'll help you get it back to that spot," Peyton said. Picking up the remote, she rewound the movie to the spot where George Bailey was checking on his daughter who had caught a cold.

"*It's a Wonderful Life*. One of my favorites," Noah said.

"Daddy, I would like you to meet Noah Wilde. He is visiting Southport to share how wonderful Christmas is here," Peyton said.

Mr. James nodded a bit absently and muttered, "It is Christmas, isn't it?"

Turning to Noah, Peyton's father said, "You like *It's a Wonderful Life*, do ya? You can watch it with me."

Noah smiled. "I'd like that."

Peyton nodded and squeezed Noah's hand as he walked past and planted himself on a small couch perpendicular to the lounge chair.

"I brought something for you, Daddy," Peyton said.

"Oh?" Mr. James leaned forward.

Peyton handed him the sand dollar wreath that Noah made.

His mouth opened wide. The slightest gloss formed in his eyes and a small smile creased his lips. "This is just like the ones Mary used to make."

"Yes, Daddy. Mom and I used to make them every year. I can hang it on the door for you, if you like?" Peyton asked.

"The door? Yes, the door. Would you do that for me?" Mr. James asked.

Peyton nodded and said, "We will do it on the way out, is that okay?"

"Yes, that's okay." Mr. James nodded. He looked lost for a moment and then blinked. With a slight wrinkle of his brow, he asked, "Can we watch *It's a Wonderful Life* now?"

"Yes, Daddy. We can watch *It's a Wonderful Life* now," Peyton said, her voice soft. Moving the ottoman to sit in between her father and Noah, she leaned on her father's armrest and clasped his hand between hers.

"I have ice cream!" Mr. James announced out of the blue as he leaned forward in his seat.

"Would you like some ice cream, Daddy?" Peyton asked.

"Yes, with a drizzle of honey on it!" Mr. James brightened.

Peyton nodded, "Okay."

"I'll get it." Noah rose from his seat and started for the kitchen.

"Bowls are in the cabinet next to the sink. Might as well dish up three, this might be dinner tonight," Peyton said.

Noah did as he was told and dished up three bowls of ice cream. Two with honey drizzle and one plain. He handed the plain one to Peyton.

"I usually use chocolate syrup. I'll have to remember to stock Daddy's cabinet next time I'm here," Peyton said.

"I like honey," Noah said as he dug his spoon into his ice cream.

"You like honey?" Mr. James asked. "On your ice cream?"

"Yes, I do, sir," Noah nodded.

"And you like *It's a Wonderful Life*?" Mr. James asked.

"I do," Noah said.

"Hot dog! I like you!" Mr. James said. "You can call me Henry!"

"All right, Henry. You can call me Noah."

"Noah… like the flood," Henry said to himself as much as anyone. "No one believed Noah. But he was right!" Henry pointed a slightly crooked finger at Noah.

"Yes, sir. He was," Noah said.

"Okay, I'm gonna eat ice cream and watch *It's a Wonderful Life* now," Henry said. Leaning back in his chair, Henry zoned out to the television screen.

Noah looked at Peyton and smiled.

"He likes you," she whispered.

"I like him, too," Noah said.

Peyton split her hands to hold one of her father's and one of Noah's. "Thank you," she mouthed to Noah.

Noah shook his head. "Thank *you*."

By the time Clarence had finally received his wings, the bowls of ice cream had been emptied and cleaned. Henry was clearly tired.

"We should go," Peyton said.

Noah nodded. Getting out of his chair and kneeling next to Henry, Noah grasped his hand in his. "Mr. James… Henry… it has been a pleasure to meet you. Thank you for allowing me to stay and watch *It's a Wonderful Life* with you."

"Thank *you*." Henry squeezed Noah's hand, if feebly. "Come by and visit anytime."

"I will," Noah said.

As Noah rose, Peyton asked softly, "Would you give us a minute?"

Noah nodded and headed toward the door. Not knowing what to do, Noah affixed the sand dollar wreath to Henry's door as he waited in the hallway. Gladys rose from her seat at the front desk and craned her neck down the hallway. Noah did his best to hide in the shadow of a ficus tree.

"I can see you," Gladys called. "I don't wanna see you, so I ain't seein' you. You get me?"

Noah pressed flatter against the wall.

"You get me?" Gladys repeated.

"Yes, ma'am. I get you!" Noah half-yelled, half-whispered in a hoarse voice.

Gladys settled back in her desk chair and mumbled audibly, "All right, then."

A few moments later, the door to Henry James' room opened and Peyton squeezed through with a look back at her father. Her watery eyes made Noah's heart hurt for her.

"You okay?" Noah asked.

Peyton nodded and sniffed. "Yeah. I, uh, I need a favor. A *big* one."

"Yeah, of course," Noah said with a fervent nod.

Leading him to the empty dining room, Peyton placed the envelope in her hand onto a table and slid into a seat. Reading her intent, he sat across from her.

Sliding a stack of papers from the envelope, Peyton said with tears welling in her eyes, "I… I need you to sign something for me. I need you to be witness that Daddy recognized me. That he was in… as sound mind as he is going to be, according to his doctors."

"Sure. He was solid…" Noah said.

"I didn't want to do this. The doctor said he isn't coming back," Peyton said, full tears began streaming down her face. "But it's the season of miracles, right?"

"It is," Noah said in a soft voice as he offered a reassuring nod.

"Our attorney said we needed to sign this. I didn't want to. I put it off, maybe a little too long," Peyton said, sliding the papers across the table.

Noah looked at the title of the document. "Power of Attorney, for your parents' estate."

Peyton bobbed as tears streamed down her face.

"Of course I'll sign it for you." Noah scribbled his signature on the witness line. Sliding the papers back, he grasped Peyton's hands. "I'm sorry you have to go through this. Your dad, he's amazing. Thank you for introducing me to him."

Peyton wiped her eyes and her face as she nodded. Her voice barely audible, she said, "We should go."

Noah nodded. As they rose from their chairs, he placed an arm around her. "Whatever your dad needs, he's in good hands with his amazingly capable daughter."

"If only that were the case," Peyton choked.

"What do you mean?" Noah asked with a frown.

Before Peyton could answer, Gladys hissed, "You two best be gettin' out of here before I lose my job."

"We're going. Thank you, Gladys. You're the best," Peyton sobbed.

Gladys looked at the sadness in Peyton and melted behind her desk. "Girl, you know I got you."

Peyton nodded and pushed through the doors.

As they ambled out to Peyton's car, she said, "This has been a lot. Do you mind if I just drop you off?"

"Of course," Noah said, his voice soft. His mind reeled about what Peyton meant by wishing the house was in capable hands.

Fourteen

Noah opened his hotel door packed with cameras ready for the day. As he allowed the door to close, something caught his eye.

A sand dollar wreath hung in the center of the door, a red bow tied on the bottom, a starfish fixed to the top. The starfish appeared to be holding a note.

Pulling it free, Noah flipped open the note and read, "Noah, thank you for humoring me yesterday with one of my dearest traditions. I wanted to leave you with the winning prize for out-sand-dollaring me. You were so great with Dad last night. It was the first evening in a long while that a spark of genuine happiness appeared in his visit with you. Today is a Christmas sale day at the shop so I might be a bit tied up. Stop in the coffee shop on Moore Street. They will have your morning coffee waiting for you. With Southport Christmas cheer, Peyton."

Noah folded the note and stuffed it in his pocket. He took a moment to admire the wreath that hung on his door.

The morning was pleasant. The slightest nip in the air created a wispy layer of fog rising up from the waterways. Pulling out his camera, Noah took several photos of the morning sun shooting rays through light mist. Water birds took flight in a line directly toward him, giving him a series of amazing shots of wildlife in action.

Slinging the camera over his shoulder, he decided to walk the half mile stroll to the coffee shop. His trek toward downtown passed by Bonnet's Creek and a little marker dedicated to the "Gentleman Pirate". Noah paused to snap a photo of the marker, which shared a brief history of the pirate and his time in Southport and the inlets of the Cape Fear River.

As cars passed, the drivers would wave. The first took Noah by surprise. He turned and waved, hoping the driver would see him returning the welcoming gesture in their rearview mirror.

Shoving his hands in his pockets, he chuckled, "Small towns… kinda nice. I like it."

He didn't miss the opportunity with the next car, give a good morning wave. While it may not have been a Christmas experience per se, it was most definitely a Southport charm experience.

Pushing his way into the coffee shop, the aroma of freshly ground beans filled the air. Walking up to the counter, the barista said, "You must be Noah."

Taken aback, Noah realized by that point he shouldn't have been. With a nod, he said, "I'm Noah."

"I'm Darian. Nice to meet you. Peyton said you'd be stoppin' in and to give you whatever you wanted," the barista said.

"That was nice of her, but unnecessary," Noah said.

"She said you'd say that, too," Darian said.

Realizing there wasn't argument to be won, Noah conceded, "I'll just have a drip with room for a splash, please."

Darian studied him for a moment before saying, "It's Christmas. Sure you don't want something a bit more festive?"

"What do you recommend?" Noah asked.

"Peyton said you're a photographer. How about I make somethin' photo worthy?" the barista asked.

"Sounds good to me." Noah nodded.

"All right, it'll just be a minute," Darian said as she set to work.

Noah browsed around the little shop. It was crammed with coffee mugs and knickknacks. Most were coastal themed or Southport monikered. A large portion was dedicated to Christmas. Noah picked up a Southport Winterfest mug. Setting it on a wooden crate with the shop's tree as the background, he took a photo.

"Here ya go. Might want to use the same spot for your drink," the barista said.

Noah went and accepted the mug of coffee. The foam art Darian etched into the beverage took Noah aback.

"This is amazing," Noah said.

"You like it?" Darian asked.

"It is definitely photo worthy," Noah said as he carefully carried the concoction over the wooden crate and replaced the mug with his freshly brewed coffee. Angling his camera just right, Noah was able to capture Darian's handiwork with the lights of the Christmas tree blurred in the background.

Moving the camera away from his eye, Noah admired the Christmas tree etched into the coffee foam in a continuous swoop. What made the design truly eye catching was the adornments of little peppermint sprinkles carefully placed throughout the tree like ornaments. At the base of the tree, a chunk of chocolate floated like its trunk. At the top, a star fashioned out of a dollop of whipped cream.

"This is truly the most beautiful coffee drink I have ever had," Noah said. "Do you mind if I take your photo with it?"

Darian blushed for a moment and then leaned against the counter where Noah placed the drink. Snapping several photos as another customer pushed through the door, he thanked her.

"Just don't go tellin' everyone. I can't do that during the morning rush," Darian warned.

"I won't tell. Thank you, again," Noah said.

"You tell Peyton 'hey' when you see her," the barista said as Noah walked out onto the coffee shop porch to enjoy his morning beverage.

Sipping his Christmas Cookie Brulee latte, Noah watched the town of Southport navigate downtown as the morning sun rose higher. Despite the warm beverage, Noah was able to keep his jacket on a little longer before ultimately needing to take off the layer.

Finishing his coffee and placing his mug in the tray by the door, Noah set off to see what other surprises the coastal town had to offer him.

Noah spent his day touring other waterfront homes. Each was gorgeous on their own and beautifully decorated for Christmas. None swayed him from his top two cover contenders. Peyton's family house and Cybil's home had the look and feel he had in mind when he was given the assignment.

While reviewing his cover shot candidates, he knew something was missing. He wasn't sure what he needed, but he hoped to be able to capture it in subsequent photo shoots.

He checked his watch — it was time for him to get cleaned up for Peyton's Southport Winterfest Flotilla viewing party along with the other waterfront row homes.

He had no idea what to expect other than watching decorated boats float by. He also knew, between Peyton and the town, there was sure to be a surprise.

On the trek back to the hotel, the evening traffic brought more friendly waves from all but one vehicle. A large black truck with a throaty exhaust shot by as it blasted Noah with a wash of hot air. *That* particular driver did not wave.

Fifteen

Peyton's car was already parked outside of her family's house. Many of the waterfront owners were busy sprucing up their porches while they were getting ready for their guests.

Noah could hear a clatter of dishware emanating through the screen door of The James House. Adding to his rap on the frame of the door, Noah called out, "Knock, knock!"

Peyton peeked around the corner, her hands draped in a dishtowel she was using to polish a punchbowl. Her smile was effervescent. "Come on in! Let me set this down real quick," she said, disappearing back into the kitchen.

Pushing into the foyer, Noah was met by Peyton scurrying back out to greet him. Yanking on a string, she loosened an apron that was fashioned around her neck and pulled it over her head, tossing it on the closest chair.

Fluffing her hair after it had been pulled through the apron loop, Peyton stopped just short of Noah. An almost nervous smile crossed her face as she looked into Noah's eyes. "Thank you again for being so wonderful last night. It meant a lot to me. And I think, to my dad, as well," she said.

Noah smiled, "I enjoyed every bit of it, especially meeting your father."

"I wish… I wish he had gotten a chance to meet you… before," Peyton said.

"I'm glad to have met him just the same. There were moments when I could see the same sparkle in his eyes that I see in yours," Noah said.

Peyton let out a breath and subconsciously brought a hand to her chest. "You say the most interesting things, Mr. Noah Wilde," she said, taking a step closer to Noah so that their toes touched.

Her chest rose and fell as she placed her hands on Noah's arms and started to pull him closer.

Heavy footfalls and a loud knock at Peyton's door shattered the moment. Peyton let go of Noah's arms and peered around him to see Ty fighting the blur the screen made to steal a peek into the house.

Seeing Peyton come into view and Noah turn to face him, Ty's eyes scrunched into a scowl.

Peyton sighed as she opened the screen door and asked, "Ty, what are you doin' here?"

"I came to give you this." Ty handed Peyton a bouquet of greenery wrapped in a pretty red bow. With a grin, he stepped close, holding the bouquet in the air as he announced proudly, "It's mistletoe!"

Peyton scowled, "That's holly, but thank you just the same." Taking a step away from the house's entrance, her eyes darted up and she took a concerted step away from the mark her eyes had targeted. "Besides, I already have mistletoe."

Ty frowned and set the bundle of holly leaves with their deep red berries on a table. "What I really came by for was to ask you one more time to join me tonight. My boat needs you. *I* need you."

"Ty," Peyton said while letting out a deep breath. "That ship has literally sailed. I'm sorry."

Ty's eyes glanced from Peyton to Noah, who paced around the inside of the foyer, trying to be inconspicuous.

"Well, the boat hasn't shipped by for *me*," Ty snapped.

"It's time, Ty," Peyton said, her voice soft but firm. "I'll wave at you from the porch with my guests. I look forward to seeing what you've done this year."

"Yeah." Ty nodded, his chin on chest as he turned to descend the steps. His shoulders were slumped as he walked down the James House walkway and through the well-functioning gate. Starting his truck, he accelerated hard, making his tires chirp as he pulled away.

Peyton stood for a moment as she watched Ty leave. With a breath, she turned and walked back inside the house.

"I'm sorry about that," Peyton said in exasperation, a hand to her forehead.

"I can… I can leave…" Noah started.

Peyton scowled and leaned her head into Noah's chest. "You aren't going anywhere."

Noah put his arms around Peyton as she lifted her chin to look at him. Slowly, they began to melt toward one another.

Knock, knock, knock.

The pair froze before slowly turning together with tiny steps to see Mabel standing at the screen door, a glass dish in her hands.

Cocking her head, Peyton opened the door. Before she could welcome her in, Mabel strode through and into the foyer.

Looking at Noah, Mabel offered a sly grin and said, "Hello, Mr. Wilde."

"Hello, Mabel," Noah said.

"Peyton, I am so sorry for barging in like this, but it is a Winterfest Flotilla emergency!" Mabel said as she made her way to the kitchen. "Jessica Crandall's oven died, and well, she had this casserole for the viewing party that barely got to room temp. I thought you wouldn't mind if borrowed your oven."

Peyton shot Noah a quick glance and shrugged, "Not at all, Mabel. Help yourself. The oven should be warm; it was just at three-hundred and fifty degrees for my cookies."

"Oh, sugar cookies. They are adorable. My goodness, they're sand dollars!" Mabel squealed from the kitchen.

Peyton blushed as she looked at Noah and said, "It was a surprise for you in honor of our foraging yesterday."

"I love it. I can't wait to see them," Noah said.

Mabel popped into the living room wiping her hands together, "Well, that's that. I have a timer set for thirty minutes, would you or that handsome young fella bring the dish over to Jessica's when it's ready?"

"Sure, Mabel. Not a problem." Peyton nodded.

"Carry on, you two!" Mabel said as she strode through the screen door, waving a hand over her shoulder. "Act as though I were never here!"

Noah and Peyton looked at each other and laughed.

"I do have a bit to do before the flotilla gets underway. Would you mind helping me?" Peyton asked.

"Not sure if it will be in my wheelhouse, but I'll do my best," Noah said.

"How are you at making cocktails? I was planning on setting out pitchers and letting folks pour their own. I have cookies to decorate and hot crab dip to toss in once Mrs. Crandall's casserole is done."

"I can do that. Anything specific?" Noah asked.

"Mom…" Peyton swallowed hard for a moment and then continued, "Mom used those cards I have set out in front of the pitchers. They were my grandmother's recipes and who knows whose before that."

"I can follow a recipe." Noah nodded.

"Careful with the measurements, I think Grandma nudged them a bit strong," Peyton said.

"Your family sounds like you really came together to celebrate," Noah said as he read the first card.

"Yeah. I was blessed. I *am* blessed," Peyton said. She paused and looked over her shoulder. "How about you? You haven't told me much about your family."

Noah shrugged. "Like I said when we met, my family was kind of like nomads. We hit all four corners of the country, my relatives lived somewhere in the middle. If it's possible to be close and not close all at the same time, that would be us. We love each other. We enjoy each other when we get back together, we just all live such different lives."

"You have siblings?" Peyton asked.

"One of each. Both older. I also have a niece and a couple of nephews," Noah said.

"You don't do holidays together?" Peyton asked.

"Sometimes. As my siblings' families grew, they separated to share Christmas with their in-laws quite a bit. I think we did more together when Grandpa was still alive. He was kind of the foundation for us," Noah said. "And of course, working for the magazine, I'm often on assignment during holidays."

"What about your parents?" Peyton asked.

"They rotate between my brother's and sister's to have Christmas with their grandchildren. When stars align and my parents host, I join them if I'm not doing a piece for Coastal Charm," Noah said.

"Must be hard, being away for Christmas like that," Peyton said as she sprinkled a layer of cheese on top of her dip.

"It is. I guess my assignments for the magazine keep me focused. I mean, the articles do put me in some incredible places to spend the holidays," Noah said.

"But holidays aren't the places. It's the people," Peyton said before covering her mouth. "I… I'm sorry. That was insensitive."

"It's okay. And you're right. If there is anything Southport… and you have taught me, it's that holidays are special because of the people around you, not the picture-postcard scenery," Noah said. Changing the subject, he waved the recipe card in the air, "So, if I'm to cut back on this recipe…"

"Ahh, I'm sure Grandma had a reason for her measurements. We should listen to our elders," Peyton said with a laugh.

"Copy that," Noah said as he poured what he thought was a handsome amount of gin into a pitcher.

By the time he had the last pitcher filled and garnished with the recommended stalk of herbs or slices of fruit, Peyton's oven timer chimed.

"Ugh, I've got to get this crab dip in. I should have done it right after the casserole, I just got… distracted…" Peyton called from the kitchen.

"I got it. Just point me in the right direction," Noah said.

"The Crandalls are two houses down in the opposite direction from Cybil's. Her gate is probably already open. Just go on in," Peyton said. As Noah appeared in the kitchen, she nodded. "There are potholders in that drawer."

Finding a set of potholders with Santa on one hand and Mrs. Claus on the other, Noah opened the oven door and pulled out the casserole that Mabel had brought over.

As he passed by, Peyton darted up to him kissed him on the cheek, "You're pretty incredible… for a Yankee."

"I'm not a…" Noah started.

"Uh, uh, you need to get over there before it gets cold." Peyton grinned.

"Hmm," Noah grunted.

Opening the screen door with his elbow and the admittedly well-functioning gate latch with his foot, Noah meandered two houses down as he was instructed. There was considerable chatter coming from inside the house, making Noah's "hellos" unheard.

As he walked up the porch, he heard Peyton's name.

"Oh, the boy is just lovely, it's just… what's the point?"

"You're right. You know Ty is still in love with that girl and he ain't goin' nowhere."

"What good is a trade-up if it doesn't last?"

"Girls, you are missing the point. This is the season of miracles and if anyone in Southport could use one, it's Peyton. Maybe that stranger is that miracle."

"I don't know, Mabel. He's gonna run off back to New York or wherever he's from. And then what is poor Peyton left with?"

Noah's head drooped as he stood by the screen door. When there was a pause in the conversation, he cleared his throat.

"My stars, it's Noah everyone!" Mabel rushed to open the door and welcome Noah into the Crandalls' house. "We were just talking about what a delight it is to have you in Southport for the holidays and now here you are with Jessica's casserole. Thank you so much!"

"My pleasure." Noah nodded and turned on his heel. "I hope you all enjoy the show. The, uh, the flotilla, I mean."

"You too, hon. Tell that Peyton we'll make our rounds after the show starts," Mabel said.

"I will," Noah said, pushing through the door.

The words he heard, the truth that he had to admit was behind some of them, made his feet feel like they were stuck in cement. He trudged back to Peyton's house with a heavy heart. Shaking his head, he muttered to himself, "What *are* you doing?"

"Hey!" a voice called. "You gonna walk around talkin' to yourself or are you gonna come in?"

Noah looked up to see Peyton's smiling face teasing him from the porch.

"Just here to take some photos, ma'am," Noah said, his heart feeling heavy with the truth in his words.

"Like I said, some things you can't get through a camera lens, mister. You have to *experience* them," Peyton said. "Come on. It's almost showtime!"

Sixteen

Noah was introduced to a stream of guests that milled about. Some bounced from house to house and porch to porch while others selected one location to camp in to watch the boat parade and visit with neighbors.

The hosts and hostesses set an array of treats and beverages on tables. Chairs, rockers and porch swings were claimed while some guests preferred to lean against the porch rails as they looked out at the water.

Peyton scurried about making sure everyone had a plate and Noah helped keep their drinks topped off as the main event of the evening began its journey from the Yacht Basin to the channel marker close to Noah's hotel and looping back again along the waterfront.

"Here it is!" one woman said with a burst of excitement.

The crowd next door on Cybil's porch began to cheer and the excited applause cascaded down the row of porches almost like the wave at a sports arena.

Peyton used the attention focused on the water to pause her hostess duties and slide in next to Noah, who had wedged himself into the far corner of her porch. Soon, light displays from boats began to come into view. The flotilla moved slow and steady, allowing the viewers to take in the colorful displays. A tidy gap between vessels kept the boats safe and the lighted decor from bleeding into one another.

Noah held up his camera and aimed it down the waterway, catching a string of lit boats and the reflections of their displays dancing off the water.

Each boat had its own theme. Some were simple, with lights strung along the rails and around the pilot houses. Some had wreaths on the doors, some had Christmas trees mounted inside the cabin, on the roof or fashioned on deck. One boat had their family dog wrapped in battery-powered lights happily wagging its tail in the bow of the boat, pointing the way.

Other boat owners took the mission to heart clearly putting a lot of time and effort into decorating their vessels. One had a lighted

Santa on the rails along the stern with eight reindeer driving his sleigh with a motion light display to make it look like the deer were running. Another had a pirate theme with a crew of swashbucklers handing out presents to one another instead of pillaging. All but the captain had swapped their hats and bandanas for Santa hats.

One boat in particular caught Peyton's eyes. The light display and music blasted from the vessel's speakers made her sigh. The entire boat was dressed in blue lights from bow to stern, including the tall masts that held the fishing nets.

A playlist made up completely of different artists singing "Blue Christmas" wailed across the water.

"Nice, Ty," Peyton grumbled.

"Gotta give the guy credit for committing to the theme," Noah whispered.

"No, no, I don't. Commitment must be a new idea he's trying on," Peyton said. "I'm not so sure it fits."

As the boat passed by, the captain, Ty Bates, looked directly at the James House, a floor-mounted light casting him entirely in blue.

Noah couldn't resist a good photo op even though it was met with a swat and a huff from Peyton.

A few boats later, the entire crowd was on its feet. From porch to porch, they watched as the final boat made its pass. Seated up high on a flying bridge towering over the top of a sleek boat, Santa himself waved to all on land, especially the school kids that had been lined up along the park's seawall to not only enjoy the boat parade, but to cast their votes for favorite displays as they passed by.

Making the loop at the easterly channel marker, the flotilla made its second pass with most porch guests refilling their plates and cups. Peyton and Noah ensured the guests of the James House were well tended to.

Peyton didn't seem to have a strong desire to watch the flotilla's second appearance and even less desire to hear another rendition of Blue Christmas. She seemed to over-focus on her guests and made several trips to the kitchen to refill platters that were unlikely to be needed.

Noah watched Peyton, snapping a quick photo of her in the glow of her porch's Christmas lights as she cared for her guests, especially the more senior ones. He smiled. Not knowing her mother or grandmother, he imagined them, in clothes from different eras, doing the exact same thing for flotillas long past.

Being caught with his lens pointed in her direction and receiving a scowl from Peyton, Noah turned his camera's attention back to the flotilla, the porches of onlookers and the crowd that had assembled near the water.

Once Santa had passed by for the second time, the porch parties began to break up. Guests said their goodbyes, and a few meandered from neighboring porches to say a quick greeting before continuing down the sidewalk.

As the crowd on the James House porch dwindled, Peyton and Noah began collecting the dishes and glassware in the glow of the Christmas lights. As they reached for the same glass, their hands grazed one another.

Peyton looked up and smiled. "Thank you for your help. I didn't mean for you to have to play host."

"It's all right. It was fun. I think everyone had a good time," Noah said.

The last straggling guest stood up from their chair and walked toward the porch steps, "It *was* a good time. The old-fashioned pitcher could have used a touch more bourbon, but an otherwise lovely evening."

"*You?*" Peyton gasped, nearly dropping the plates in her hand. "What are you doing here?"

The man in a well-tailored suit grinned. "Just checking on my investment. Magnificent view, by the way."

Taking a step down, he called out over his shoulder, "Good night, y'all. Make sure you lock up this time, Ms. James. Don't want looters rifling through your… I mean, *my* house."

Sliding his hands in his pockets, the man sauntered away whistling "Jingle Bells" and disappeared down the sidewalk.

Peyton set her plates down, her hands trembling.

Noah squared up with Peyton, setting down the glasses he was toting back to the kitchen.

"What did he mean by that? *His* house?" Noah asked.

Peyton looked at the water, her eyes oscillating between angry, sad and defiant. The flash of the Oak Island Lighthouse danced in the distance.

"Peyton, who was that man?" Noah asked.

Peyton said, "He's a real estate attorney out of Charlotte. He claims my family has no actual deed to the James House. He's forcing a sale since I can't prove ownership."

"What do you mean? This is a historic house," Noah pressed.

"A historic house with no proof of its lineage," Peyton said.

They both looked out at the water.

"I'll help you," Noah said suddenly, though he had no idea how to hold to his words.

"How? I've torn the house apart, searching for some kind of evidence. Noah, I can't even prove my family *existed*. The James House was supposed to be my great, great, great-grandfather's house. Our family records seem to start with my grandfather," Peyton said.

"There has to be some way to fix this. I mean, your family should have rights just for the time you've lived here and taken care of the James House. It's *named* after your family," Noah said.

Peyton's deep breath turned into a choked sob. "The house has been in my care for only a few months and it's already at risk of being taken away from the family. It's all that I have left."

Noah wrapped his arms around Peyton. At first, she wriggled in frustration before giving into a full cry, burrowing into Noah's chest.

"We'll fix this," he whispered.

When Peyton's breathing returned to normal, she pulled back, and the meek look on her face turned into a scowl. "The moment Daddy went into the nursing home, that guy, Chauncey Craven shows up. He has a stack of court papers two inches thick on why there is no claim to the house. Daddy didn't have an attorney. No papers regarding administering the James House if he isn't able to himself. No will…" Peyton said, the thought of her father needing a will nearly broke her.

With a sniff, she said, "It's like Craven was ready and waiting."

"Taking advantage of your father being ill." Noah shook his head.

"I got an attorney. He said I couldn't even represent the family without a power of attorney signed by my dad," Peyton said.

"The document I witnessed the other night," Noah said.

"Yes. He said even *with* that, if I don't find proof that my family owns the James House, there is an old provision that it would become the state's and a sale could be forced. He said the easiest way to protect the James House and my family's legacy is to buy it so that we can have a recorded deed. Buy a home we *already* own! I couldn't afford a home a tenth of today's prices on Southport waterfront," Peyton said.

"I can't help you there, but I can dig into the history. See what I can find," Noah said.

"I have searched *everywhere*," Peyton said.

"Maybe a fresh pair of eyes will help." Noah placed a comforting hand on her back.

Wiping her tears, Peyton offered a feeble nod.

"I'm sorry you have to see me like this. All the drama," Peyton said.

Noah took a stride forward and planted a solid kiss on Peyton's forehead.

"I am grateful to get to know you this Christmas," he said.

Peyton wrapped her arms around Noah and leaned her head on his chest.

Seventeen

Noah awoke early. His fitful sleep left him yearning for coffee, and a lot of it. Peyton's dilemma with the James House kept running through his head.

The moment he was back in his hotel room after the Winterfest Flotilla, he was poring over web searches, real estate case law and tracing as much history on the James family as he could find.

His reading of laws regarding unrecorded deeds did little to help him sleep, as the precedent was not in Peyton's favor. With the rising sun peeking over the barrier islands, Noah was eager to get to work.

Visiting the local coffee shop, he hastily grabbed his liquid breakfast and found a quiet corner to work. The first item on his list was calling the *Coastal Charm Magazine* historian.

After he explained Peyton's situation, the historian agreed to help. Next on his agenda was walking across the street to the Southport Maritime Museum. Following the gravel walkway that wrapped around the museum and led to a second historical center, Noah pushed his way into the Garrison House, a grand, brick and columned colonial building that had been a central hub for Fort Johnston and now a museum dedicated to the fort and the town's history.

Mabel looked up from the reception desk she was tidying and smiled. "Well, if it isn't Mr. Wilde. Thank you for bringing over Mrs. Crandall's casserole last night. You should have stayed for a bite yourself."

"I wanted to help Peyton with her viewing party. It seemed like she had her hands full," Noah said.

"You are so kind," Mabel said. "So, what brings you in for this visit? Want to learn more about the town's history?"

"I do," Noah nodded.

"Southport, then Smithville, and Fort Johnston were key hubs for both the maritime trade and military defense. While the fort was initially built by the British in 1749 to defend against the French and the Spanish, the start of the Revolutionary War spurred the patriots to burn the fort down. Recommissioned by George

Washington and the first Congress, the site became pivotal in the Civil War. You heard of the Blockade Runners? They were fortified cargo ships used to slip past Union vessels that tried to block the waterways.

Anyway, over the years, the fort served as a meeting place for the citizens of Southport. Military parades, the North Carolina Fourth of July Festival, Christmas galas… this place was the center of much of Southport's past. It was also where the notorious 'Gentleman Pirate' Stede Bonnet was captured after being double—crossed by Blackbeard himself," Mabel said, pride oozing from her voice as she shared the story.

"It sounds like this sweet little town has seen its share of adventure as well," Noah said. With a slight squint in his eyes, he asked, "What do you know about the James House and how it came about for the James family?"

"Well, their story seems to begin after the Revolutionary War in 1801, when the house was built. Thomas James, Peyton's great, great, great grandfather, was the initial owner. The house was presented by Benjamin Smith himself, a Revolutionary War soldier and governor of North Carolina. Southport was Smithville, once upon a time, named after Benjamin. So, no one questioned him giving Thomas James the James House and the piece of property it sat on," Mabel said.

Noah leaned forward with interest. "So… the James family has a clear claim to their long- time home."

Mabel winced. "Records weren't great back then and over time, they just get even muddier. Sometime in the early 1900s, Peyton's great-grandfather had to enter a plea to the court to receive a title. The title was given with a contestation clause due to the lack of records. If the judge certified a deed at that time, that would be the most likely record of true ownership."

"Where would I find evidence of that deed?" Noah asked.

"If it was recorded, it would be in county records," Mabel said, and frowned. "Why are you asking?"

"Just trying to deliver Peyton an early Christmas present," Noah said.

"Hmm." Mabel studied the photojournalist. "If I think of anything or dig anything up, I'll let you know."

"Thank you, Mabel," Noah said as his phone buzzed. Stepping out of the Fort Johnston Museum, Noah answered. His eyes swept over the wide lawn that overlooked the water. Neat little rows of Adirondack chairs awaited guests to pay vigil over the sea.

"Vivian, thanks for getting back to me," Noah said, greeting the *Coastal Charm Magazine* historian's call.

"I'm not sure if I'm delivering the news you want to hear, Noah. That attorney's contestation claim has legal merit. If there wasn't a deed recorded, a buyer in good faith can purchase the home. It is an ugly process, but he being a real estate attorney, I'd bet his hooks into the property are solid. Maybe you should exclude that house from the article? We don't want our Christmas piece embroiled in a controversy," the historian said. "I'm sorry, Noah."

"Thanks for looking into it for me," Noah said as he ended the call and slipped his phone back into his pocket. He looked off over the water, his heart sinking into his stomach.

Before he could contemplate his next step, his phone buzzed again.

"What are you doing right now?" Peyton's voice asked through his earpiece.

"Just… working on my article," Noah said.

"Where are you at? Can I come by and pick you up?" Peyton asked.

Noah hesitated. The news from the historian had soured his mood and his mind churned over what he could do next to help Peyton.

"Come on. I need a mood changer, and I promise, I have just the thing," Peyton said.

Noah figured if Peyton could put a cheery spin on the day, then so could he. "Yeah, of course. I'm at the Maritime Museum."

"Perfect! We'll make our first stop downtown. See you in a few!"

Noah leaned against the back of one of the Adirondack chairs lined across Fort Johnston's lawn and chuckled. There was an infectiousness to that woman that he struggled to resist. Her ability to lean into adversity and still smile, still be warm and charming… it was a trait he had not seen before.

Peyton pulled to a stop in front of the Southport Maritime Museum. Noah rose from the bench he had been sitting on and watching a pair of squirrels bicker.

"Ready for another Christmas adventure?" Peyton asked.

"Absolutely," Noah said, falling in stride next to her along the sidewalk. "What's today's mission?"

"I call it… Operation Christmas Joy," Peyton said.

"Well, you're pretty good at that," Noah said.

Peyton smiled. "This is bringing joy to those who really need it."

"Sounds like a worthy mission," Noah said.

Crossing the road, they walked into Bullfrog Corner. A freshly printed sign declared that the store was the winner of the Winterfest Storefront Showcase for their window displays.

"We must have come to the right place," Noah said.

Entering the store, they were greeted with Christmas carols being played through the store's speakers. A Christmas tree was the centerpiece of a well-decorated store.

Toys, games and books littered the shelves and walkways. In the front of the store was a section dedicated to North Carolina. Books and shirts about Southport, pirates, lighthouses and just about anything else you wanted to learn about the state and the coastal region.

"We need toys," Peyton said as she perused the aisles.

"Who are we buying the toys for, or is that a mystery?" Noah asked.

"The Village Shoppes is throwing a party for foster children and their families. We started it last year and are hoping to make it an annual tradition," Peyton said.

Noah picked up a stuffed dolphin and inspected it. "Boys? Girls? What ages?"

"Yes. All of those." Peyton giggled. "We need a pretty broad range of toys. Almost every age. I need to buy thirty of them."

"Wow. That's a big order." Noah flexed his fingers together. "Let's get to work!"

Working side by side, they walked each aisle. Noah fiddled with a sea turtle that was wrapped in a rescue tarp. "Look, they get to learn about sea turtle rescue and a portion of the proceeds go to a sea turtle rescue fund."

"They have manatees and dolphins, too. Let's get one of each," Peyton said as she moved along the aisle.

Peyton winced as something grabbed her arm. Turning, she found Noah holding a hungry shark. With a grin, he pulled a trigger that made the shark's mouth open and close. Grabbing a nearby alligator with the same function, she parried and snapped back at Noah.

Plunking a pair of hats off the shelf, she jumped and put one on Noah's head before pulling one on her own.

"Santa hats, good idea," Noah approved.

His eyes went large as he made a beeline toward a display. Picking up a toy, he began pressing the buttons. A burst of air propelled a ring through a clear plastic tank of water. "I used to have these when I was a kid," he said.

"That's 'cause you're in the classic section," Peyton said.

"Classic? How can it be classic if I had one as a kid?" Noah twisted his face.

Peyton laughed, "Tell me about it. I had one of these Real-Life Susie Dolls. You'd feed a bottle you filled with water. A few minutes later, you'd get the joy of changing her diaper."

"Sounds more like work than play," Noah said.

"I loved it," Peyton said, studying the doll. "Mine even wore the same dress."

"Get it. Maybe it will bring the same joy to someone else it brought to you," Noah said.

Peyton nodded as she placed the doll in the basket.

Turning a mini-tabletop air hockey game on, Noah flicked a paddle toward Peyton. "Winner gets to choose dinner. I mean, if you're available for dinner."

"I'm available for dinner." Peyton giggled. "You like vegetarian?"

"Oh, no. *Now* it's on," Noah slid his slider into the puck and sent it past Peyton's paddle.

"It's like that, is it?" Peyton rolled up her sleeves. With an angled shot, she sent the puck off the side, just bouncing off Noah's paddle into the goal.

"One to one. This is serious. I am *not* eating tofu today." Noah sent the puck across the board. At first, Peyton caught it but as she moved her paddle, the puck fell into the goal.

"You win!" Peyton smiled. "I'm glad, too. I don't like tofu either."

"We're getting this, right?" Noah asked.

"Oh, yeah. Get that Connect Four and Toss-Across too," Peyton said.

"Look at you going traditional," Noah teased.

"I like to think of it as nostalgic," Peyton said.

Tilting his head, Noah said, "That is why I like traditional. It triggers memories from the past. A simpler time. Happy."

With their baskets full, they made their way to check out. Peyton asked, "You're going to join us, aren't you?"

"I'm invited?"

"I may put you to work, but yeah. You're invited," Peyton said.

The store manager plunked four boxes of candy canes on the counter, "All these toys are for the foster kid event, right? These are on the house."

"Thank you, Deb!" Peyton said.

"Let me know if there is anything else you need," Deb said.

Peyton looked thoughtful for a moment, "We could use some wrapping paper. We had some donated, but it hasn't arrived yet."

"Yeah, sure. Pick some out right over there," Deb pointed toward a display of tubes of wrapping paper.

"Reindeer, the North Pole, bears ice skating and gingerbread men," Noah called out.

"Take one of each. Just post a good word about the shop online," the store manager said.

"Thanks, Deb. You can come out, too, if you want," Peyton said.

"Leave the store this close to Christmas? I wish I could. Post photos," Deb said with a smile.

"I will. Merry Christmas, Deb!" Peyton said as she and Noah gathered up as many packages as they could carry.

Eighteen

On their way back to the Southport Village Shoppes, a call came in over Peyton's dashboard. The caller ID read "Edward J. Milton, Esquire".

Peyton studied the call for a moment and smashed the red decline button on the console with her finger.

"No time for bad vibes today," Peyton said, almost to herself as much as anyone.

"It could be important." Noah winced.

"Not as important as the kids who are coming to celebrate Christmas," Peyton said.

Noah nodded.

Pulling up as close to her shop as she could, Peyton parked her car. Seeing them arrive with arm loads of toys, Krista leaned out of her coffee shop, "Looks like I need to brew a fresh batch of coffee stat!"

Jolene burst through the doors of her bakery. "I've got snacks!"

"All right, we are going to have an old-fashioned wrapping party!" Peyton laughed as she set several bags onto a series of folding tables they had set out in the courtyard.

With all of the toys laid out and several wrapping stations set up, the middle of the Village Shoppes started to look like Santa's workshop in the final days before Christmas. Paper, ribbon and bows seemed to whirl in the air as presents were neatly wrapped.

An assembly line of gift preparations began to take shape. While the ladies wrapped presents, Noah would grab the completed packages and set them under the tree that had been decorated and placed next to Santa's throne.

They had scarcely finished the last presents when vans and cars began arriving. The wrapping stations were hastily replaced with cocoa, cider and eggnog. Next to the beverages, Christmas cookies and cakes lined festive trays. A bowl of chocolates was ringed with candy canes and added to the table just as foster parents and volunteers escorted the children into the Village's courtyard.

In between trips delivering beverages from her coffee shop, Krista received a phone call. Her face showed she was clearly in a panic, and she shot Peyton a desperate look. With a frantic wave, she beckoned her friend over.

Noah watched their exchange as he snapped a few photographs of the event and spoke to the foster coordinator for permission to use non-identifiable photographs of the event. He didn't like the expression on Peyton's face as she made a beeline across the courtyard toward him.

"Hey, Noah…" Peyton wore a coy smile as she rocked back and forth. In a whisper, she leaned in, "Uhm, our Santa seems to have thrown out his back. Poor guy can't even let out a Ho-ho-ho without receiving a shockwave of pain. Is there any way that you could, you know, play the big guy?"

Noah patted his belly. "I'm not sure if I'm the right person for the job. The kids might notice."

"True, you'd be the most fit Santa I ever met. The costume makes up for that. Plenty of padding options. Hand out candy canes. Chat with some kiddos. It'll be fun," Peyton said.

Noah raised a brow.

Peyton smiled. "Come on. Do it for the kids. Do it for yourself and the article. Talk about experiencing the joy of Christmas. I mean, you'd be Santa. What do you think? Put the suit on. Give those kids some joy, Noah."

Noah looked flustered. Peyton's deliberate flurry of words didn't allow him to slip in any form of a protest.

With a shake of his head, Noah let out a sigh and said, "Where's the suit?"

Peyton broke into a wide grin as she nodded across the courtyard to Krista's coffee shop and beckoned with her finger. "Krista has it in the back of the coffee shop. Go get 'em, Santa!"

Peyton gave Noah a swat as he reluctantly trudged across the courtyard. As he headed toward the coffee shop, he was escorted by Krista, who joined him and quickened the pace in a light jog.

"You are a life saver!" Krista said as they climbed the steps to her coffee shop.

"For the kids," Noah said, his voice almost robotic.

Opening the door to her small office, the coffee shop owner said, "There it is. Don't worry, fresh from the cleaners. You'll do great!"

"Thanks!" Noah said, giving the suit a reluctant once over.

"See ya outside, Santa!" Krista said, her smile nearly audible in her words.

Glad that the suit could fit over his clothes, Noah only had to swap out his shoes for boots. Slipping on the jacket, he found the padding in three sizes. According to the paper that came with the suit, the smaller you were, the higher the level of padding you were to wear.

After sliding on the beard and glasses, the final touch was Santa's hat and white gloves.

"What have I gotten myself into?" Noah asked himself as he glanced in the mirror. With a deep breath, he mumbled, "Here goes not ruining a bunch of kids' Christmas!"

Walking through the coffee shop, he flung open the screen door and stepped out onto the porch. The courtyard had been abuzz with excited children enjoying sugar cookies and cocoa.

"Look, it's Santa Claus!" a tiny voice said.

Noah saw a little girl with freckles and red hair tied into a ponytail looking up at him with wide eyes.

The children froze. Turning, they stared at the man in the fur-lined red suit. Suddenly, the chatter in the courtyard stopped. All eyes were on Noah.

"Uh… Ho, ho, ho!" Noah bellowed. As he looked out onto the crowd, he called, "Hello, everybody! Look who we have here."

With pointed fingers highlighting each child he could see, Noah said, "You've been good. You've been good and you've been good. Ho, ho, ho. I've never seen so many wonderful children in one spot."

Peyton stifled a giggle and pointed to the chair by the tree.

"Right. Who would like to tell Santa what you want for Christmas this year?" Noah asked as he made his way down the porch steps and to the makeshift throne. "Come on. Get in a line. Who's first?"

The little girl who saw Noah first raised her hand, her big green eyes never blinking.

"Hello…" Noah started. Looking up, he saw an adult behind the kids silently mouthing a name. "Lucy. Yes, come on up, Lucy!"

Lucy walked slowly up to Noah and gasped, "You know my name?"

"Ho, ho, of course I do," Noah said. Accepting Lucy's wide arms, he picked her up onto his lap. "Hello, Lucy. What would you like for Christmas this year?"

"I… I want a home for Christmas, Santa," Lucy said.

Noah looked into the little girl's eyes. "I know, Lucy. I've been hoping for that, too. It isn't something I can bring you directly, but I have the most talented elves that are certainly trying."

"Thank you, Santa," Lucy said.

"Is there a toy that you would like this year, Lucy?" Noah asked.

"A puppy dog!" Lucy said. "It doesn't have to be a real one."

"A puppy dog," Noah said in an extra loud voice. "Let me see…"

Peyton handed Noah a package.

"Here you go, Lucy," Noah said.

The little girl inspected her present.

"Don't, uh… don't stop hoping, Lucy. It may not be tomorrow, it may not be Christmas but keep hoping. Your family will find you," Noah said.

"Thank you, Santa," Lucy said, giving Noah a hug.

"Merry Christmas, Lucy."

"Merry Christmas, Santa."

Noah lifted Lucy and gently set her down. As he picked the next child up and sat them on his lap, he glanced at Lucy as she carefully ripped the wrapping off her present. Her eyes went wide, and she squealed as she squeezed her gift tight to her chest. "A puppy! Thank you, Santa!"

Turning his attention to the child in his lap, he said, "Hello, Michael."

Twenty-nine children and twenty-nine hugs later, Peyton stood in front of Noah. "Children, let's give Santa a big round of applause. He came a long way to visit with you today. Let's show him how much we appreciate him!"

The children cheered.

"We are going to let Santa go back to the North Pole. He still has lots to do before Christmas Eve!" Peyton said.

"Bye, children!" Noah waved.

"Bye, Santa!" the kids said in a chorus.

Lucy broke from the crowd and darted across the courtyard. Wrapping her arms around Noah's leg, she looked up and said, "I love you, Santa."

Noah froze. Looking down, he felt his eyes water as he smiled through his puffy white beard. "I love you, too, Lucy."

Lucy's foster mother touched Lucy's shoulder. "Come on, Lucy. We need to let Santa finish his work."

Lucy nodded. Her foster mom mouthed "thank you" to Noah.

Noah nodded as he gave a final wave to the children and disappeared into the coffee shop. Once out of view, he removed his hat and beard and leaned against a counter. Wiping his face, he stared at the ceiling. His heart felt a strange volume of weight. It wasn't sad, it was hopeful. But it was heavy.

The screen door screeched open.

Looking up, Noah saw Peyton standing in the doorway.

"Now *that* was Christmas!" Peyton beamed.

"That was the hardest, most wonderful thing I have ever done. I probably messed up kids' minds, I don't know," Noah said, shaking his head.

"You were wonderful," Peyton said. "Best Santa we have ever had."

"You've only had one other," Noah said.

"Yeah, well, don't tell Frank what I said. He loves playing Santa." Peyton laughed. Her face sobered and she said, "You spent time with the kids in ways that they don't often get. Sure, we couldn't give each child the present that they specifically asked for, but we made it work pretty good."

"We did," Noah said with a nod.

Peyton cocked her head at Noah's sullen mood.

"You made their day. Their season. For some of them, probably their year," she said, walking up to Noah.

Resting her wrists on his shoulders, she said, "You were the most genuine, the most caring, the most *handsome* Santa I have ever met."

Noah picked up the beard. "Want me to put this back on?"

"No. I like *this* version of Santa," Peyton said.

"I could wear it to dinner. I mean, you called me handsome. I'll take it," Noah teased.

"The man under the suit and the fluffy beard. That's what made this Santa so handsome," Peyton said.

Leaning close, her lips had just brushed Noah's when the screen door screeched open.

Krista stumbled as she tried hard to put on the brakes. "Sorry, guys. Ms. McKenzie wanted to see you to thank you for helping to put this on, Peyton. I can tell her you're busy with Santa."

Cocking her head, Krista wrinkled her nose. "I'm sorry, that did *not* come out right!"

Peyton laughed, "It's okay. I'm coming. Get changed, Santa! I'm taking you out for a well-deserved, carnivore-pleasing meal tonight!"

Nineteen

Noah and Peyton helped clean up after the foster event. Finding a spot looking over the water, they ate an early dinner and clinked holiday beverages together.

The town tree, the Oak Island Lighthouse and all the Christmas lights strung from the houses along the waterfront row were aglow as they strolled along the sea wall.

"Thank you, you really didn't have to buy dinner," Noah said.

"You won our air hockey tournament fair and square. Besides, you saved the day, Mr. Kringle." Peyton nudged Noah before slipping her arm into his.

"As you have taught me time and time again on this trip, some things you just have to experience. There are things that might not show up in the photos or even in the article, but I'll carry them with me," Noah said. He glanced out at the water. His heart was flipped upside down and he didn't understand why.

"Well, Southport, especially Southport at Christmas, has a way of growin' on you," Peyton said.

"It's not just the town," Noah said, wishing he could reel the words back in.

"Really. What else is growin' on you? White fluffy beards? Cybil? Warmer-than-usual Christmases?" Peyton teased.

"Yeah, *those* things," Noah said and continued to stare at the water.

"I can see about getting you that beard…" Peyton giggled. Her phone buzzed in her pocket. Taking it out so that she could decline the call, she froze. With a sigh, Peyton said, her voice tinged with anxiety, "It's my attorney again. I should take this."

"Of course." Noah nodded and walked a few paces away so she could have her call in relative privacy.

He couldn't hear the conversation, but he could hear the tone of Peyton's voice. It was clear her attorney was not delivering good news.

When the call ended, she stayed where she was. Her arms were crossed tight against her chest, and her head was drooped.

Arms pushed down at her sides, Peyton flexed her fingers back and forth. Taking a deep breath, she spun and walked back toward Noah.

He didn't say anything. Trying to be as steadying a presence as he could muster, he waited for her to collect herself.

"He said… he said the loss of the James House looks imminent. Deadlines to produce a recordable deed are placed by court order. That crooked attorney timed court submissions to coincide with the holidays, knowing it would be that much more difficult to refute anything," Peyton said. "As of Christmas Day, the James House will no longer belong to my family."

"Is there anything we can do?" Noah asked.

Peyton shook her head. "Show proof that my great, great, great-grandfather already had a recorded deed. It would supersede anything the real estate attorney submitted."

"Then that's what we have to do," Noah said.

Peyton looked cross. "My attorney has scoured every county office in the state of North Carolina. There aren't recorded deeds by anyone in my family for that property or any other properties in Southport."

"There's still hope," Noah said.

Peyton pulled away from his consoling touch.

"There's more," she said. Peyton's eyes narrowed. "The attorney submitted his petition the day of my father's stroke."

"What do you mean?" Noah frowned.

"That vulture was just circling. That snake! He was lying in wait, ready to strike the moment my father was ill," Peyton said.

Noah could see the anger in her eyes. Her cheeks glowed a fiery red. Angry tears began to flow.

Not knowing what to do, Noah stepped forward and hugged her.

To his surprise, she didn't fight it. She leaned into the hug.

All at once, she broke away. Looking up at Noah with teary eyes, Peyton apologized. In sudden embarrassment, she excused herself and walked away.

"Peyton…" Noah called.

With her hands flailed at her side, she sniffed, "I just can't right now! I'm sorry, Noah. Goodnight."

Noah nodded to himself and watched her walk away.

His heart broke for her. He knew there was next to no chance that they could find any evidence that would help her family's claim on the property. Still, moving forward and trying was the only thing he knew to do.

Letting Peyton have her space, Noah watched from the edge of the seawall.

When she climbed into her car and drove away, Noah began walking to his car where he left it that morning near the coffee shop. As he passed by an alley, a figure stepped out.

Ty Bates stood in front of him, blocking the sidewalk.

He looked almost featureless with the glow of the streetlight behind him. His hands were shoved into the pockets of his worn leather jacket.

"Peyton's a good woman," Ty said.

"She is," Noah admitted.

"She doesn't need someone to come here and shake up her world just to leave it. She needs someone who can and *will* be here for her. I'm not even saying it's me. It might be too late for me. But I have something you don't. I *love* her. I'm not just some fly-by-night Christmas fantasy," Ty said. "She's had enough heartbreak. I know my part in that. She doesn't need you adding to it."

Noah's eyes quivered as he tried to refute Peyton's ex-boyfriend's words. The problem was, he couldn't refute them. He wasn't wrong.

Instead, Noah sighed.

"Then we agree. Peyton doesn't need a broken heart. She doesn't need you," Ty said. Satisfied with his message, Ty smiled to himself and walked past Noah down the sidewalk.

Noah stood in the glow of the lights shimmering from the trees along downtown Southport. His mind was numb. He knew there were thoughts and feelings that were screaming to be let out. But they never came.

With a sigh, Noah kicked at the sidewalk and found his car.

Part of him wanted to track Peyton down. As he turned the ignition and pulled away from the waterfront, he found himself heading toward the hotel. The lights of downtown Southport disappeared in his rearview mirror.

Twenty

Noah woke with a headache. The kind brought on by his mind not shutting off while he tried fruitlessly to sleep. In stumbling automatic movements, he made his way down the hotel steps and trudged along the road toward downtown Southport.

Mindlessly waving at the cars that streaked by, his mind continued to roll in his head. Like a clothes dryer with a heavy, imbalanced load, his thoughts churned and hit hard with each revolution. Ty Bates' words as he cornered him on the sidewalk the previous evening had plagued him all night.

Noah enjoyed his time with Peyton. He was *really* enjoying his time with Peyton. He also knew his assignment was up in a few days and he would be off to another town right after Christmas.

As he walked up the steps into the coffee shop, Noah shook his head as though it would provide him with some magical clarity. He needed to focus on the article and if he could, help Peyton along the way. Any other notions of getting swept up in the moment he would hold at bay.

"I just need to avoid mistletoe…" Noah mumbled to himself as he made his way up to Darian who was manning the counter once again.

"Hmm?" the barista asked.

Noah looked sheepish. "Sorry, Darian. Just running through my to do list with a serious need for a cup of coffee."

"Well, *that* I can help you with." The young barista smiled as she adjusted her apron. "What'll it be today?"

"Big and caffeinated. No frills this morning," Noah said.

"All work and no play day, huh?" the barista asked as she started the process of making his coffee. "How about just a splash of vanilla and a hint of cinnamon? Still down to business but with a subtle note of Christmas."

"That sounds perfect." Noah nodded. "Thank you."

With cup in hand, Noah thanked the barista and stepped out onto the coffee house porch. It was the chilliest start to a day since he had arrived in Southport. With the hot cup in his hand contrasting with the cool, it was even starting to *feel* like Christmas.

Inspired to track down some shots that embodied the spirit of Christmas in a manner that was unique to Southport, or at least to the South, he took his coffee and his camera on a morning tour of the waterfront.

One of the restaurants that featured fish fresh from the local fleet had a sand-sculpted snowman, complete with a top hat and a red scarf wrapped around its sandy neck. Noah snapped a photo and smiled.

A shrimp boat headed out with the tide, its rails strung with red garland glistening in the slivers of the morning sun that made fingerlike beams through the light cloud layer.

Another restaurant had an evergreen tree decorated completely with shells and little glass balls filled with sand. Snapping a photo of the tree, Noah moved in closer. Finding the right angle, he was able to capture a shot of the harbor through one of the glass balls.

Feeling as though he was hitting his stride, Noah tossed his empty coffee cup and searched for the next Christmasy shot.

Feeling his phone buzz, he pulled it free from his pocket. Hesitating to answer, he finally said, "Hello?"

"What are you doing today?" Peyton asked. "I was hoping you could join me on a little Christmas errand."

"I, uh. I have to work on some shots and get them to my editor. She's kind of pressing me, hoping I can find the right angle for the piece," Noah said.

"I can help with that," Peyton said.

Noah's heart did a flip in his chest. "I really think I should just hammer it out."

"Okay. I mean, it is pretty busy at the store. I'm just having a hard time focusing," Peyton said. "But I will put on my Santa hat and pour all of my energy into raising the spirits of my wonderful customers."

"You are good at that," Noah said.

"Well, see you later?" Peyton asked.

"Yeah, sure. Thank you for calling, Peyton," Noah said before slipping his phone back into his pocket.

He didn't feel right about the conversation. Walking numbly back toward downtown, he stood in front of the row of waterfront houses. The James House gleamed in the morning light. The sun's rays sparkled off of the red bows and garland contrasted against the white columns and porch rails.

Taking a shot, he looked at his photo. It was a cover-worthy shot. Letting his camera hang from his shoulder, he studied the house. The idea that the real estate attorney could swoop in and take it away from Peyton and her family made his blood boil.

Walking into the Maritime Museum, Noah wandered its displays looking for inspiration. He perused the vignettes of Southport's past and the town's deep connection with the Cape Fear River and Atlantic Ocean. He read about the impacts of hurricanes reshaping the coastline of the town and the barrier islands.

He read of pirates. Blackbeard and Stede Bonnet were steeped in the town's history and lore. Bonnet, the "Gentleman Pirate", was captured off Southport's coast, effectively ending the golden era of piracy in North Carolina.

Flipping through a book in the museum gift shop, Noah read that while Blackbeard and Bonnet were the most famous pirates, piracy continued to some level through the early 1800s.

Noah tapped the book in his hand.

With sudden inspiration, he thanked the museum volunteer manning the front desk and made his way out of the Maritime Museum and back to the Garrison House of historic Fort Johnston.

Pushing his way in, he found a familiar face behind the desk.

"Good morning, Noah."

"Good morning, Mabel."

"What brings you in today? More sleuthing? I think I exhausted all of my resources," Mabel said.

"Maybe. Maybe there's another angle. What if Peyton's great, great, great-grandfather was a pirate? Records would be a bit sketchy, wouldn't they?" Noah asked.

"Unless there was a recorded bounty, they likely wouldn't exist at all," Mabel said. "At least not unless they retired and found a way to be an upright citizen. But their records would only begin then."

"Find a way to become an upright citizen… like helping in a war effort?" Noah suggested.

"That would be one way to absolve yourself of your crimes. If you were helpful enough, you might even be gifted land and a home by a grateful Colonel in the Continental Army. Perhaps even given a new name," Mabel said, leaning into the conversation.

"Like James," Noah suggested.

Mabel grinned. "Like James. That gives me an idea. Wait here."

The historian ambled off into the bowels of the Garrison House.

Noah leaned against the counter, mulling over the idea that perhaps Peyton's family's history seemed to begin with the house because they came from a line of pirates.

The door to the Garrison House opened and Peyton strode through, causing Noah to nearly jump. His cheeks glowed red as he took a stumbling step backward.

Peyton cocked her head. "What are you doing here?"

"Just… learning more about the history of Southport," Noah said meekly.

Setting a package on the counter, Peyton studied Noah, sensing something was off.

Mabel's voice carried into the room, "Thomas James. The earliest document I could find in our records is 1846!"

Peyton scowled, "Are you looking up my family?"

Noah stuttered. "I… I had an idea I want to ask Mabel about."

Scurrying excitedly into the room, her eyes on a book she was brandishing, Mabel said, "Thomas James owed a lien on the house. That is the earliest record indicating ownership."

Looking up from the book, Mabel stopped in her tracks. "Oh. Hi, Peyton. We were just… we were…"

"Snooping around my family tree?" Peyton finished for Mabel.

Peyton snatched the book and leaned over the counter. Flipping the yellowed pages of the handwritten ledger, she saw that the line was signed by the court clerk. "This provides a legal document presuming ownership to 1846. That is better than the 1917 title that my great, great grandfather petitioned for."

"It doesn't satisfy the original ownership claim, but it gets us an entire generation closer," Noah said.

"Anything more like that, from earlier?" Peyton asked.

Mabel shook her head. "No. There was a fire in what was the county records in 1823. It wiped out most local documents. We lost quite a few more in Hurricane Hazel."

"Another dead end." Peyton dropped her head sullenly.

"Maybe. But we are seventy years closer than we were a half-hour ago," Noah said.

Peyton smiled in appreciation for Noah's enthusiasm before glancing at her watch. Her face fell into an anxious scowl.

"I have to go," she said. With a glance toward Noah, she added, "I could use the company."

Noah hesitated. The look in Peyton's eyes was profoundly convincing.

"*Please.*" Peyton bounced on her heels.

Noah nodded. With a final glance at the book, he thanked Mabel. "Keep that somewhere safe. It could be useful!"

"I'll keep it under guard," Mabel assured him as Noah escorted Peyton out of the Garrison House.

Twenty One

"Back to see your dad?" Noah asked as Peyton pulled up to the nursing home.

"Something like that." Peyton nodded. Getting out, she opened the back hatch of her car. "Mind helping me with these?"

Noah spied bags full of presents and treats.

"We're going to a Christmas party," Peyton announced with an enthusiastic smile.

"Can't say no to a good Christmas party," Noah said, gathering packages in his arms.

The nursing home was filling up with guests bringing in holiday cookies and cakes. Coffee, cider and cocoa were warmed and ready in large carafes. A tree in a corner of the community room was quickly filling with wrapped presents under its boughs.

The air was festive as guests and staff wheeled and escorted residents from their rooms to the party.

Peyton looked at Noah. "Come with me to get Dad?"

Noah nodded and followed Peyton to her father's room. Giving the door a loud knock, she cracked it open, surprised to see her father standing in the foyer. He was dressed in a suit with a tie in the shape of a Christmas tree complete with lights.

"You look ready to go." Peyton admired her father.

"Someone said there was a party," Henry said, a mischievous smile on his face.

"Yes, there is," Peyton said, holding her arm out for her father to take.

"I've got the prettiest girl with me," Henry said. With a glance toward Noah, he winked. "Am I right?"

"Yes, sir. You are most definitely right about that," Noah replied.

Henry suddenly paused and frowned at Noah. "Who are you?"

Noah opened his mouth, not sure how to respond.

Peyton let out a concerned sigh.

"Just kidding. You're my *It's a Wonderful Life* watching friend. Good to see you again, Noah." Henry grinned.

"Good to see you, too, sir." Noah smiled.

Giving his daughter a yank, Henry urged, "Come on, we have a party to get to!"

Falling in line with other guests ambling down the hallway, they entered the community room where an old record player was set up playing songs from aged, etched vinyl.

"May I get you two something to drink?" Noah asked.

Henry patted his pockets and said with a pivot toward the hall. "I forgot my hooch!"

"*Dad!*" Peyton scolded.

"Party pooper," Henry said. "I guess I'll just have a coffee. I like it like the coal in my stocking: black."

"Yes, sir." Noah nodded.

"I'm fine for now," Peyton said.

Noah poured Henry a cup of coffee and brought it to the table where Peyton had seated her father at.

A bell at the front of the center rang, announcing that more visitors had arrived.

"Someone got their wings," Henry said with a finger in the air.

"Yes, they did." Noah nodded.

"I'm going to check out the dessert table. Want anything?" Peyton asked.

"See if they got any shortbreads," Mr. James said.

"I know they do. I brought your favorites," Peyton said.

"Should have brought them straight to my room," Mr. James teased.

Peyton stood up from the table. "I'll grab us a selection."

Both Noah and Henry watched as Peyton moved across the room, greeting people as she walked by.

"She likes you," Henry said.

"Excuse me, sir?" Noah looked surprised to hear Peyton's father declare that.

"She likes you. She hasn't brought anyone by since I been here other than you. She didn't even bring boys by the house other than school dances when it was customary for them to come and escort them proper-like," Mr. James said. "She's a special girl, my Peyton."

"Yes, she is," Noah agreed.

"You should marry her." Mr. James said, his voice deadpan straight.

"What?" Noah was glad he hadn't grabbed a beverage for himself since he would have choked and spilled it all over the table.

"I don't know how much I've got left in this world. I'd like to see her with a good man before I go. Someone like you," Mr. James said.

"I, uh…" Noah stammered.

"What are you boys plotting over here?" Peyton asked as she set a plate of cookies down on the table. She looked at Noah's red face and turned to her dad.

"Just swappin' tales," Mr. James said. Seeing the plate, his eyes widened, "Ooh, shortbread cookies!"

Peyton glanced at Noah, who shrugged.

The nursing home director greeted the residents and guests. Staff dressed like elves began passing around gifts. When each resident received one, the packages were opened.

The chatter in the room elevated as presents were revealed.

Each resident received a classic game or toy. Guests and staff encouraged the residents to play. Some made art with Spirographs and Play-Doh, others teamed up to play board games. Mr. James tapped his box, looking expectantly at his daughter and Noah.

"Let's do it!" Peyton said, taking her father's gift out of its packaging.

"Toss-Across, huh?" Noah asked.

"Our foster kids shopping trip inspired me. I figured you are never too old to have some good old-fashioned fun. I figured if any party needed a reminder like that…" Peyton said, and her voice drifted for a moment. Her voice returned cheery. "The nursing home director thought it was a great idea. So, we sent word out to the families and people who pledged donation gifts to come up with a classic toy or game."

"No air hockey?" Noah asked.

"Wasn't sure I could afford to lose another bet, but if you're game, I can probably find one. I need a redemption match," Peyton said.

"Let's see your hand at Toss-Across," Noah said, setting the board with its swiveling X's and O's ready for a match.

"What do you think, Dad? Can we take him?" Peyton handed her father a bean bag.

"Poor kid doesn't stand a chance!" Mr. James grinned. "Loser buys dinner!"

"You're on!" Noah said.

Peyton and her father alternated tosses while Noah was on his own. It didn't take long for the game board to be dotted with X's and O's. With the game down to one final blank, either team had a chance to win.

Noah readied his shot. With a glance at Peyton and her father, Noah let loose with his shot, glancing off the edge of the board and sliding across the floor. "I thought I had that one."

Mr. James' throw sailed through the air. In a soft arc, it hit the square, spinning the tile to complete the row.

"Looks like I owe you two dinner," Noah said.

"You sure do." Mr. James grinned.

As carolers dressed in period clothing paraded through the room, the mood of the nursing home was high as residents tapped into their more youthful, playful sides with the nostalgic toys.

Noah noticed a man sitting by himself, tinkering with a set of Lincoln Logs.

"You two mind if I go and say hello?" Noah asked.

Seeing where Noah's eyes had landed, Peyton smiled. "That is a great idea. I'm sure Charlie would love to visit."

Noah excused himself and walked over to the man who was diligently constructing something on the table in front of him.

"Whatcha working on?" Noah asked, casually walking up to the table, his hands shoved in his pockets.

The man looked up. After studying Noah for a moment, the man declared, "A pirate ship!"

"Ah, that's sounds fun," Noah said.

"Want to help?" the man asked. "The name's Charlie."

"I'd like that, Charlie. I'm Noah."

"Noah. Like the flood. Guess you're the right man to help with building a ship," Charlie said.

Noah laughed. "I guess so."

Pointing across the table at a pile of wooden pieces, Charlie asked, "Hand me one of those connectors, would ya?"

"I was just learning about pirates today," Noah said, handing a piece to the man.

"Were you? All about Stede Bonnet, I imagine," Charlie said as he worked on his build.

"Yes, and others. I was curious about any that might have been around here *after* Bonnet's capture," Noah said. "Tough to find any information."

"Where you been lookin'?" Charlie asked.

"I was at the Maritime Museum and the Fort Johnston Museum," Noah said.

"Well, Mabel is a good place to start, but you're more likely to find stuff about citizens with good standing there," Charlie said.

Noah frowned. "What do you mean?"

Charlie laughed as he worked on assembling a mast for his ship, "You wanna find stuff on pirates, you gotta look where people write stuff about pirates."

Noah frowned at Charlie as he twirled a construction piece in his fingers.

"Pirates are criminals. You want to know stuff about them, you gotta dig through the criminal records and the jail logs. Places where crimes and bounties are posted," Charlie said. "Hand me that napkin, would ya?"

Noah handed the Christmas napkin to Charlie, dumbfounded by the man's logic.

Spreading it out, Charlie poked slits in the napkin and fashioned it to the wooden piece of his mast. His pirate ship was complete.

"That looks pretty good," Noah said. "Mind if I take a photo of it?"

"Not at all. Let's call her H.M.S. Noel for Christmas," Charlie announced as Noah took a photo.

"Give me that camera and slide next to him," Peyton said as she stood over to witness Charlie's creation.

Noah rounded the table and knelt next to Charlie.

"Thank you, Charlie. This was fun. And you've given me a lot to think about," Noah said.

"Anytime, kid. You know where to find me," Charlie said.

Noah nodded. "Merry Christmas."

When Noah found Peyton and her father, they were finishing a small puzzle. "That looks nice," Noah said as he admired the Christmas scene of a horse-drawn carriage driving through the snow, a wreath around its harness and glowing lanterns shining through the night attached to the carriage frame.

"Yeah. What do you think, Dad? Should I get you a puzzle for Christmas?" Peyton asked.

"Will you two come and help me finish it?" Henry asked.

Peyton looked at Noah and placed a hand on her father's shoulder. "I'll definitely be there, Dad."

"How about that dinner you owe us? We won fair and square!" Henry said.

"Absolutely. Where would you like to go?" Noah asked.

Henry looked thoughtful for a moment and then he looked up, his eyes very deliberate. "I want to have dinner at my house."

"Your room?" Peyton asked.

"My *house*. Our family home. With you and Noah," Henry said.

Peyton shot a glance at Noah. "We can grab some take out and eat there."

Henry nodded, looking very pleased. "Something Italian. Oh, and red wine."

"Sure, Dad." Peyton giggled. "I know a place. They'll deliver right to the door."

"Here's my card, I need to make good on our deal," Noah said.

Peyton called in the order and handed Noah his card back.

Swiveling her head around the room, Peyton said, "I should check in with the staff. Let them know we're borrowing Dad for a bit."

"You know," Henry said, "I'm suddenly feeling really tired. I think maybe I should just go to my room and watch *It's a Wonderful Life*."

Peyton cocked her head at her father.

Henry looked at Noah, "Have you seen that movie?"

"It's one I could watch again and again, Mr. James," Noah said.

"I think I'll go back to my room, now," Peyton's father said.

Peyton shrugged at Noah, "Okay. I can probably have the delivery moved here..."

"No. I think I'll take a nap. You two go on and have the dinner without me," Mr. James said as he started walking down the hall toward his room.

As he shuffled down the hall with Peyton in his wake, Peyton's father looked up and said, "I had a fun day."

"Me too, Dad. Me too," Peyton said, with an arm around her father.

Twenty Two

Noah waited for Peyton outside of her father's room.

Peyton opened the door. Leaning into his room with one foot in the hallway, she called softly, "I love you, Daddy!"

"Is he okay?" Noah asked.

Peyton frowned, "I think so. I think maybe we just tuckered him out. It's like he flipped a switch."

"You can stay with him. I can catch a ride…" Noah said.

Shaking her head, Peyton said, "He was adamant. He wanted a nap and wanted us to make good on our deal."

As they climbed into Peyton's car, they waited for the heater to kick in as the evening had a crispness to it. Glancing through the windshield, they watched in shock as Mr. James walked back to the community room to rejoin the party.

"I think we've been swindled," Peyton said.

Noah laughed. "I think we have been, too."

"Well, we have dinner waiting for us, if you're up for it," Peyton said.

"Dinner…" Noah rubbed the back of his neck. With a shrug, he smiled. "I mean, we shouldn't let it go to waste."

Putting the car in gear, Peyton backed out of her spot in front of her father's nursing home and headed to the James House.

Winter's early sunset allowed the Christmas decorations affixed to each light pole along Southport's main streets the chance to be lit. The trees and houses along the drive were aglow. The James House, its porch wrapped in evergreen boughs and white lights looked like a Christmas postcard. It was warm and welcoming.

A young man had just made his delivery and waved at Noah and Peyton as they got out of their car.

Peyton studied her family's house and sighed. "It's not just the house. It's the memories," she said.

"No one can take those away," Noah said.

"Yeah." Peyton glanced at Noah and nodded. "Come on, let's eat."

Noah held the gate for Peyton as she led him up the porch steps and into the house.

"I'll grab some plates and silverware. Would you bring that into the dining room?" Peyton nodded past the living room and toward the far corner of the front of the house. "There's a wine opener in the credenza and you'll see the wine glasses there too."

Noah navigated the house with just the glow of the Christmas lights. He hated to spoil the effect by turning on additional lights.

Finding glasses shimmering from the porch Christmas lights, he set a pair on the table. Pulling open credenza drawers, he found a wine opener and set to work on the bottle that had been delivered.

"You can turn on lights, you know," Peyton said as she joined him with plates and silverware.

"There is just something nice about the Christmas lights…" Noah started.

"I think so, too," Peyton said. With a raised brow, she asked, "Would it ruin the ambiance if I added a couple of candles?"

"I think that'd be all right." Noah nodded, pouring Peyton a glass of wine.

Lighting two tall candles, Peyton set them on the table. Noah pulled out a chair at the head of the table for Peyton.

"Why, thank you, good, sir," Peyton said as he helped her slide her chair in.

Slipping into the closest seat across from her, Noah bellied up to the table.

Through the glow of the Christmas lights and the flicker of the candles, Peyton looked at Noah. "Thank you for coming with me today."

"I had fun. It was a privilege to share a piece of Christmas with your father and the other residents," Noah said.

"He had a good day," Peyton said.

"He seemed to." Noah nodded.

Peyton's eyes narrowed, "I can't believe he rejoined the party after we left."

"He was adamant about dinner," Noah said.

"I think he had a plan," Peyton said.

"A plan?" Noah asked.

"Yeah." Peyton nodded. "I think he wanted this. For us."

"Dinner in the dark," Noah teased.

Peyton leaned slightly across the table toward Noah.

Noah was drawn to her. She was always beautiful. In the soft light, she was stunning. The moment made his heart do flips inside his chest.

Trying hard to resist the temptation to kiss her, Noah leaned back in his chair. Raising his glass, he said, "To a Henry James Christmas party!"

Peyton moved her glass to meet his. "The little conniver."

"Let's see what we've got here." Noah opened the containers. With the silverware Peyton brought to the table, he served their plates.

Peyton watched him work the way she watched him with her father and with Charlie. She tapped her wine glass with her finger as she mulled his affect with her throughout the day.

"Did I do something wrong?" Peyton blurted.

"What?" Noah leaned back in his seat.

"You suddenly seem afraid to be alone with me," Peyton said. "Don't think I haven't noticed you avoiding doorways with mistletoe hanging from them."

"I'm not afraid…" Noah winced. "I'm… yeah, maybe a little."

Peyton tilted her head to the side and studied Noah.

"Peyton… I like spending time with you. I *really* do. But, what happens next week?" Noah asked.

"I don't know what happens next week. I can't control what happens next week," Peyton said. Her eyes looked around the dining room of the James House. "Clearly. But, like you said, memories can't be stolen from you."

"Hearts can be broken," Noah choked.

"You're worried I'm going to break your heart?" Peyton asked. She sighed. "You're worried you'll break mine."

"I ran into Ty…" Noah started.

"You're taking relationship advice from Ty?" Peyton blurted. "I can take care of my own heart, Noah Wilde."

Peyton looked across the candlelight at Noah.

"You broke his heart," Noah said.

"He broke his own heart by being stupid and selfish," Peyton said. "You don't seem to be either of those two things."

"Well, thank you," Noah said, not sure what to do with the statement.

"I'm not going to push you into anything. I like you, Noah. My dad likes you. There you have it. What you do with that information is up to you…" Peyton said.

Leaning over the table, Noah pressed his lips against hers. There they danced together as Peyton's fingers wrapped around the back of Noah's head to keep him close.

When dinner was finished and the plates were put away, Noah and Peyton moved to the front porch. Holding their refilled wine glasses, they huddled under a blanket as the night air had become properly chilly.

There was a crispness in the air that seemed to make the night sky over the water that much more clear. The Christmas lights reflecting on the water and the steady presence of the Oak Island Lighthouse beam looked surreal.

"You should take a photo. It's beautiful," Peyton said.

"I'd just as soon own this moment in a memory," Noah said.

His words brought a smile to Peyton's face as she moved her lips to his.

Peyton took a deep breath and nodded. "You're right. I am going to make the most of whatever time I have left with the James House. Instead of being lost in worry, I'm going to capture as much joy as I can."

Noah wrapped his arm around Peyton and nodded.

"Hey, don't let on about the James House. I mean, they'll all find out soon enough, but I just want to get through the Holiday Home Tour first. It is such a big deal to all the neighbors, and I don't want to be a cloud on their Christmas," Peyton whispered.

"Of course." Noah nodded. His mind drifted back to his search for the proof that the house was awarded to the James family many generations ago.

"I used to sit with my mom out here. We'd stare out over the water and into the night sky and search for shooting stars," Peyton said. "Once in a while I'd catch Daddy in the corner of my eye watching us. It looked like he wanted to join, but he'd walk away. Let us girls have our moment."

"He is a sweet man," Noah said.

"He is. Losing Momma was hard on him. It was hard on all of us. I think it broke Daddy's heart and it broke his health," Peyton said. "To be honest, he's had more moments as himself in the past few days than I've seen in months."

"Maybe he is getting better," Noah suggested.

"I like to think so. His doctor was very clear with me. Daddy may have some good days, but…" She nestled in close to Noah.

"The good days are the ones that matter," Noah said, his voice soft.

Peyton nodded against Noah's chest.

Twenty Three

Noah had barely taken a sip of vanilla and peppermint latte before his phone rang. Glancing at the screen, he scowled. It was rarely a good thing when his editor called the second it was eight o'clock.

"Good morning, Jennimay," Noah wanted to guzzle his coffee, but instead had to take care with cautious sips until it cooled down.

"How's it going down there, Noah?" Jennimay asked.

Taking a breath, Noah said, "I think I'm starting to get the Southport Christmas vibe."

"Your photos look great. I mean, *really* good. Without the décor, I'm not sure I was looking at our December spread or July's, but you've captured some great shots," Jennimay said.

"Yeah. You know my style, I focus on the landscape, the water, the buildings, wildlife…" Noah started. "But I'm going to send you a different set that I've been working on. Because all that is beautiful, but I think to share Christmas in Southport, I've got to capture the people."

"That's a twist for you. I gave up asking for people shots from you a dozen assignments ago," Jennimay said.

"I think not having snow on the ground, barely needing a jacket during the Christmas season has forced me to look a little harder. Dig a little deeper. I've needed to find the heart *behind* the shot," Noah said.

"Okay…" Jennimay's voice was skeptical. "Tell me about the story, Noah."

"Well, there's the charm of a Southern town, for sure. The way they all come together to celebrate. It is pretty magical. But there is something else. The house I want to use as the cover, the generations of ownership by a local family are in dispute, and a real estate attorney is threatening to rip it away from the family because of a legal loophole on Christmas Eve," Noah said.

"That's sounds like a *sad* story, not a Christmas story, Noah," Jennimay said.

"I would agree. But there is a chance I can help save it for the family. It sounds crazy, but I stumbled across what might be the key, and it leads to pirates from the 1800s," Noah said.

"Vivian said you had her dig into something. It sounds like that dispute is not going well for the current owners. I'm not sure we want to bet our cover on something that might be a black mark for that town. You have several great cover options. I'd rather we play it safe," Jennimay said.

"I mean, tales of pirates and town lore that goes back generations…" Noah started.

"Christmas. It is a *Christmas* issue, Noah. Readers want warm and fuzzy. Not swashbuckling and mysteries," Jennimay said. "I want you to focus your time on the Thomas House. I think *that* is your cover, Noah."

"Okay." Noah sighed.

"Cheer up. I'm working on your next assignment. You're going to love it. Sunny and warm January escapes an hour from the U.S. mainland," Jennimay said.

"Sounds great, Jennimay," Noah said, playing with his coffee cup.

"The Thomas House! Go get me that winning cover!" Jennimay said as she as she ended the call.

Noah felt a bit numb as he watched Southport slowly wake up.

Finishing his coffee, he walked to the Thomas House. Not wanting to disturb Cybil, he worked quietly outside. Through his lens, Noah looked for fresh angles that would capture the beauty of the colonial home, Cybil's deft touch at decorating and even a reflection of the water against the windows which were teased with golden sunlight.

It was a lovely home. It would make a spectacular cover. Yet, he was drawn to the James House. It wasn't a better design or in any better repair. It wasn't decorated as carefully as the Thomas House. But, yet, it called to him.

Shaking his head, he tried to separate his feelings from what his eyes were seeing through the lens. For the first time in his career, the object in the photo seemed to be living and breathing. Somehow sentient.

Standing at an angle, he captured both homes in a shot that he felt was one of his favorite photos of the trip.

"It's a bit chilly out here this morning," a voice called from the Thomas House foyer. Cybil's cheery face was poking through the screen door out to the porch. "You need a hot coffee or tea?"

"I'd take a warmup of coffee." Noah nodded. Opening the gate to the Thomas House, he marched up the steps, subconsciously blowing warm air onto his hands.

"Come on in." Cybil held the door open for Noah.

"Thanks. It *is* a bit chilly out there," Noah said, rubbing his arms.

"Chilly enough I was enjoying sunrise from my chair at the window. Nice, though, with the tree right there. I love Christmas trees," Cybil said as she led Noah into her kitchen. "I was tryin' to decide if I needed one more, for the Holiday Home Tour."

"Where would you put it?" Noah asked as he scanned the already well-decorated living space.

"Now you sound like my husband. He always said we'd have a forest in here if he didn't tell me to stop putting up Christmas trees," Cybil said.

"From an objective eye and my professional opinion, your house is beautiful. In fact, my editor really wants the Thomas House as the cover for my spread," Noah said as he accepted a cup of coffee. "Thank you."

"Your editor. What about you? What do *you* want for your cover?" Cybil asked.

Noah hesitated and said, "I love your house. It's an excellent example of Southport at Christmas. The love, the charm…"

"But?" Cybil smiled over her coffee cup.

"I'm drawn next door," Noah said.

Cybil's smile turned into a grin. "There's nothing wrong with the James House. But are you sure it's the house that's drawing you?"

"No," Noah said, his voice soft yet pointed.

"Love has a way of shining through things. Houses, ornaments, photographs…" Cybil said. "You could take a hundred photos of my house and not one of them would shine like one you would take of the James House."

Noah suddenly looked anxious. Setting his cup down, he asked, "Would you mind if I come back later? There's something I really need to do."

Cybil's eyes flashed to the James House and she let out a smile, "You do what you need to. This house isn't going anywhere."

Noah hurriedly made his way toward the door and muttered to himself, "Neither is the James House, if I can help it!"

Twenty Four

Noah burst into the Fort Johnston Museum and Southport Visitor's Center with such fervor that Mabel nearly fell out of her chair behind the front desk.

Clutching her chest, the historian scowled. "My stars, Noah. You nearly gave me a heart attack."

"I'm sorry, Mabel. I thought of another path to the answers I need," Noah said, panting as he leaned against the desk.

"Well, once my nerves settle, let's see what we can do," Mabel said. Looking Noah in the eye, she squinted. "What is all of this about? Your article?"

"In a way," Noah said.

Mabel eyed Noah carefully. "There's something else…"

"Just trying to help a friend," Noah said.

"A friend, as in Ms. Peyton?" Mabel pressed. Taking Noah's nervous rocking back and forth as an answer, Mabel smiled. "Anything for our Peyton! How can I help you?"

"When I was visiting the nursing home, I spoke to a very nice gentleman named Charlie," Noah said.

"Charlie Banks. He *is* a very nice gentleman," Mabel agreed.

"He suggested that if I wanted to learn about pirates, I needed to dig into the town's criminal logs," Noah said.

"That *is* a good idea," Mabel said. "I don't have those here. Some of the old records like that were stored in the Brunswick Jail. I don't have access to them, but I know who does."

"Great!" Noah leaned in.

"Sweet young lady, though she enjoys digging into the more macabre and mysterious side of the town's history. I'll put you two together," Mabel said.

After making a quick phone call, Mabel smiled, "She'll meet you at Whittler's Bench in half-an-hour."

"Thank you, Mabel. You are wonderful." Noah beamed.

"Silver-tongued sweet talker," Mabel teased, as Noah burst out of the museum.

Noah anxiously waited by Whittler's Bench near the town's waterfront. He had no idea what to expect from this new contact.

As he paced around the little circle that was a prominent meeting point, a golf cart fashioned like an old 1950s pickup truck pulled up. It had worn red paint and was hauling a fake Christmas tree strapped at an angle between the bed and the roof of the buggy.

A woman in a green satin period dress bolstered by a hoop skirt hopped out of the buggy. She cast a scrutinizing eye through a lacy veil that playfully cascaded off her dress-matching hat.

In a grand and proper Southern accent lacing through her words, the woman said, "Mr. Noah Wilde, I presume."

"I'm Noah. Nice to meet you." He nodded, holding out his hand.

"Mabel says you have some questions about Southport. When they involve the town's less written-about history, I'm your girl," the woman said. Pulling off a delicate glove, she shook Noah's hand. "The name's Katie."

"Thank you for meeting me on such short notice, Katie," Noah said, beguiled by the woman's authentic aura and dazzling Southern charm. He suddenly felt like he was thrust into the antebellum period.

"Not at all. This is what I do. Besides, I hear it's to help one of our own," Katie said. "But before we get into the nitty-gritty of your specific questions, let me give you a quick spin around town. It will give us a foundation to build off of."

"That sounds great," Noah said, welcoming any information that might help him help Peyton.

"Climb in," Katie said as she slipped behind the wheel of the custom golf cart. When Noah climbed in beside her, she smiled. "All right, off we go."

Navigating the buggy through the streets of downtown Southport, Katie stopped outside the Christmas House. "No doubt you've already been in there," she said.

"I have. It's amazing. I don't think I've ever seen so many decorations in my life," Noah said.

"It is a tourist favorite. What they don't know is, under all that holiday cheer, there are mysteries to be solved. It was built in 1885. There are nooks and crannies the current owners themselves probably haven't found yet... and maybe the spirits of a former owner or two hangin' around, as well. That's the thing about these old homes, they were cleverly designed to with little cubbies in which to stash things, sometimes whole rooms that you wouldn't know were even there," Katie said.

"1885, that's too recent," Noah mumbled.

Katie studied Noah for a moment. "You like *really* old stuff. All right. Onward it is."

Letting her foot off the brake, Katie moved along the waterfront homes that Noah had begun to become familiar with.

"All these beautiful, Southern homes have a ton of history, perhaps none more than this one, the Brunswick Inn," Katie shared. "This was the summer mansion for Benjamin Smith, one of North Carolina's earliest governors. The home changed hands a few times, becoming Inn Brunswick, one of the oldest businesses in Southport that still rests on its original foundation."

"Benjamin Smith has come up in a few conversations," Noah said.

"Sure. He was a colonel in the Continental Army. The town that was built around Fort Johnston was named after him. The name stuck for just shy of a hundred years before becoming Southport. You'll still see the name around, like the Smithville Burial Grounds we'll be passing by," Katie said.

"Any connections to pirates?" Noah asked.

"Pirates? Well, Blackbeard and Stede Bonnet, the Gentleman Pirate, spent their fair share of time using the Cape Fear River estuary and protective barrier islands to hole up, resupply and make repairs to their ships. The area served as a base for Bonnet," Katie said.

"I saw the plaque near Bonnet Creek," Noah said.

"He was ultimately captured by the government right off our shore after a bit of a double-cross by former co-conspirator Blackbeard," Katie said.

"Were there others?" Noah asked.

"Piracy lasted for most of the next century to some diminishing degree," Katie said.

"A new friend of mine suggested records of some of them would be kept in criminal logs?" Noah asked.

"Possibly. Record keeping wasn't exactly iron-clad back then, but there are probably some," Katie said. "Mabel said you had some interest in the Brunswick Jail. We'll head there next."

Rolling along the tree lined streets, Spanish moss draped over branches like ghostly fingers, Katie pulled to a stop outside a two-story brick building. "Welcome to the Old Brunswick Jail. Lots of stories here, and perhaps one of the more haunted sites in Southport.

Inside the jail and even outside have a storied past of sorrowful events."

"The plaque says 1904," Noah said.

"Sure, the jail itself postdates most pirate activity, but there would have been a time some of the criminal records would have been stored there," Katie said. "Along with the ghosts, of course."

"Ghosts?" Noah sighed. "I don't think that is going to help me with what I need."

"Are you kidding me? Looking for documents from the 1800s? It sounds like you are very much chasing ghosts, Mr. Wilde," Katie said. Pointing to the building, she added, "If there's anything left after the fires and hurricanes, it would be in that basement there."

"Hmm." Noah studied the sedate building, deep in thought. "Can you get me in there?"

"I can arrange that," Katie nodded. "I'll reach out and set a time to get us in there tomorrow morning."

"Tomorrow morning," Noah mumbled out loud.

Katie laughed. "I have an event to attend. I didn't dress up like this just for you, Mr. Wilde. Though this is my formal guide attire. You should come back to visit for Halloween. You can join my haunted walking tour. Some would say it's to die for."

"That sounds like it might be worth a whole other article." Noah smiled.

"Of *that*, I have no doubt," Katie said as she put the buggy into motion again. "I'll get you back to Whittler's Bench and then I'm off for caroling, unless you'd like to attend. Your modern-day attire might be a little off-putting, though."

"Probably less so than my singing," Noah said. "Thank you for the tour. You've given me a lot to think about."

"I hope I can help you find what you're looking for," Katie said.

Noah's eyes drifted to the row of waterfront homes and the James House that he was trying to protect. "Me too."

Twenty Five

"I thought I might find you down here," Peyton said as she pulled around the loop that circled Whittler's Bench along Southport's waterfront. "You up for a little afternoon interlude?"

"I think I'm done working for the day." Noah nodded.

"Get some good photos?" Peyton asked.

"Yeah, I think I did," Noah said, biting his lip on his quest for James House documents.

Peyton pulled along the sidewalk out in front of the Maritime Museum.

"We didn't go far." Noah laughed.

"Southport isn't all that big," Peyton said.

Noah watched as several men and women in period dress walked into the museum. "I'm not sure I'm dressed for this."

"You'll be fine. Just stick with me," Peyton said, holding her arm out for Noah to take.

Notes of Victorian Christmas music were heard wafting through the building as guests arrived and were welcomed by staff and volunteers in period dress. Christmas cookies were accompanied by cider and cocoa.

Handing Peyton a cider as he was satisfied himself with a candy cane, they walked through the museum. A group of carolers in hoop dresses, hats and gloves stood in front of the crowd and began to sing in tune with the music. In their hands, each held what looked like well-worn leather books of Christmas carols.

Played by a live band using violins, flutes, a box drum and a concertina, the music reminded Noah of watching a movie set centuries ago. Flashes of a Dickens story ran through his head.

Katie, in her bright green dress, stood out. She gave a little smile and wink at Noah who gave a friendly nod back.

"I see you met Katie," Peyton said.

"She's kind of hard to miss around town. Mabel introduced us. She gave me a brilliant tour of the history of the town, stopping at some of the sites I hadn't seen yet," Noah said.

"She's a firecracker. Sharp, too," Peyton said. "Outside of Mabel, I don't think anyone knows the town better."

They stopped to watch and listen to the carolers as they sang a song or two before meandering on and allowing other guests to filter into their space.

"Well, look at you two." Mabel smiled as they stood in front of a station manned by the historian.

"What do you have here, Mabel?" Noah asked.

"A Victorian Christmas paper ornament. You select your favorite Christmas carol sheet music, and I'll teach you to fashion it into an angel, a star or snowflake to hang from your tree," Mabel said.

"What do you think? Feeling crafty?" Peyton nudged Noah.

"I'll give it a go," Noah said. Sitting next to Peyton, he rifled through the Christmas music. Each was a carol or hymn that was popular in the 19th century.

Noah worked with the Coventry Carol while Peyton used Holly and the Ivy.

"Wonderful selections," Mabel said. "Now, what design would you like to make?"

Noah looked at Peyton for inspiration. "I think maybe an angel."

Mabel smiled. "And you, Peyton?"

"Snowflake," Peyton said.

One by one, Mabel demonstrated how to craft their paper ornaments. Each shape was cut with four identical sections so when put together in a cross pattern, they formed a sort of three-dimensional ornament.

When they were done, they admired their handiwork.

"Well done, you are ready to decorate your vintage Christmas tree. Add strung fruit, nuts and cookies and you are there. Minus the actual candles, which I do *not* recommend," Mabel said.

"Thank you, Mabel," Noah said. Holding his angel by her string, she danced through the air in a twirling circle. "Really kind of pretty."

Handing the angel to Peyton, he said, "I made this for you."

Peyton smiled and held up her snowflake. "Why do you think I chose to do a snowflake? I didn't want you to go all the way through Christmas in Southport without a little snow."

Noah's cheeks glowed red.

"*That's* the tree I'm missing. A Victorian tree!" a familiar voice said behind Noah.

Turning, he found Cybil admiring their new decorations.

"You two are so good at that, I should host a vintage tree decorating party," Cybil said. "Are you two free tonight?"

Peyton nudged Noah. "I'm game if you are."

"Sure," Noah said.

"I'll have dinner and cookies. Mabel, would you bring any leftover craft supplies from the event?" Cybil asked.

"You had me at cookies, Cybil." Mabel laughed.

"See you later," Cybil sang as Noah and Peyton continued to meander.

A group of guests began dancing a Viennese Waltz in front of the band and carolers, making the event feel even more like a surreal twist in time.

"Care to dance?" Peyton wrapped an arm around Noah.

"Not if you want to keep your toes," Noah said. "How about a stroll?"

Peyton nodded. Slipping her hand in his, she let Noah lead her out of the museum.

"It's like every day there is some new Christmas event in this town," Noah said.

"If there isn't, we make one. Like Cybil needs another tree. That woman just wants an excuse to mingle," Peyton said.

Noah squeezed Peyton tighter. "I like mingling. With the right audience."

The December air had brought in a breeze at least cool enough to make the remaining leaves turn. Peyton leaned into Noah to ward off a chill.

By the time the two had made a circuit and stood at the James House, Cybil was waving from her porch.

"I could use a strong, young man to help move a tree!" Cybil called.

"Duty calls," Noah said, leading Peyton through the gate of the Thomas House.

Cybil welcomed them in. She stood by the banister of her stairs and spread her arms wide. "I was thinking right about… here."

"It would be lovely for the Holiday Home Tour," Peyton said.

"That's what I was thinking. It would help to carry the theme," Cybil said.

"What theme?" Noah asked.

"Don't worry about it," Peyton said and immediately turned to Cybil. "So, this tree…"

"Right. Follow me, if you don't mind." Cybil walked to a door between the kitchen and the foyer. Opening it up, she flipped a light switch.

"I don't know how I would ever do this without your help," Cybil said.

"No worries. Where can I find this tree?" Noah asked.

"At the bottom of the steps, hook a steep curve to the right. You'll find the Christmas corner mostly empty right there," Cybil said. "The extra tree will be in a green bag."

"Extra tree. Got it," Noah said.

Peyton raised a brow. "You don't have an extra tree? What are you, a Scrooge?"

"No. One just always seemed to be enough. I may have to rethink that, though." Noah laughed.

Descending the steps, he found the basement of the old home more of a deep root cellar. With the low water tables, most homes in the South didn't have basements. The waterfront homes built on top of a little hill afforded enough usable space.

Noah made his way to the section Cybil had directed him to. Brushing off some dust, Noah hoisted the tree over his shoulder. As he began to turn back toward the steps, he paused. In the now empty space that had held the tree, he noticed a section of the brick wall was missing.

Taking a closer look, he found there was a thin brick façade over a portion of the wall. A small square cubby had been intentionally built into the wall.

Noah carried the tree up the steps and to the banister that Cybil had selected as its home for the holiday, then set it down.

Looking at Peyton, he said, "There is a section in the root cellar that looks like it was a cubby. Katie was telling me about hidden alcoves in these old homes."

"Yes. Our house had them too. I've plundered each and every one," Peyton said, knowing where Noah was going with the suggestion.

"Oh," Noah nodded, crestfallen.

"I appreciate the thought, though," Peyton said.

"I'm sorry you're going through this," Noah said, his voice soft.

Peyton smiled, "I have decided if this is going to be my last Christmas in the James House, then I'm going to enjoy it the best I can."

Noah nodded.

Cybil entered the room with a tray of eggnog, just in time to greet Mabel at the door. "Come in, come in. We were just about to get festive!"

Mabel set her wares on a table and accepted an eggnog.

"All right. Noah, if you will set the tree up, we ladies will get to work on the décor. I brought my samples from the museum to get us started," Mabel said as she took a sip of her eggnog. "Ooh, that packs a punch!"

"I said it was a party." Cybil grinned.

Twenty Six

Katie was already at the Old Brunswick Jail when Noah arrived. It took a moment to recognize her in a pair of jeans, a sweater and a pair of tall, red boots in lieu of her period dress and hoop skirt.

"Good morning, Mr. Wilde," Katie said, her Southern accent strong.

"Good morning, Katie," Noah said.

"So, you ready to dig through some old criminal records?" Katie asked.

Noah shrugged and offered a meek smile. "That's the plan."

"What exactly are you looking for?" Katie asked as she unlocked the front door.

Noah was almost disappointed as she turned a modern lock with a contemporary key.

"I'm not one hundred percent sure. Ideally, documents from the early 1800s," Noah said.

Katie snorted. "If anyone had done anything too exciting, I'd be sharing the stories on my tours."

"I'm just trying to find evidence that someone existed," Noah said.

Katie led Noah down into the jail's basement, which was used as storage. A documents room kept stacks of ledgers, books, and papers free of damage from the elements.

"Sad to think that some people might have gone through life and just disappeared. No stories. No records. No families," Katie said.

"Maybe some went into the pirate business just to *become* anonymous," Noah suggested.

"As sound a theory as I've heard. Other than revenge and riches, that is," Katie said.

"Here you are. Can I help you look? The records are kinda all over the place. You probably heard, on account of fires and hurricanes, what you are looking for, even if it did exist once upon a time, might have been lost anyway along the way," Katie said.

"Yeah. It's worth it if I can find what I'm looking for," Noah said.

"I'd be more helpful if you'd share in your mystery," Katie said, moving a stack of documents from the period Noah had designated. She eyed Noah for a moment and asked, "This for the article you're writing, or about Peyton? I saw you two gettin' along at the museum yesterday."

"Both," Noah admitted. "I don't want to get too much into it, but records on the James family don't seem to exist until the James House was built. And even then, it's pretty spotty, with huge gaps in between."

"You think the lack of history isn't an accident? That Thomas James might have been hiding something like maybe he was a pirate?" Katie looked thoughtful. "That's not a bad theory, Mr. Wilde."

"You can call me Noah."

"I know. My head gets stuck in the antebellum etiquette sometimes," Katie said.

Having a better idea of what she was looking for, Katie dug in alongside Noah, poring over documents from a bygone era.

Hours passed by, as did boxes of documents. Out of the mix, only two documents were recovered. One was a fine issued to Thomas James in 1803 for his part in a bar brawl. The other, dated 1799, was a redacted warrant for unspecified crimes prior to the end of the Revolutionary War.

Katie held the document in the light for Noah to see. "Look, in both cases, he was pardoned by Benajmin Smith."

Noah looked at the document and took a photo of it.

"It shows Thomas James was here during the time the James House was built, *and* he was an associate of Benajmin Smith," Noah said, his mind racing. "It's not enough."

"That's all you're going to find in the criminal records that were left here and not destroyed." Katie shrugged. "I'd say as far as needles in haystacks go, finding two was pretty darned good."

"I suppose you're right," Noah said. "We're so close…"

"We're?" Katie cocked her head. With a mischievous smile, she nudged, "You and Peyton?"

Noah couldn't suppress a smile himself. "She has made this a Christmas that I'll never forget."

"That's the people of Southport for you," Katie said. "Come on, let's get out of this dusty old room."

Twenty Seven

Noah looked nervously across the table in the waterfront restaurant.

"You look fit to be tied," Peyton said, her eyes warily sweeping over Noah.

"I found something today, with a little help," Noah said.

"You *found* something," Peyton cocked her head.

He produced photocopies of the documents he had found earlier that day, and scooted them across the table toward Peyton.

Picking the papers up, Peyton studied them, her brows dancing as she tried to decipher what she was reading.

"Where did you find these?" Peyton asked.

"The Old Brunswick Jail," Noah said.

"What were you doing in there?" Peyton asked.

"Following a lead Charlie at the nursing home gave me the other night," Noah said. "What if your family really started their journey in Southport as pirates? He said records would be found in criminal records, not public records. I found these."

"In the Old Brunswick Jail." Peyton stared across the table.

"Katie let me in and helped sort through all this stuff," Noah said.

Peyton looked cross, "I appreciate what you're trying to do, but I don't really want the town digging through my business. It's hard enough. The one challenge with a small town is personal stuff doesn't stay personal for long."

"No one knows anything about the trouble with the James House," Noah said, his voice low.

Peyton sighed. "I know you're just trying to help. What does this mean? It doesn't exactly say my great, great, great-grandfather was a pirate. *Or* that he legally owned the James House."

"No. It doesn't," Noah agreed. "But it shows that we're close. It shows your Thomas James *was* here during the time the house was built and that he *was* a known associate of Benjamin Smith's."

"So, the story of Smith granting my family the house has merit," Peyton said, a glimmer of hope in her eyes.

With a sigh, she said, "Thank you, for trying to help."

After a moment of reflecting on the documents, Peyton brightened, "You really think I come from a family of pirates?"

"I don't know. The little scraps that we have gleamed point to maybe something like that," Noah said.

"Well, what are we waiting for? We have more plundering to do!" Peyton announced by raising a finger in the air. "What's next? Where do we hunt for clues?"

"Where else does pirate lore in Southport take us?" Noah asked.

"We can check in at the Royal James. The owners tend to be pretty spun up on pirate lore," Peyton said.

"Sounds as good a place to start as any," Noah said.

The pirate-themed bar named after Stede Bonnet's ship was quiet, given the early hour of the day.

"Is Pat here?" Peyton asked the lonely bartender.

"He's around, let me get him for you. Pour you something in the meantime?" the bartender asked, tossing a bar towel over her shoulder.

"I'll have a winter ale and…" Noah nodded toward Peyton.

"A cider?" Peyton said.

The bartender whipped out two glasses and filled them up to a frothy finish.

When she was gone, Peyton clinked her cider against Noah's beer glass. With a wink, she growled, "Arr!"

Noah laughed.

A joyful man lumbered toward their table. "Hey, Trina said you wanted to visit?"

"Yes. Thank you for coming down, Merry Christmas," Peyton said. Turning to Noah, she introduced, "This is Noah Wilde. He is doing a piece on Southport at Christmas. And… he's helping me on a little project."

"Sure, I'm not sure how I can help, but happy to," Pat said.

"It has to do with pirates," Peyton said.

"Oh, then I can definitely help," Pat said.

Noah leaned in, "What can you tell us about pirates closer to the 1800s?"

"Well, the hundred or so years after Stede Bonnet and Blackbeard certainly saw a drop off of piracy off the North Carolina coast, but there were a few, less notorious ones that continued to plunder the high seas up until the Revolutionary War. A few of them took advantage of and even aided either side of the war," Pat said.

"Any put roots down in Southport?" Noah asked.

"Not that you would know. To return to good-standing civilian life, you would need to be summarily pardoned or magically just appear," Pat said.

"And if you did that, you wouldn't have a recorded past," Peyton said.

"No, you wouldn't," Pat said.

"How would they own land?" Noah asked.

"I mean, during that time you could head out west. There were programs where you could receive a government grant if you cultivated the land. You slink off to an island in the Caribbean. Then, maybe you'd be granted rights to land somewhere, or they'd steal it. I mean, they were pirates after all," Pat said.

Peyton shook her head. "Or steal it."

"Could they have done that in town?" Noah asked.

"At Fort Johnston or Smithville at the time?" Pat shook his head. "Not likely. I mean, like I said, outside of the stealing thing. They'd have to be pretty crafty to manage that or have some help in high places."

"Got it." Noah sipped thoughtfully on his beer.

Peyton looked a bit dejected as she finished her cider. "I wonder what Christmas was like for pirates."

"Pirates *loved* Christmas," Pat said. "It was a time for celebration. Pirates liked to party. The town didn't mind them so much around Christmas time, either."

"Really?" Peyton asked.

"Sure, where do you think they got the rum for the nog?" Pat grinned. "In fact, if you aren't in a hurry, I could have Trina whip up a Royal Nog for you."

"Thank you, we'll have to put that on the list to come back for," Noah said.

"Be sure you do," Pat said.

Slipping out of his barstool, Noah reached his hand out. "Pleasure to visit with you."

"Likewise. Come by anytime!" Pat said.

"Merry Christmas, Pat," Peyton said.

"Merry Christmas, Peyton."

Peyton huddled close to Noah as they left the Royal James. With a twinge of defeat in her voice, she said, "I think I should have taken up his offer on the nog. Maybe a double."

"We learned some stuff. It's not all bad," Noah said.

"My family might have been pirates that stole the land where the James House sits," Peyton said.

"The prevailing history is that Benjamin Smith granted the land and the house to your family. We just need to prove it," Noah said.

"That seems less and less likely. Even if Smith did give the land to my great, great, great grandfather, there may have been a reason it was never officially recorded," Peyton said. "Which means that vulture from Charlotte can swoop right in."

"There's still time," Noah said. Giving Peyton a squeeze, he said, "Come on. I have an idea that might cheer *everyone* up."

Twenty Eight

Peyton shot Noah a curious look as he drove her through Southport.

Turning into the nursing home parking lot, Noah smiled. "Come on. What a better way to spread Christmas cheer than with family?"

With a nod, Peyton smiled back.

Walking through the nursing home, they swapped a chorus of Merry Christmases with Gladys before knocking on Henry's door. The sand dollar wreath with its red bow and starfish topper was still in place.

"Hi, Daddy!" Peyton called as she pushed into his room.

"Wha… Oh, hello, Peyton," Henry James said.

"Hello, Mr. James." Noah followed Peyton into the room.

"I think it's high time you call me Henry," Peyton's father said.

Noah nodded. "Henry. I thought I'd come and make good on the Toss-Across bet."

Henry tilted his head toward his daughter and said, "I thought you already had."

Noah laughed. "We had a wonderful dinner together. We wanted *you* to share in the spoils of victory. Would you come to dinner with us? At the James House?"

Henry looked at Peyton who shrugged and smiled.

"I'll get my shoes on!" Henry said as he shuffled in his chair to swap his slippers for shoes.

The moment they walked into the James House, Henry's eyes were wide as a child's on Christmas morning. He swept the entire house, touching furnishings as he walked by.

Stopping at a ceramic tree that was placed on a credenza, his fingers lightly followed the slope of the boughs. "This was my mother's. We knew it was Christmas time when it came out. Used to sit right here."

Henry's head tilted as he stopped in front of a display of brass angels. "This was my grandmother's. I would sit for hours, listening to her sing Christmas carols and watch these spin around," Henry said.

"I can light that for you, Daddy," Peyton said.

"Would you?" Henry asked, a hint of excitement in his voice.

Lighting a series of candles that sat underneath the angels, they gathered and watched as the flames flickered and began to heat up a little windmill at the top of the decoration. Slowly, the wheel began to spin. As it did, the little angels began to fly in a circle. Passing by bells, they rang a soft tune powered by the candles' flames.

Seeing Henry's smile in the glow of candles warmed Noah's heart. Seeing Peyton's face in the same glow, completely enamored with her father's enjoyment, made his heart do flips.

A knock at the door turned their attention. Noah left them with the display so that he could grab their food order. Handing over a tip and a Merry Christmas, Noah started to carry their dinner to the dining room.

Henry turned and pointed to the sofas. "If it's okay, I'd like to have dinner in here. So, we can see the tree."

"That's a great idea, Dad," Peyton said.

Noah found enough space amidst the little Christmas village to place their food on the table.

"I'll go get dishes," Peyton said, pivoting toward the kitchen.

"I can get them," Noah offered.

"I just need a moment. Stay here with Dad," Peyton said as she disappeared down the hall.

Noah joined Henry, who had moved to the tree.

Peyton's father's eyes surveyed the tree, seeming to delight in every unique ornament that was hung. His fingers cradled a ceramic figure of a girl on a rocking horse. "This was Peyton's first Christmas ornament. Her mother and I must have spent an hour trying to pick out just the right one. I didn't think it was all that important at the time. Now I know just how precious each of those moments is. It isn't the ornament. It's the time you spend with someone you care about as you search for it. It's the look in your daughter's eyes when it is opened. It's the years of memories that that one little thing carries with it."

"That might be the most profound thing about a Christmas ornament I have ever heard, sir," Noah said.

"This tree. It's all… memories," Henry said as he looked up. At the very top, his eyes landed on the angel. He brought a shaky hand to his lips. Taking a moment, he just stared at the angel. "That was Mary's. She loved that angel. Now, she's *my* angel. And Peyton's. Looking down on us. Sharing in this moment, right now."

Peyton stood with a stack of plates and silverware carried against her belly as she watched her father.

"Life took her from me. From us. But it can't take away the memories. I miss you, Mary," Henry said. Seeing Peyton with an armload of plates, Henry shifted gears jarringly quickly, "Let's eat. I'm hungry."

Noah looked into Peyton's eyes that were such a violent storm of pain and sorrow and fear. In the center of the storm was the joy and peace of watching her father. In one of his lucid moments just being Henry James.

Settling into the sofa seats, Peyton helped Henry dish up a plate.

Henry looked at Noah. "Thank you for this night. It means the world to me."

Noah nodded.

"Grandma would never let us eat in here. Always in the dining room. Mom made exceptions, for special occasions. She liked to spend time by the tree as well," Henry said. Turning to Peyton, he said, "You would spend hours in here. In the tree light, staring down on this little Christmas village. I always wondered what stories ran through your head."

"I think I pictured being in that little village. With family and friends, in the perfect snowy Christmas," Peyton said.

"We had one, back in 1989. Thirteen inches that Christmas day!" Henry said.

"It was Christmas miracle," Peyton said. "No one had sleds or snow shovels. We used trash can lids as toboggans. Garden spades as shovels. I built a snowman. His eyes were made with starfish and his buttons were little sand dollars. Daddy helped me make him. Momma found us a scarf of hers we could use and Granddad's old fishing hat. He had PVC pipe arms, work gloves and was holding a fishing pole."

"At a glance, I would have swore my dad was out on our lawn," Henry said. "This house has given us some wonderful memories, hasn't it?"

Peyton went stone cold. She said in a soft voice, "Yes, Daddy. It has."

"We'll look back on nights like this, years from now and reflect on it, too. Well, you young 'uns will," Henry said. "I'll have my arm around your momma and we'll both be looking down."

"Daddy…" Peyton sighed.

"You can't stop the train of life from coming. But you can be determined to make the most of what track you've got. Enjoy every moment," Henry said, his voice sharp and determined.

Gazing around the room, Henry seemed to take stock in his surroundings. Suddenly, he looked right at Peyton and said, "I want to live here."

"What?" Peyton asked, almost choking.

"I know I need help. I know I ain't gettin' much better. But I also haven't gotten any worse," Henry said. "There are those visiting nurses I seen on TV. So, I can be at home."

Peyton sat open mouthed, trying to devise the words.

"I won't be any trouble," Henry said, almost pleading.

Peyton rocked her head back and forth. "It's not that, Daddy."

With a heavy sigh and glassy eyes, Peyton started, "Dad, there's something I need to tell you…"

Henry cocked his head at his daughter, who clearly seemed distressed.

Peyton's lips begin to quiver as she fought to try to get out the words.

"That we were hoping to spend Christmas together. Here," Noah blurted, surprised at the words coming out of his own mouth.

Peyton's eyes grew wide as she shot a disapproving glance at Noah. "Right. Christmas. All together. Here. All of us. At the James House."

"That would be nice." Henry smiled about as big as Noah had seen in his short time knowing him.

Peyton got up from her seat on the couch. "Excuse me, Daddy. I need to borrow Noah for a moment. To clean up these dishes in the kitchen."

As soon as they were in the kitchen and their dishes and food trays were safely on the counter, Peyton grabbed Noah by the arm and spun him around. Looking him directly in the eyes, she scowled.

"What did you just promise my dad? Christmas? Together? The three of us? *Here?*" Peyton made a circle with her finger. "I can't imagine a more heartbreaking Christmas for my dad than to show up Christmas morning to find the locks on the family home are changed. Oh, and by the way, Daddy, our whole family history has been a lie."

Noah looked despondent. He shook his head, "I didn't want you to give up. Not just yet. I see how much you both love this place and if there is even a shred of hope, I want you to keep fighting for it. For your family."

"Why? Why are you so invested in my problems?" Peyton asked, an icy edge to her voice.

"Because *I* can't imagine a more heartbreaking Christmas than to see you… and your dad… heartbroken on Christmas," Noah said.

The room fell silent. The air in the kitchen was thick.

"The reality is, I am going to wake up on Christmas Day and this house won't be ours anymore. I'm going to pick up my dad at the nursing home and after a tough conversation, have Christmas at my little house. Because it is *mine*," Peyton said, her voice defeated. "Besides, I don't have a stocking for you."

Noah cocked his head. "I don't need a stocking. I just need you and Henry… to be okay."

Peyton paced around the kitchen for a moment. With a hand slapped to her forehead, she said, "I should just tell him. So it isn't a shock."

"You said, even if you were going to lose the James House, you were going to enjoy it as much as possible. Let's do the same for Henry. You saw him with the memories tonight. We still have the Holiday Home Tour and we have Christmas Eve. We'll deal with after that, well… *after that*," Noah said. "Build a few more memories in this place with your dad. In your family home."

Peyton wiped a tear and nodded.

Henry popped his head into the kitchen. "Is everything all right in here?"

"Everything's fine, Daddy," Peyton sniffed.

"I wanted to see if anyone was up for *It's a Wonderful Life*," Henry said.

"I was hoping you would ask, Henry," Noah said with a smile. Behind his back, he interlaced his fingers with Peyton's.

Twenty Nine

Noah and Peyton escorted Henry back to his suite in the nursing home.

Peyton got Henry settled and ready enough for bed so that when he was done with the movie, he could crawl right under the covers or conk out in the recliner under his blanket.

Noah got the movie going, and the room welcomed a conversation on the screen that took place amongst the blinking stars.

By the time George Bailey jumped into the frozen pond to save his brother, Henry was deep asleep.

Peyton adjusted her father's blanket. Nodding towards the door, she whispered, "I think he's done for the night."

Noah nodded and waited as Peyton kissed her father on the forehead.

"Goodnight, Daddy," Peyton whispered.

Grabbing Noah's hand, she tiptoed toward the door.

Nudging Noah with her shoulder as they walked down the nursing home hallway, Peyton looked up at him. "Thank you. It may not seem like much, but tonight might have been the nicest thing anyone has ever done for me."

"I can't believe that. I enjoy spending time with you and your father," Noah said.

"I'm sure you have other things to do," Peyton said.

"There's nothing I'd *rather* do," Noah said.

Peyton shook her head and said, "This was setting up to be such a challenging Christmas, and it is. It's just… a lot more bearable with you."

"I make things bearable. Now, *that's* a high compliment." Noah laughed.

"I mean great. You made a below-average Christmas great," Peyton said.

Noah nodded. "I can take that one."

They climbed into Noah's car and he frowned. "You know, since the first time I met you, you were boiling over with Christmas spirit. I mean, it's infectious. *You* are infectious. I never would have known you were struggling."

"Yeah, well, dwelling on things isn't the James family way," Peyton said. "I think that is why the town has been such a special place. My grandparents and parents were so generous and so kind."

"And now, so are you," Noah said. "Not very pirate-like, if you ask me."

"I didn't ask," Peyton rolled her eyes.

As Noah drove toward downtown Southport, he was diverted.

"What's going on down here?" he asked as he peered out his windshield.

"Oh, my gosh!" Peyton exclaimed. "I can't believe I forgot! It is the Light Up the Night Christmas Parade. It is an over-100-year tradition. Park at my house. We'll walk to downtown."

Following Peyton's instructions, Noah parked in Peyton's driveway.

"Come on, we're going to miss it!" Peyton grabbed Noah's hand and jogged the four blocks to the waterfront.

Snaking through the crowd, they scurried up the steps to the James House.

"Good evening, Peyton and Noah!" Cybil called from her porch. A chorus of ladies chimed in behind her.

"Good evening!"

"Did we miss much?" Peyton asked.

"Just started," Cybil said. "We have parade watching libations if you want to pop over."

"Thank you. We had an early dinner," Peyton said.

"I saw that Henry was over. Nice to see him home, even if for a bit," Cybil said.

"Yeah," Peyton said almost under her breath.

The South Brunswick Middle School band marched in step to lead off the parade with the town mayor waving from a convertible.

Behind the band were floats from various businesses and institutions from around the area.

The Maritime Museum staff waved from the bow of a large boat that was towed along. Fort Johnston Museum and Visitor's Center followed close behind in an old VW van with its doors open. Mabel waved from one of the open bays.

"That doesn't look like it was from the Revolutionary War," Noah said.

"It was from a movie that filmed here called *One Summer*," Peyton said. "Cute movie. You'd probably like it."

"I'll have to check it out," Noah said.

The Old South Tour Company buggy drove by with Katie tossing candy canes to the children watching from the sidewalks. Seeing Peyton and Noah, she gave a hearty wave.

"In her period dress," Noah said.

"I can hardly picture her without it," Peyton said.

Olde Southport Villages had a float with a miniature set of the shops towed atop a flatbed.

"That is adorable," Noah said. Waving at Krista the barista, he glanced at Peyton. "Shouldn't you be on there?"

"Normally, yes. With everything going on, I was excused for the evening," Peyton said.

"Christmas parade flu?" Noah asked.

Peyton waved at a smiley Krista. "If that was the case, I'd say I was more than busted."

Darian from the downtown coffee shop waved from a float supporting the business near the waterfront.

The South Brunswick High School marching band played Christmas carols as they moved along the parade route. The school's football team tossed little foam footballs while the mascot Cougar danced along and high-fived every child with their hand up.

The police and fire departments made a showing with Santa riding on the back of a ladder truck.

"Winterfest. Something to celebrate every night," Peyton said.

Noah turned to Peyton and smiled. "If not, we make one."

Peyton said softly, "Now, you're learning."

Taking Noah's hands in hers, she looked up with a grin, "Oh, what's *that?*"

Noah's eyes followed Peyton's. With a chuckle, he said, "That looks like mistletoe everywhere."

"I wasn't going to let you avoid it this time," Peyton said as she pushed up on her toes and wrapped her arms around Noah's neck.

Noah leaned in, letting her lips meet his. "I like mistletoe everywhere. With you."

They could hear giggles from the opposing porch.

"I think we're giving your neighbors a show," Noah whispered.

"Might as well leave a lasting impression," Peyton said.

"I think you already have," Noah said.

Thirty

Noah's morning began with a walk into town and a quick exchange with Darian and one of her creations at the coffee shop.

He had all but expected the phone call. "Good morning, Jennimay."

"How is my photojournalist elf today?" Jennimay sang through the phone.

"I'm doing good as long as you never call me that again," Noah said.

"Fair enough. I like some of the recent photos you've sent in. I think you are starting to hit your groove in Southport," Jennimay said.

Noah sipped his coffee and nodded to himself. "The locals said that would happen. As one of them puts it, you have to *experience* Christmas in Southport, not just see it."

"Smart local. Your photos seem to be capturing that experience, good work," Jennimay said.

"The people here know how to celebrate the holiday," Noah said.

"Have you put more thought into the cover house? I have to admit, I am torn myself. The Thomas House fits it to a 'T'. It's kind of what I pictured when I sent you down there. *But*, I have to say, there is something about the James House that tugs at me. I can't quite put my finger on it," Jennimay said.

"I am leaning toward the James House," Noah admitted.

"I read your notes on it," Jennimay said. "So, the family might actually descend from pirates?"

"It isn't definitive, but the evidence is starting to point that way," Noah said.

"That is interesting. Coming from a pirate lineage. And for generations, the Jameses have been a prominent, upstanding family in the town of Southport," Jennimay said.

"They have. The community loves them, and it is mutual," Noah said.

"And you've found proof of the rightful owner of the house?" Jennimay said.

"I have found proof that the original James family owner *did* reside in Southport, or Smithville, during the time the house was constructed and he was a known associate of Benjamin Smith, Continental Army Colonel and post-war governor of North Carolina," Noah said.

"They were friends and neighbors," Jennimay said.

"It seems that way. But I still don't have definitive legal proof of original ownership," Noah said.

"Which means the James family could still lose it. At the very least, they could be embroiled in a messy legal battle when the article is published," Jennimay said.

"Yeah," Noah said, his voice coming out as a sigh.

"Well, follow it. We'll have the option to swap covers and tweak the article when it goes to print," Jennimay said.

"What about the digital version that comes out on Christmas Day?" Noah asked.

"I'm going to let you make that call. You've got boots on the ground. Use your gut. I don't like the lack of symmetry between the print and digital editions if we need to make changes, but the story is intriguing and both houses would make a great cover," Jennimay said.

"Thank you," Noah said. "And thank you for trusting me."

"You've always been good, Noah. Your work is technically flawless. But I am seeing some vision this time around. I'm seeing real heart in your photos," Jennimay said. "Keep up the good work. You're almost done there."

"Yeah," Noah said.

"I'll talk to you on Christmas Eve. I'll need your final call," Jennimay said.

"That's tomorrow," Noah realized out loud.

"Yes, it is. Talk to you then, Noah," Jennimay said and ended the call.

Slipping his phone in his pocket, Noah debated his next step. The search through the bowels of Southport's ancient justice system verified Thomas James was there and connected to Benjamin Smith.

His real estate legal expert at *Coastal Charm Magazine* told him that wasn't enough to save the house. He needed to find a recording of the deed or the deed itself, or the house would legally be claimable.

Noah shook his head as he surveyed the streets of downtown Southport. He tried to think of where he might find a record of the original transaction.

A pair of raised voices caught his attention two doors down from the coffee shop. Peering down the block, Noah found two familiar faces. Chauncey Craven and Ty Bates were squared off in front of the town newspaper.

Ty shoved the smug attorney against the brick wall of the newspaper. Pointing a finger at Craven's chest, Ty snarled, "You stay away from Peyton and the James House."

The attorney was unmoved by Ty's threatening presence, "That ship has nearly sailed, son. No amount of fist swingin' is gonna change that."

"It might not change anything, but I swear I'll feel a lot better," Ty said, his fingers balled up in a fist.

Another man that Noah recognized from the parade came around the corner and walked toward the newspaper.

"Everything all right here, boys?" the man asked.

Ty paused for a moment as he scowled at the attorney. "We're all right. Just explain to Chauncey here that we take care of our community."

"We do. But we also deal with our problems in a civil manner. At least out on the sidewalk in broad daylight, Mr. Bates," the man said.

"Yes, sir," Ty said, taking a step away from the attorney.

Chauncey Craven brushed the wrinkles out of his suit and checked his cuffs. With a snap of his lapel, he grinned, "I *am* part of the community now."

"Not yet, you aren't," Noah said, striding up to the men.

Chauncey squinted, "You've been hangin' around the James House. *My* house."

Noah squared up with the man. "The fight for that house hasn't even begun. I'm going to do what I can to ensure you never step foot in it."

"Y'all don't know nothin' about real estate law. But, you will by Christmas mornin'," Chauncey said with a wicked grin as he walked off toward his shiny Range Rover.

Noah sighed, "I really don't like that man."

"That's something we can agree on," Ty said. He squinted at Noah slightly as he walked off, still seething.

"You must be Noah Wilde, the photojournalist from the magazine," the man said. Sticking his hand out, he added, "Mayor Clemmons."

"Mr. Mayor. I recognize you from the parade," Noah said.

"A fine evening it was," the mayor said.

"I'm a bit surprised you know me," Noah said.

The mayor laughed. "Not much gets past me in this town. I take it you know about the little situation we have with one of our waterfront homes? The James family has always been an exceptional part of the community, from my perspective. As far as the house and the house's history, well, I'd like to see the history remain, but not if it's a false history. Wish there was something I could do to help Henry and his daughter."

"I can place Thomas James, that is the original resident of the James House, as a confidant of Benjamin Smith in Southport at the time the house was constructed and its original occupation," Noah said.

"Occupation don't hold up in a property deed dispute," the mayor said.

"No sir, it doesn't," Noah said.

"I'm sure the Jameses attorney has scoured high and low for a recorded deed," Mayor Clemmons said.

"He has. I've scoured every resource in the county and had my national team look into it as well. They found nothing," Noah said.

The mayor looked at the entrance to the newspaper, "You got a moment? I'd like to introduce you to someone."

"I've got time." Noah nodded.

Following the mayor into the State Port Pilot newspaper office, Noah was greeted by a young girl at the front desk.

"Ms. Adams, this is Noah Wilde. He is doin' a magazine article on the town and he stumbled onto a little mystery. We were hopin' to run past Ms. Jordyn," Mayor Clemmons said.

"I'll see if Jordyn is available," the girl said and scurried down the hall.

A well-put-together woman strode confidently behind the young lady manning the front desk.

"Mr. Mayor, Merry Christmas," the woman said.

"Merry Christmas, Jordyn," the mayor said. "This is my new friend, Noah Wilde. I was hoping you might have a minute or two for him. He's kind of diggin' into a little Southport mystery."

"I do like mysteries." The woman smiled. Holding out her hand toward Noah, she said, "I'm Jordyn Nelmark, editor of the State Port Pilot."

"Pleasure to meet you, Ms. Nelmark," Noah said.

"I'm in the people business, please, call me Jordyn."

"All right, Jordyn," Noah replied.

"Come on. Follow me, we can talk in my office," Jordyn said. "See you later, Mr. Mayor."

"Take care of our friend there, Jordyn," the mayor called.

"I'll do what I can!"

With a hand extended, the newspaper editor motioned for Noah to slip into the office and to take a seat. Sliding behind the desk, the woman instinctively grabbed a pen and tapped it on a notepad. "What can I do for you, Mr. Wilde?"

"Noah's fine," Noah said, leaning forward in his seat.

"I've been helping a friend," he began.

"Peyton James," Jordyn said to Noah's surprise. Jordyn fanned her hands out over her desk. "It's a small town."

"Right," Noah suddenly looked nervous to share.

"Anything we say here will be held in confidence unless you or Ms. James gives me explicit permission to share," Jordyn said.

"Okay." Noah rubbed his hands together. "Peyton's family home, the James House, is under legal dispute. An attorney from Charlotte claims there was never a recorded deed on the property and therefore it can be purchased and claimed under some convoluted real estate law."

"I see. The James family has an attorney?" Jordyn asked.

"They do. They haven't been able to find proof of original ownership. My resources have come up dry as well," Noah explained. "I can place Thomas James in Southport at the time the James House was built and occupied and that he was an associate of Benjamin Smith."

"Who reportedly gifted the house and property to Thomas James," Jordyn said.

"Correct," Noah said.

"From a story perspective, it lines up. From a legal perspective…" Jordyn paused.

"The James family is in trouble," Noah said.

Jordyn clasped her hands together and tapped her index fingers to her lips. "They are a sweet family. I'd love to help. But I'm not really sure how I can. The property grant goes back to the early 1800s. The newspaper was started in 1928. We don't have records that go back that far. Not even close."

"Records for the entire family don't seem to exist until after the Revolutionary War. There is a theory that Thomas James may have been a pirate," Noah said.

Jordyn's eyes went wide. "Now *that* would be newsworthy."

"Newsworthy, but not helpful to the cause," Noah said.

"No, I suppose not," Jordyn said. Her eyes narrowed as she mulled over the situation. "Let me rummage through the archives. I may have a few other contacts who might be able to help."

"I'd appreciate that. Peyton and her father would appreciate it," Noah said.

"Give me some time. I'll see what I can dig up," Jordyn said.

"They have until midnight Christmas Eve," Noah said.

Jordyn shook her head and gasped, "Of course they do."

"It was a legal ploy by the attorney, knowing it would confound the James family in seeking additional help," Noah said.

"Yeah, well, that attorney didn't plan on Southport stepping up to take care of our own," Jordyn said, her voice defiant. "I need to make some calls. Clear my schedule and get dusty in the records room."

"Thank you," Noah said.

Jordyn began marking through her calendar. "Ugh, I'm supposed to be working the Candy Cane Garden event. We're a little short-staffed with the holidays and all."

"I'm a photojournalist. I can cover the event for you," Noah said.

After studying Noah for a moment, Jordyn nodded, "All right. You're on."

"Thank you for doing this," Noah said.

"Thank you for caring for our people," Jordyn said. With a wave of the backs of her hands, she smiled and said, "Now get out of here. We both have work to do!"

Thirty One

Noah arrived at Keziah Park in the heart of downtown Southport not knowing what to expect. The park's centerpiece was an oak tree nearly a millennium old with little gardens maintained by the Southport Garden Club that added splashes of color around the otherwise open space.

On Candy Cane Garden Party day, the park was filled with visitors displaying, admiring and bidding on decorated wooden candy canes and silk wreaths. Pulling out his camera, Noah took shots of the event from the periphery. He wanted to capture how well attended the garden party was while showing off the festive holiday wares of the event.

Carolers stood under the massive tree while hot cocoa with candy canes hooked to the rims of their cups were served.

Noah smiled to himself as he stared through his lens. "Yet another Southport reason to celebrate."

A voice from behind him said, "Are you going to walk around talkin' to yourself or are you goin' to say hi?"

Letting his camera drop, Noah turned to see Peyton standing behind him, the hook of a candy cane sticking out of her mouth.

"What are you doing here?" Peyton asked.

"Celebrating Christmas Southport style," Noah said.

Peyton smiled. "Look at you sleuthing out our holiday secrets all by yourself."

"I had a little help," Noah admitted. "I'm on a freelance assignment for the Pilot."

"I see. And how did that come about?" Peyton asked.

"I ran into the mayor, who introduced me to Jordyn, who shared with me she was a little short-handed today. I figured I could help out and see this Candy Cane Garden Party for myself and see if there was a Coastal Charm-worthy shot in the mix," Noah said.

"Careful, Noah. You're starting to become a small towner. That's how it works around here," Peyton teased. "You show up and folks put you to work."

"Yeah, that might not be so bad," Noah said. "So, what am I looking at?"

"Okay, the Garden Club puts this on every year. Artists, businesses and anyone handy decorates the wooden candy canes. You can hang them on a wall. Buy a stand to plant them in your yard. First you gotta bid on them and hope you win the auction. You win, you get to take your candy cane or wreath home and add it to your décor. It all helps the Garden Club sponsor events throughout the year," Peyton said.

"The community coming together to support the community in supporting the community," Noah said.

"Don't try to do small town math, it doesn't always add up," Peyton said.

Noah laughed as he admired the scene. "No, I think it does."

"I shouldn't hold you back from your work," Peyton said.

"I got the shots I needed. You helped me fill in the story. I'm ahead of the game," Noah said. "Mind if I join you?"

"Mind? I'd be offended if you didn't," Peyton said. Perusing the displays of candy canes, she seemed to be on a mission.

"Looking for something in particular?" Noah asked as he walked past traditional canes with red and white stripes, canes with intricately painted winter scenes and one painted to be reminiscent of the Southport water tower.

"I am." Peyton nodded. "There is a very special candy cane out here somewhere. I need to find it."

"Hmm." Noah studied the canes. "Any clues as to what I'm looking for?"

"Look for a sunset view that could have been stolen from our front porch," Peyton said.

"All right." Noah narrowed his focus.

Suddenly, Peyton darted ahead of him and stood by a wooden candy cane. With a gentle swipe, she ran her fingers along the smooth finished edges.

Noah caught up and eyed the candy cane with a water view and sunset colors, seabirds in the pink and orange sky heading to shore for the night. In the lower right-hand corner, the initials MJ were scrawled in white paint.

Noah sighed and placed a gentle hand on Peyton's shoulder. "Your mother's?"

"Yeah," Peyton nodded. "The ladies at the Garden Club couldn't bear to sell it. There is a new volunteer this year running the warehouse. I only thought of it when a customer at the shop talked about coming here today."

Swallowing hard, Peyton picked up the bid sheet. "Hope Daddy is fine with only one gift this year."

"Those are generous bids," Noah said.

Peyton nodded. "Momma was amazing at all things crafty."

Writing in her bid to top the previous bidder by a reasonable margin, she admired the candy cane.

"Oh, that's beautiful," a bidder said as she scribbled her name and dollar amount on the paper.

Peyton sighed and picked up the pen as soon as the previous bidder moved on. Hovering nervously, Peyton stared at the sheet, almost warding off other bidders.

"Come on," Noah said. "Let's get you some candy cane cocoa and circle back. Otherwise, you're just going to be bidding yourself up."

Peyton nodded and reluctantly walked away from her mother's candy cane.

As they reached the cocoa table, Noah's phone rang.

"Noah, it's Jordyn. How's it going out there?"

"It's really nice. I'll send photos and a write up in about half an hour," Noah said.

"Sounds great. I wanted to tell you, I was rummaging through the archives, keep in mind, our records are off by nearly a century and a half from what you are needing. I didn't find the Golden Ticket that you are looking for, but I did find a lead. There was an article a military historian submitted to the paper back in the thirties. Some sort of an expert on the Revolutionary War and had an archive on Benjamin Smith. I have a contact running that archive down," Jordyn said.

"Thank you, that is great news!" Noah said.

"Don't get your hopes up yet. It is still a shot in the dark," Jordyn said.

"I appreciate it just the same," Noah said.

Ending the call, Noah found Peyton near the cocoa table, anxiously trying to break away from a conversation.

"Noah!" she blurted. Handing him his cocoa, she glanced at her watch. "Noah, this is Purdy Myers. She is next year's Garden Club president. Maybe you would like her to share the club's plans in the new year for your article."

Purdy's eyes grew wide, and she placed her hand on Noah's non-cocoa arm and began excitedly sharing a month-by-month detail of the club's planned activities.

While trying to listen and not seem uninterested, Noah craned his neck to try to follow Peyton's frantic sprint to the bidding sheet. Seeing her halfway across the park, an announcement was made that all bids were closed and the sheets were about to be tallied.

Noah watched as Peyton spun, and her face shared her heartbreak. "Excuse me, Ms. Myers. This is so good and detailed, maybe the paper can make an appointment. Take you to tea or lunch and get the full scoop," Noah said as he spun and made a beeline toward Peyton.

As Noah neared her, Peyton dropped her head. "I didn't win. Some ridiculous bid came in after my last entry. I missed it."

The current club president stood in front of a microphone, "Ooh, this is exciting. Too good to wait for the end. We have an all-time high bid. Can you imagine, a thousand-dollar candy cane? It is for a truly special piece."

The garden club president held up the sunset candy cane that Peyton's mother painted.

"The winning bid goes to Peyton James! Congratulations, Peyton. And thank you for your generous donation. Your family has always been so kind to us," the garden club president announced.

Peyton looked confused. Her eyes met Noah's.

With a sheepish smile, Noah shrugged. "I didn't want to take a chance on you missing out."

Not knowing how to respond as her eyes began to pool, Peyton said, "How much is Jordyn paying for your freelance gig?"

"If she gives me what I asked for? A fortune," Noah smiled.

Peyton hugged Noah. Over his shoulder, she whispered, "Thank you."

"Let's collect your winnings. I have an article I need to submit," Noah said, taking Peyton by the hand.

Peyton accepted her prize and admired it. "This is going out front for the Holiday Home Tour," she announced proudly.

"This is good stuff," Jordyn Nelmark said as she clicked through Noah's article. "*Really* good. And your article was surprisingly poignant for an event piece."

"You never know how a simple decoration can impact someone's day or even their entire holiday season," Noah said.

"I did get a call from Purdy Myers. I'm supposed to have tea with her to get the scoop on the entire year of club activities?" Jordyn asked.

Noah grinned. "It was a deal struck for the right reasons. Sorry about that."

"It's all right, these shots are worth it," Jordyn said. "You held up your end of the bargain. I wish my end had more meat on the bones. My contact was able to reach the current archivist that chronicles the Revolutionary War period. There are letters from Benjamin Smith. It shows Smith's intent to grant the property to a mystery confidant that was described as an ally in the war. Someone who was close to Smith when he was a colonel."

"Well, that's interesting," Noah leaned forward.

"It is, but…" Jordyn seemed to hesitate. "The contact scribed only in initials- T. M."

"T. M.?" Noah frowned. "That's not Thomas James. Who is T. M.?"

Jordyn shrugged. "They found a thread and are going to keep pulling at it. I'll let you know if they find anything else."

Noah nodded numbly. "Thank you."

Leaving the newspaper, Noah's mind reeled. Maybe the pirate Thomas James *did* steal the property.

Thirty Two

Noah's mood as he arrived at the James House was mixed. The search for proof of ownership to remain in Peyton's family continued to uncover new information about her family's past, but none of it was imminently helpful to the cause at hand.

With each new string they pulled, they got closer to the right time period, but the latest bit of information might have turned out to be the house's undoing. If Benjamin Smith had intended to bestow the property to someone other than Thomas James, the James family would not only have no legal recourse, but their entire history could be rewritten.

Noah stood outside the gate, looking at the historic home in its festive holiday grandeur. It looked welcoming and full of the personality and love of the family that lived there for generations. It pained him that he couldn't have done more.

Pacing, he reviewed the conversation with Jordyn in his mind, trying to make sense of it. A voice called from the porch, "Are going to stay outside talkin' to yourself or are you gonna come inside?"

Noah looked up to see Peyton standing on the porch. A kitchen towel was slung over her shoulder.

"Just admiring," Noah said.

"The house or the lady of the house?" Peyton asked.

"Both," Noah said. Swinging open the gate, he marched up the steps. Pausing, he swiped a smear of flour from Peyton's cheek.

Peyton's eyes danced as they looked into his. "Hmm, don't try leading me astray, mister. We've got work to do!"

"Like baking cookies?" Noah asked.

"The Holiday Home Tour starts in two hours. I have to clean up and then I have to clean myself up. I must look like a wreck!" Peyton said. "If you can manage the last few trays of cookies, I can tidy up the house."

"What should I expect tonight?" Noah asked, as he followed Peyton into the kitchen.

"You ever watch one of those movies with the grumpy old man and the ghosts?" Peyton asked.

"*Scrooge*? I mean, *A Christmas Carol*?" Noah asked.

"Yes!" Peyton exclaimed. "You remember those scenes with young Scrooge at the Christmas party in the old barn or tavern, or whatever it was? It is a lot like that. Just stretched across every house long the waterfront."

"We're having a Scrooge party?" Noah scoffed.

"More like a Dickens party. The real celebration is the homes. People get to mingle and visit while they admire each house's flavor of Christmas décor. Eat some cookies or canapes…" Peyton said.

"Canapes?" Noah frowned.

"Appetizers. Sometimes we call 'em canapes in the south," Peyton said as she began ensuring the house was ready for visitors. "And each house makes a family recipe cocktail. Some make Tom and Jerrys, mules, hot buttered rum… I'm making Glogg."

"Glogg?"

"A type of mulled wine. I really like it for the aroma that fills the house when I make it. Warm spices, orange and cranberries. It fills the air with Christmas *and* guests can serve themselves," Peyton said.

"Aromatic and practical," Noah replied.

"Oh, I almost forgot an important detail," Peyton said as she caught a reflection of herself and paused to tease her hair. "The house families get gussied up in period dress."

"I look forward to seeing you as a Dicken's character," Noah said.

"Oh, you get to take part in the fun, too," Peyton said.

Noah shrugged. "It turns out I didn't pack any period clothing."

Peyton grinned. "No worries. I have something for you already pressed."

Noah frowned.

"Mom used to make Dad dress up. He hated it, but he did it anyway," Peyton said.

"Just like I'm going to," Noah said in a sullen tone.

"Yes, you are," Peyton said. "Good thing you and Daddy are about the same size."

"Good thing," Noah mumbled, swapping a pan of baked cookies for the final sheet of raw ones.

Noah helped Peyton clean up the kitchen before heading to his hotel to shower and change.

Unzipping the garment bag that Peyton thrust into his arms as he left, he revealed his ensemble for the evening. A white, wing-tip collar shirt laid the foundation for his evening attire. Fitted stirrup pants followed, tight around the high waist and at the foot, they were certainly different from any other pair of pants that Noah owned. Sliding in front of the mirror as he tucked his shirt into the pair of trousers, he studied the ensemble.

"So far, so okay," he mumbled, and thought the word "good" might have been a bit too high praise.

Layering an ornate vest that gleamed with a blue on black silk jacquard over his white shirt, he buttoned it and smoothed out the shirt's wrinkles underneath the vest.

Hung around the neck of the hanger was a tie. Though he owned more ties than he would have liked at home, this misshapen, oddly sized tie had him mystified. Setting it aside, he told himself, "I'll deal with that later."

Pulling the last item from the garment bag, Noah slipped into it. A tailcoat with the front tapered and open toward his waist had long tails covering his backside.

Noah twisted in the mirror. He had to admit, it didn't look *bad*. It felt like he should grab his lantern to hitch it to his wagon for the ride back to the James House.

Settling on sticking with modern transportation, Noah left his hotel room for his rental car. Passing by other guests coming and going for the evening, he offered an embarrassed wave with his head down.

Pulling up to the James House, he got out of his vehicle. He felt his cheeks flush as heads on the sidewalk and neighboring porches turned toward him and watched him push through the James House gate.

"Good evening." Noah nodded, happy for not having to fiddle with the latch on the gate to make his escape into the confines of the James House as quickly and efficiently as possible.

Ladies on nearby porches waved and giggled as Noah rapped on the door and waited, continuing to give self-conscious little waves as he rocked back and forth amidst the chatter and occasional catcalls from ladies who were assembled from a wide range of ages.

Finally, the door to the James House swung open.

Noah's jaw dropped, and his lips parted, but no words escaped. For a long moment, he just stood in the doorway, staring at the hostess.

Peyton had slithered into her Victorian era dress. An impossibly deep blue with black lace filigree, it flowed from her shoulders to her feet with a tight taper at the hips. Lacy frills accented an open, but modest square cut at her chest. Her hair was pulled back with ringlets cascading to her shoulders, allowing pearl earrings to dangle unfettered.

Bringing a hand to her chest, Peyton frowned, "Is there something wrong?"

"No," Noah said, shaking his head. "You are… breathtaking."

Peyton's cheeks glowed red. "You look pretty handsome yourself. Come in before we make a scene for the neighbors."

"I dare say they will find that suggestion disappointing," Noah said as he held up his hand in a quick wave to Cybil who was observing every moment of his entrance.

Peyton gave Noah a once over in his borrowed suit. She smiled and said, "I think it's a pretty good fit. You look dashing."

"Thank you. I'm sure your father wore it better," Noah said.

"I don't think so," Peyton said, cocking her head at him as took in another look.

Noah winced. Pulling the tie from his pocket, he said, "I did have a little trouble with this."

Peyton laughed. "Daddy could never figure that tie out, either. Mama would have to tie it for him. Let me have a go at it."

Taking the tie, Peyton wrapped her arms around Noah. Tugging at the silk, she pulled him close. Their eyes danced together as their chests began to beat in rhythm. Her lips parted and her mouth met his. For a moment, they stood together embraced.

"Yeah, that's how your mother used to tie mine, too. Never could figure out the darned thing myself. Didn't much mind the help, though," Henry said as he ambled by on his way to the kitchen. "Don't mind me, I was just going to sample the Glogg!"

Peyton and Noah laughed together as they pulled apart.

"All right, serious business with this tie," Peyton said. "This is a puff tie. We'll connect this strap behind your collar, tuck the tails and… excuse me while I reach into your vest… and voila! Now you look like a proper Reconstruction era southern gentleman."

"Thank you," Noah said as he caught a reflection in the evening windows. The blue satin tie was a near-perfect match for the color of Peyton's dress.

"Now, you look even dapper-er," Peyton smiled.

Setting up his camera on a shelf roughly chest high, Noah pointed it at the Christmas tree. Wrapping his arm around Peyton, he allowed the automatic shutter to rifle off countless shots as they posed and laughed in front of the lens.

Henry stood in the entrance to the living room, admiring the pair. His eyes wore a sheen as he watched them. "You two look magnificent. Mary would have been over the moon watching you two tonight," he said.

"I'm honored to be part of the festivities," Noah said.

"You're lookin' pretty good in my suit, too. Might as well consider it yours, Noah," Henry said.

"I… couldn't," Noah started.

"You can and you will," Henry said. "It's done."

"Would you join us in a photo?" Noah asked.

Henry nodded and allowed himself to be positioned with Peyton in between him and Noah.

When the camera completed its round of photos, Henry held his cup of Glogg up in the air. "I'm going to sit for a bit."

Looking through the shots he had recently taken, Noah froze on a photo of the three of them.

Peyton peered over his shoulder and gasped, "That's beautiful."

Noah nodded. "Yeah. I take so many photos. Once in a while, one grabs me. Like this one."

Henry looked sharply dressed on his side of the photo. His own tailcoat, darker than Noah's, was accented by a burgundy ribbon tie.

Peyton looked up at Noah and said softly, "Thank you for being here."

"I wouldn't miss it for the world," Noah said.

Doing a little dance around the house, Peyton admired the home and said with a sigh, "I guess this is the last night of the James House."

"I tried everything I could think of. I'm sorry," Noah said.

Peyton strode close to Noah and looked at him. "Don't be sorry. I'm grateful for everything you've done. And don't think I don't know all the stones you turned over. Remember, this is a small town. I hear things."

"Yeah." Noah nodded. He watched her flit about, surprisingly light on her feet.

Peyton caught him watching her and shrugged. "Someone once said they can't take away the memories. So, I'm not going to let them."

Taking Peyton by the hand, Noah smiled. "Well, let's make some more memories!"

Thirty Three

The Holiday Home Tour kicked off with carolers parading down the block. Stopping at each house, they would sing a Christmas carol to the applause of the owners and often their guests would filter in.

At first, they admired the front of the house and the porch decorations. Some homes even decorated their fences with ribbons, garland or wreaths. Many had wooden candy canes crafted by local artists. Some had collections that spanned nearly a decade of Candy Cane Garden events.

Each homeowner was dressed in period attire, while most of the guests wore contemporary clothing. Guides would escort guests through the properties as they shared the history of the home while weaving in tales of Christmas parties over the centuries.

Some guests landed at a friend's home and never strayed. Others bounced from house to house, enjoying the personality and splendor that each had to offer.

Peyton welcomed guests as she stood on the porch with Noah at her side. She winced when the historian guiding a group of guests launched into her family's history. She wondered what future years' stories would sound like. Stories of pirates and scandals replacing tales of her mother's and grandmother's generous philanthropy and stewardship.

Still, the familiar faces fended off gloom as Peyton hugged her friends as they came to visit. Several winked and nudged her seeing Noah by her side.

As guests milled about, Peyton moved the party inside. Noah checked in on Henry. Grabbing a plate of treats and a glass of eggnog, he ensured Peyton's father was in good spirits as he visited with friends and neighbors who came to call for the event.

Stealing a moment to take a few photos of the gala, Noah stared through the lens. If it wasn't for the guests in normal clothes, the shots could have easily depicted another era, especially those of Peyton in her party gown.

He admired her as she moved with elegance and grace. Ever the dutiful hostess, she moved effortlessly from guest to guest. It was clear she loved the town and the town loved her.

The festive mood inside the house became a contrast with the sound of voices out on the front porch.

Moving to investigate, Noah slipped out the front door to see Chauncey Craven peering through the windows.

"Hey!" a voice called from the sidewalk.

Noah and Chauncey turned to see Ty Bates push through the gate, his temper worn clearly on his face. As he stomped up the steps, he paused as he gave Noah and his attire a once-over, "I guess I'm glad I don't have to wear that get-up."

"I told you to stay away from Peyton and her family," Ty snarled as he turned his attention to Chauncey Craven.

"Tomorrow, this house will be mine," the real estate attorney said.

"It's not yours yet," Noah said, his voice even as he stifled his own anger. He didn't want to alarm Peyton or her guests and detract from their party.

"And it may never be," another voice called from the sidewalk.

Jordyn Nelmark walked through the gate and looked up at the trio of sparring men. "Mr. Wilde, can I steal you for a moment?"

Noah glanced at Ty and Chauncey. "Sure. I think my friend here can send Chauncey on his way."

Ty gave Noah a reassuring nod.

"Thanks," Noah said to Ty and turned to follow the *State Port Pilot* newspaper editor to a shadowy corner of the house out of earshot of the others.

"My contact found something. Deep in the archives, information that Benjamin Smith himself tried to keep quiet. There was a confidant during his time in the war. It wasn't a pirate. It was a spy working on behalf of the Continental Army. He was a businessman who had solid ties to the British traders and suppliers. He used those ties to support the efforts of his neighbors, most notably, Benjamin Smith," Jordyn said.

"It correlates to the earlier redacted note that they found," Jordyn continued. "The house was indeed intended to be given to the spy, Benjamin Smith's close friend, James Montgomery."

Noah paced a few steps as he mulled over the information that the reporter was sharing with him. "So, this Montgomery family owns the home?"

"That was the intention." Jordyn nodded. "Look at these. They are old, but… tell me what you see."

Jordyn swiped her finger on her phone and toggled back and forth between two photos.

"This is a photo of Benjamin Smith and Thomas Montgomery. Here is a photo of Peyton James' great, great, great grandfather," Jordyn said.

"They're the same person," Noah said.

"Thomas Montgomery became Thomas James after the Revolutionary War to avoid persecution from British loyalists due to his, in their eyes, treasonous acts to the British crown," Jordyn said.

Noah stepped away, his eyes fixating on the mingling guests inside the house conversing in front of the Christmas tree. Peyton smiled as she entered their conversation.

"The house *was* intended for the James family. The James family didn't exist until the war's end. Before that, I give you the Montgomerys," Jordyn said.

"That's… amazing," Noah said. His face fell. "That is a key thread in Peyton's family history, but it won't settle her legal problem. She still needs a deed."

Jordyn nodded and said, "There is something else my contact suggested. It's a long shot, but if there was time for a miracle, it would be Christmas."

Noah leaned in.

"Documents pertaining to the house that was being built, if not delivered and recorded with the courthouse, would likely have stayed with the granter for safe keeping," Jordyn said.

"Benjamin Smith, not the Jameses… or Montgomerys would have the deed," Noah said.

"*If* it actually exists at all," Jordyn nodded.

Noah frowned and asked, "Does that mean it would be in Raleigh at the Governor's mansion or Benjamin's Smith's personal home?"

"If he was conducting business in Southport, like granting his good friend a piece of property, he likely would have kept the documents at his summer home," Jordyn said. Her eyes pivoted down the street.

"The Old Brunswick Inn," Noah said.

Jordyn nodded. "The summer mansion for Governor Benjamin Smith."

Noah paced excitedly, trying to figure out his next step.

"Despite being in the throes of the Holiday Home Tour, I have already talked to the owners. We have permission to pay a visit," Jordyn said. "You should go get Peyton."

"What if there's nothing there? What if we just get her hopes up for nothing?" Noah asked.

"What if there *is* something there? She'd want to be a part of it," Jordyn said. "There is a saying in my family, 'the truth is the truth'. Sometimes it gives you the answers you want, sometimes it doesn't. Either way, it is what it is."

Noah nodded. "Okay."

Noah walked up the steps of the porch and entered the festive home. Christmas carols played over an old record player. Guests swapped stories while sipping wine and Glogg. Henry was holding his own as he caught up with friends and neighbors.

Peyton was holding court as a proper Southern belle should, entertaining her guests and rekindling stories of their childhood together and Christmases past.

Noah hated to steal her away from the moment. She looked happy. In her home, with her friends and her father, she *was* happy.

With a deep breath, Noah slipped through the crowd. During a break in the conversation, he excused himself and extended an outstretched hand. Offering a sheepish smile, he asked, "Mind if I steal Peyton for a moment?"

The ladies in the circle of friends giggled and shooed Peyton away with the gallant man in his Victorian suit.

Surprised he was leading her out of the house, she frowned and looked at him. "Where are we going?"

"To find the truth, whatever that is," Noah said as he led her down the steps to Jordyn, who was waiting for them on the sidewalk.

"Peyton, do we have a story for you," Jordyn said as she began walking briskly toward the Old Brunswick Inn.

Thirty Four

The Old Brunswick Inn stood as a stalwart in the town even as the building changed names and ownership over the years. The historic property was always full of life.

As a home, it was a place of magnificent parties. It was full of music, dance and even a bit of frivolity as it operated as a tavern. From private residence to bed and breakfast and even reputed home to a spirit or two, the grand estate with massive, white columns supporting its wide porch served sentry as a focal point of Southport's waterfront row.

The owners, Sandra, Kevin, and their daughter Megan met them at the door.

"Merry Christmas, Peyton," Sandra said as she swung the door open and gave her neighbor a hug. Repeating the process with

Jordyn, the homeowner paused as she eyed Noah. "You must be Mr. Noah Wilde. The town has been sharing so many wonderful things about you. Merry Christmas!"

"Merry Christmas," Noah said.

Suddenly, arms were wrapped around him in a festive holiday hug.

"Oh!" Noah exclaimed. "It's nice to meet you."

Extending a hand to Kevin, Noah nodded and said, "Merry Christmas. I'm Noah Wilde."

"Kevin Warner. But, please, call me Kevin," the man said.

"And who is this?" Noah asked as he offered a grin to a beaming young lady in a wheelchair.

"This is our daughter, Megan. It also happens to be her birthday," Kevin said.

"Well, happy birthday, Megan," Noah said. Patting his pockets, he produced a small package wrapped in tissue. "I just so happened to be carrying a present that I knew would find the right home."

Handing the tissue-wrapped gift to the young woman, Noah stood back. Peyton gave him a smile and a wink.

Megan unwrapped the tissue to reveal a porcelain sea turtle Christmas ornament. She offered Noah a big grin.

"May I?" Noah asked.

Megan nodded.

Kneeling , Noah gave the young woman in the wheelchair a hug. "Merry Christmas and happy birthday, Megan," he said.

Megan blushed. "Merry Christmas! Thank you."

"So, what is this about some hidden documents in our basement?" Sandra asked.

"It's only a theory, but it's worth a shot," Jordyn said.

"By all means." Sandra held her arms out for them to move from the foyer and down the hall. "Kevin, how about you be a dear and fetch our friends some flashlights? They might need them down there."

"I'm on it," Kevin nodded as he snaked his way through their gala crowd.

Peyton and Jordyn shared countless hugs and hellos as they made their way through the crowd. Noah nodded sheepish Merry Christmases as he wedged past.

Sandra led Noah, Peyton and Jordyn through the party to the cellar door. The owner smiled. "When we were kids, we used to play in the basement. There was a little alcove that we never dared to enter. We all thought it was haunted. Silly kid games. To be honest, we kind of forgot about it. I can't guarantee anything you need is down there, but you are welcome to poke around and take a look."

"Thank you," Noah said as he led the procession with a flashlight gifted to him by Kevin as they headed down the steep steps.

"Will one of you tell me what we're doing here?" Peyton asked, holding Noah's hand while hiking up her dress with her other hand.

"Your friend Noah has been scouring Southport for clues to save the James House. While, I'm sorry, that seems a task too far, we did uncover some amazing news," Jordyn said.

Stepping onto the basement floor, Jordyn opened her phone. "An expert on the Revolutionary War, and Benjamin Smith specifically, found these photos."

Scrolling through her phone, Jordyn showed Peyton the pair of photos she had shown Noah earlier. With a frown, she asked, "That's my great, great, great-grandfather?"

Jordyn nodded. "Thomas Montgomery, or as he came to be known after the war, Thomas James."

Peyton took the phone to take a closer look.

"Your ancestor was a war hero who helped liberate the United States of America," Jordyn said.

"That… that… I don't know what to say," Peyton said as she covered her mouth in shock.

"There's more. There is a redacted letter that states Smith's *intent* to gift the waterfront property and the subsequent home to be built on it to Thomas Montgomery, which also happens to be Thomas James," Jordyn said.

Peyton squinted and asked, "What are we doing here in my neighbor's basement?"

"The letter shows intent. The connection between Smith and Thomas James… or Montgomery is amazing news. They muddy the legal waters of legacy for the James House, but we still need proof of ownership. My historian with the magazine reran the search with Thomas Montgomery, but still came up empty. The deed for the house was never recorded," Noah said.

"I've searched everywhere at my house for anything that would show my family owned it," Peyton said.

"That's why we're here. My researcher friend suggested that if there were any documents stored and not filed with court, it's because they were being held by the executor of those documents. Thomas James' good friend Benjamin Smith," Jordyn said.

Noah played with the flashlight in his hands, "You can't store documents in a house that is still being built."

"So, you think they might be here?" Peyton asked.

"It is the last place we can look," Noah said.

Peyton took a deep breath. "Let's do it!"

Panning the light around the basement, Noah looked for the alcove the current owners spoke of.

"My house is full of cubbies and places where things could be stashed. I bet you this house has the same," Peyton said, moving to the far corner of the cellar.

"Storing things in stone and masonry foundations was often used in old houses as they offered the best hope of surviving a fire," Jordyn said.

"Can you move this?" Peyton tapped on a shelf full of empty Christmas decoration boxes.

"I think I can do that." Noah hoisted a corner of the shelf and pivoted it away from the wall.

A piece of board was held to the masonry wall with a ring of plaster.

"Think they'll mind?" Noah asked.

Jordyn leaned over Noah and Peyton's shoulders, nearly as interested as they were, "I have a friend who can repair that. Let's see what's in there!"

Looking around, Noah found some dusty tools that he could use to chip away at the plaster and pry the board away. Freed from the wall, it revealed a narrow passage.

Noah looked at Peyton and Jordyn.

Hesitating as he knew the dusty alcove would soil his borrowed clothes, he received a nod from Peyton.

Dropping to his hands and knees, clutching the flashlight as he crawled forward, Noah wriggled into a tiny room no bigger than a coat closet. Shining the flashlight around, he found a single, lonely shelf in an otherwise empty room. The shelf held but a small leather pouch. Holding the pouch to the light, Noah inspected it. Lined with tin and fitted with leather ear flaps at the edges to provide some protection against the weather, it was thick with dust. Crawling back through, he handed the pouch to Peyton as he rose to his feet and dusted off his knees.

Looking over Peyton's shoulders, Jordyn said, "It's a cartridge box. Soldiers used them to store ammunition in during the Revolutionary War to protect them from the elements."

Peyton shot the newspaper editor a glance.

Jordyn shrugged. "We did an article on a military display that visited the Fort Johnston Museum a few years back. These pouches were kind of a big deal."

Setting the cartridge box on a shelf, Peyton gingerly slid free the leather clasp and carefully opened the lid. Instead of the usual drilled holes in a block of wood to hold paper ammunition cartridges, the pouch contained several rolled pieces of parchment tied with leather strings.

Untying the first one, Peyton rolled the ancient paper open as Noah shined the flashlight beam over handwritten text.

"It's a pardon for a man who went AWOL during the war," Peyton read. "It cites, action taken during a difficult time, the man left his post to grieve his family that had been killed in tragic incident at his home."

She handed the scrolls to Jordyn, who read it and gently rolled it back up and tied it together with the leather band.

"A deed to a tavern in Smithville. Looks like Benjamin Smith was going into business with his brother," Peyton read.

Freeing another parchment, she froze. Her hands began to shake so much that she lost grip on the scroll, allowing it to spring closed again.

Noah picked up the document and read, "I hereby bequeath Smithville parcel B-32 to Thomas Montgomery for his servitude and loyalty to the Continental Army and the people of the United States of America."

Handing the deed signed by Benjamin Smith to Peyton, Noah said, "The James House is yours."

Peyton flung her arms around Noah and leaned into him with an emotional hug.

Noah could feel her body shake against his.

"Your great, great, great-grandfather wasn't a pirate," Noah said, his voice soft as he held Peyton tight. "He was a spy for the Continental Army. He was a war hero."

"He was a right-hand and confidant for Benjamin Smith. He gave Thomas Montgomery, who *is* Thomas James, the land," Jordyn said.

The intrigue of the mystery had brought an audience from the party upstairs. Gathering around, they peeked at the contents retrieved from the forgotten alcove in the basement.

Peyton pulled back. Looking Noah in the eye, she pressed her lips against his. Pausing for just a moment as she realized the gathering of spectators, she smiled and moved in for another kiss.

"Congratulations, Peyton Montgomery. I think you have your Christmas miracle. Nice work, Noah Wilde," Jordyn said. Turning to the owners of the Brunswick Inn, she said, "As for the rest of this, it is yours, though I think Mabel might like to talk to you about preserving the pouch and documents properly at the Fort Johnston Museum."

"Thank you. Thank you all!" Peyton said, giving Noah's hand a squeeze.

Thirty Five

Noah's arm was locked with Peyton's as they walked back to the James House.

Overcome and dazed by the information she had just learned, Peyton walked almost as if she sampled too much of her own mulled wine. Stopping outside her fence, she froze with her hands resting on the pickets. Her eyes swept over the house that she and her family enjoyed so many memories in.

"It's so unbelievable," she whispered.

"It was your family's all along," Noah said.

With a nod, Peyton pushed through the gate as Noah held it open. Ascending the steps, they found Ty Bates in one of the porch chairs, maintaining vigil.

"Most of your guests had left. I wanted to make sure that real estate guy didn't come back," Ty said as he stood up.

"Thank you, Ty. I appreciate it," Peyton said.

Ty nodded and started to walk away.

"Make sure and tell your mama I said 'Merry Christmas'," Peyton said. "And let's talk about her Pirate Rum Cake in the New Year. Come by yourself once in a while and say hello."

"I will," Ty said. Turning to Noah, he held out his hand.

Noah reached out and shook it.

"Thanks for lookin' out for her," Ty said and walked down the steps after receiving a nod from Noah.

"Merry Christmas, Ty," Peyton called.

Ty held his hand in the air as a reply as he slipped through the gate and down the sidewalk without a glance back.

Peyton rubbed her arms. "It's getting chilly, let's go inside."

A few straggling guests remained. Peyton's friend Krista was collecting glassware that had been scattered throughout the house during the party.

Mabel and Cybil sat with Henry as they chatted about Christmases past. Despite being clearly worn out, Henry seemed to be holding his own in the conversation, even if his words sometimes took a moment to develop.

Seeing Peyton and Noah, the ladies stood up.

"Well, I should be tending to my own guests, but I had to come over and say hello. It was good catching up, Henry," Cybil said.

Henry waved goodbye as the ladies departed the James House.

"I can stay and help out more if you like," Krista offered.

"Thank you, but I've got it. It's been a long night and I just need to get Dad settled," Peyton said, giving her friend a hug.

Krista smiled at Noah as she grabbed her coat and left.

The room was suddenly silent. The record player had long stopped playing Christmas tunes as it reached the end of the recording and the arm returned to its holder.

The clatter of glasses clinking and dishes rattling intermingled with conversations that had been scattered through the house had ceased.

The stillness with the cool white lights of the Christmas tree was only broken by the flickering of candles that were a fraction of their original size at the beginning of the evening.

Henry smiled at his daughter and at Noah.

"Did you have a good visit, Daddy?" Peyton asked.

"I did." Henry nodded. His face suddenly fell, "This mean I need to go back to the nursing home?"

"No, Daddy. You *are* home," Peyton said.

Henry looked confused.

Peyton sat on the edge of the seat next to him and clasped his hands in hers. "I have some news for you, if you're up for it," she said.

Henry's eyes went wide. "You're getting married!"

Peyton choked and shot Noah an embarrassed glance. "No, not *that* kind of news, Daddy. But it is *big* news just the same."

Noah pointed a thumb over his shoulder. "I should, uh, go."

"No, stay," Peyton said. "You are part of this. We wouldn't have this if it wasn't for you. Any of this."

Noah nodded and took a seat across from them.

"There's been a man poking around, asking about the house," Peyton said. "He was filing a claim that our family didn't actually own it. There was never a deed recorded with the county or the state."

Henry looked confused.

"I was afraid he had a case. Noah helped find the information that would keep the house in our name, sort of," Peyton said. "There's more. Your grandfather's grandfather was a hero in the Revolutionary War. He was a spy for Benjamin Smith. As a reward for his service and friendship, Smith gave him the house and the property. Here's the thing. Thomas James didn't exist until after the war. Benjamin Smith's friend, my great, great, great-grandfather, was named Thomas Montgomery."

Henry looked at Noah for help in comprehending the spectacular story.

"Your great, great-grandfather was a spy. A respected gentleman and trader to the British, he was able to provide the Continental Army with key information that helped aid the liberation of the United States of America and win the Revolutionary War. To protect him and his family, he changed his name from Montgomery to James," Noah said.

"Maybe I should go back to the nursing home…" Henry said, wincing as he tried to make sense of the information. "I think I must be having an episode."

"If you are, Daddy, I'm having one right along with you. It has been a crazy Christmas, but Noah helped save our home. *Our* home, Daddy," Peyton said.

Henry pointed at Noah, "I knew I liked you."

"I like you both, sir," Noah said.

Peyton squeezed Noah's hand.

"It sounds like we might have a big day ahead of us in court. Would you come with me? I think I could really use the support," she said.

"Of course," Noah said.

Peyton breathed a sigh of relief as she continued to cup Noah's hands in hers.

Despite the welcome news, she looked exhausted.

"I, uh, need to make sure Daddy's room is ready for him. Stay for a nightcap?" Peyton asked.

"I should probably go. Like you said, it's been a long night and we have another long day tomorrow," Noah said.

Peyton nodded, "Let me walk you out."

Noah lifted Peyton's coat from the coat rack and laid it over her shoulders as they stepped out onto the porch.

Taking a deep breath in the cool night air, Peyton surveyed the porch and said, "I was so scared. We could have lost everything."

Noah turned to face Peyton. Looking into her eyes, he said, "Not everything. You would still have had your family and its legacy. Whether a swashbuckling pirate, simple sea merchant or wartime spy, it didn't really matter. Because after that, you had generations of caring, giving people that loved this town and the town loved back. And you and Henry still have each other."

Peyton cast a look toward the closed door.

"Yeah, we do. And because of you, I get to give Daddy the gift he really wanted most this year. He gets to come home," Peyton said.

"You two good staying here tonight?" Noah asked.

Peyton nodded. "Yeah. I thought it might feel weird after staying at my cottage, but I'm kind of excited about it. It feels like coming home. And I'll have my dad here. It feels right."

"Good," Noah smiled. "Well, I should…"

Before he could get out another word, Peyton launched herself toward him. Despite the speed at which she closed the gap, her lips met his softly. Pressing closer, Peyton kissed him like she had never kissed anyone before.

Pulling away in a gasp, she whispered, "Thank you."

Following Peyton's arms with his fingers until they met hers, Noah held her hands.

"You said Southport Christmases were magical," Noah said.

Peyton laughed despite tiny tears having formed in her eyes, "I did say that."

"You were right," Noah said, as he let Peyton's hands go.

"I was," Peyton said with a smile. "Good night, Noah."

"Good night, Peyton," Noah said. As he took a few steps back, "I guess, I'll see you in court!"

Peyton's eyes went wide as her lips flattened into a wary grimace.

"It'll be *fine*," Noah said, his eyes sparkling in the porch Christmas lights before slipping away into the night.

Thirty Six

The scene at the Brunswick County Courthouse was raucous on Christmas Eve. Chauncey Craven wore a crisp, pin-striped suit. An entourage of men and women followed in step. They were similarly clad in dark suits, each clutching a brown leather satchel to their sides.

As Noah escorted Peyton into the courthouse, Chauncey grinned across the room at them as he patted his own satchel.

Noah paused to hold the door open as Peyton met with her attorney. With a guiding hand placed gently on Henry's back, Noah helped him navigate the building and led him to a seat up front in the nearly empty courtroom.

The judge walked into the room, giving a nod to the bailiff as he adjusted his robe and took his seat behind the bench.

Chauncey's team of lawyers was neatly assembled in the row behind him as the real estate attorney adjusted the folder he pulled out of his satchel to ensure it was perfectly square on the desk before laying a gleaming gold pen perfectly centered on top.

Noah caught up with Peyton and her attorney as Peyton frantically waved at him to join them.

Peyton asked in a hoarse whisper, "Will you sit with me? I need all the support I can get."

"Of course." Noah nodded.

As they were let in through the gate separating the audience from the proceeding floor in front of the judge, the doors to the courtroom opened wide once again.

The judge looked up to see a stream of people enter the room. Every owner along the waterfront who had early ties to the area filtered in, including Cybil, who gave a friendly wave to Peyton and Noah. The current owners of the Brunswick Inn where Benjamin Smith's documents were stashed arrived with their video account of the prior evening in their basement.

Mabel from the Fort Johnston Museum and her counterparts from the Maritime Museum walked through the doors together. On their heels, Katie from the Old South Tour Company slipped through the door.

Ty Bates escorted his mother through the courtroom door and gave Peyton and Noah a quick nod.

The judge's mouth dropped as what seemed like most of Southport, including the mayor, came pouring through the doors to the point that all of the seats were taken and the last few observers had to stand in the back of the courtroom. Jordyn Nelmark was the last to filter in and stood in the back of the proceedings.

The clerk of the court hustled down the aisle to hand a stack of printouts to the judge, who shuffled through them with a frown.

As the noise in the courtroom rose with its over-capacity crowd, the judge cleared his throat and rapped his gavel. "All right. All right!" The judge scanned the crowd. "This case clearly has the community's interest. If y'all will settle down, we'll begin this emergency hearing that Counselor Craven filed to disrupt, what *was* a peaceful Christmas Eve with my family."

Chauncey shuffled in his seat. Rising, he said, "If I may, honorable Judge Medlin, the timing of the petition is critical in order to…"

"The timing of the petition was advantageous to take advantage of the declining health condition of the homeowner and placing burden on the homeowner's proxy by power of attorney, Ms. Peyton James knowing access to time and resources during the holidays would be especially burdensome," Judge Medlin said. "While I'm impartial, I do have eyes and ears and I am a part of this community, as well, Counselor Craven."

"Yes, sir." Chauncey sat back in his seat.

"Fortunately, given the evidence provided by Ms. James and backed by expert historians, this proceeding shall move on fairly briskly and we can all get back to our holiday celebrations," Judge Medlin said.

The near-permanent cocky expression that Chauncey Craven wore began to melt off his face and was quickly replaced with a scowl.

"You have filed a petition to make a claim and file a deed with the court regarding the property of 299 East Bay Street," the judge said.

"That is correct, your honor. There was never a recorded deed filed with the county or state government at any time in the property's history," Chauncey said. "Nor has the current resident provided a copy of a deed for the property."

"Until today," Judge Medlin said.

Chauncey's face fell and he stammered, "Excuse me, sir?"

"Ms. James and her counsel have provided the *original* deed granted by Benjamin Smith to the home's original and rightful owner, Thomas James. The property would have been handed down to Franklin James to Harry James and then to Henry James who sits in the court before us. Ms. Peyton James, according to power of attorney has authoritative claim on the property," Judge Medlin said.

"Your honor." Chauncey shot up out of his seat. "I had no prior knowledge that such a document existed. May I visit the bench and review it with my team?"

"You can come up to the bench. Your team can remain seated right where they are," Judge Medlin said.

Chauncey walked up to the judge's bench, his cheeks starting to glow red.

As he inspected the document, the real estate attorney frowned, "This document says Thomas Montgomery. I do not see a representative of the Montgomery family here, sir. In that light, I petition that we continue with the proceeding."

"Thomas Montgomery and Thomas James are one and the same. That fact has been summarily supported by historians at the University of North Carolina, Coastal Charm Magazine, the Fort Johnston Museum and Ms. Jordyn Nelmark, editor of the State Port Pilot newspaper. The deed for the property was recorded with the county as of this morning. While it may have been a couple of centuries overdue, the record stands. Petition to make a claim on the property on Bay Street is summarily dismissed. Given how your legal-on-a-technicality assault on a family rich in the town's history while taking advantage of the property owner's health condition would sit with your neighbors, I'd consider this an early Christmas present, counselor," Judge Medlin said.

Looking up at the audience that had filled his courtroom, Judge Medlin slammed his gavel down and declared, "Case dismissed. Merry Christmas!"

The crowd roared into a crescendo with the audience leaving their seats.

Peyton stood and wrapped her arms around Noah. Giving her father a wink, she pulled him into a hug from across the barrier.

Looking at Noah, Peyton said, "Thank you."

Noah pulled back from the hug and with hands sweeping the courtroom, he said, "We did it. This town loves you. They love your family and I can understand why."

Peyton cocked her head at Noah for a second before being swallowed up in what seemed like a record-setting bear hug as the town of Southport rallied behind her and her father.

Chauncey glared at the original deed and the recorded document accepted earlier in the day one more time before leaving the bench. His eyes glanced over at Peyton briefly before nodding to his team to pack up and leave.

Judge Medlin pointed toward the bailiff and told Chauncey, "You might want Mr. Grainger to escort you out the side door, Counselor Craven."

With a defeated nod, Chauncey followed the bailiff, his in-shock entourage following in line like woozy baby ducks out of the courthouse.

The judge took off his robe, revealing a Christmas sweater with blinking Christmas lights. He too, sneaked out the back of the courtroom.

Outside the courthouse, the crowd slowly began to dissipate as they had the chance to congratulate Peyton and Henry and wish them a merry Christmas. Cybil escorted Henry out of the courthouse and promised to get him settled in back at the James House.

Peyton turned to Noah, a tear threatening to drip from her eye. "I am so grateful for you. I don't know how I can ever repay you."

"You don't need to repay me. I'm glad to have helped. I am relieved that you have your family's home intact. For good," Noah said.

"You saved our home," Peyton gasped, wiping a tear from her cheek.

"I don't know about that…" Noah began before Peyton shut him up with a deep kiss, her arms slung tightly around his neck.

Pulling back, Peyton blushed. "I'm sorry. That wasn't very lady-like."

Noah gently pulled her in by her waist in a twirl to bring her closer. Looking into her eyes, their lips hovered. Slowly, he pressed into her with a kiss that left them both dizzy.

As the world slowly came back into focus, they realized they were still standing on the courthouse steps.

"Let's… we should…" Peyton panted.

"Yeah." Noah nodded, slipping his hand into hers and walking her back to the car.

Thirty Seven

As they pulled up to the James House, Peyton frowned as a small gathering accumulated on the sidewalk. "What's all this?"

"I have a surprise for you," Noah said.

He rushed around the car and opened Peyton's door.

Holding her hand, he escorted her to the James House front gate. Woozy from the courtroom experience and overwhelming support, she was grateful for his steadying arm.

As they arrived at the porch steps, Cybil escorted Henry onto the porch to join them.

Jordyn stood by the sidewalk with her photographer.

Mabel walked up with a man in a brown suit that Peyton didn't recognize. He was holding something wrapped in craft paper.

With all other eyes on the James family and their home, Noah looked at Peyton and Henry, "You two are so special. It is clear, your family history is special. Not just in the heroic things Thomas James did to help liberate this nation, but every life in Southport your family has touched throughout the years."

Taking a breath, Noah scanned the crowd and continued, "I had my team at the magazine pull some strings to expedite, making a few things official. I wanted it to be my Christmas present for you both."

"With the recorded deed and verified historical documents, we deem this home a house of great historical significance," the man in the brown suit declared. "From this day forward, with the blessing of the James family, this house on 299 East Bay Street in Southport, North Carolina shall be in the official record of historic homes. Its preservation will be forever secured."

Pulling the craft paper off the item he was carrying, the man held it for Henry and Peyton to read. The bronze embossed plaque read James — Montgomery House 1801.

Peyton brought her hand to her mouth and wrapped an arm around her father. Henry stared at the plaque, his eyes welling with tears.

"Do you accept the designation of the National Register of Historic Places? There are a few rules…" the man in the brown suit started.

"Yes! We accept the designation," Peyton said. "The James… Montgomery family home… *our* home."

Hugging her father, Peyton squeezed him tight as her eyes looked up and locked on Noah's. She mouthed the words "Thank you".

"Merry Christmas," Noah said.

Stepping away so that Jordyn's photographer could have a clear shot of father and daughter, Jordyn waved him back into the frame for a final photo and winked.

"If it's okay, we can go inside and sign a few papers to make it official. Besides, it's getting a bit chilly out here," the man in the brown suit said.

Peyton nodded and escorted her father, Cybil, Mabel and the man into the house.

Noah stood with the plaque ready to help a handyman Cybil had hired to affix the plaque next to the door of the James-Montgomery House.

Jordyn walked up to Noah and said, "I think you have your cover house. Your editor should be thrilled."

"Thank you. The house… the town… the people… really deserve all the credit," Noah said.

"This place would be flattened and turned into a modern art déco vacation rental if it wasn't for you," Jordyn said. She smiled, "You ever been in a picture in any of your articles?"

"No. I'm never the subject," Noah said with a laugh.

"I'll have to send you the photos we shot. While they might lack your artistic flair, they tell one heck of a Christmas story with a photojournalist from Coastal Charm Magazine at the heart of it. Who, in fact, saved Christmas for one Southport family," Jordyn said.

Noah squinted. "That's pretty good. Maybe you should write the article."

Jordyn laughed. "I think I'll stick with community news. But I do have a number of ideas in the area that would make fantastic Coastal Charm subjects."

"I think I'd like to hear those," Noah said.

"Hang around after the holiday and we'll chat," Jordyn said as she waved goodbye through the window at Peyton, who was reviewing documents with the man from the historic register.

The words Jordyn said before bounding down the steps stung at Noah. His editor already had his next assignment ready to go and he was to report by the new year.

Glancing in through the James-Montgomery House window, his heart fluttered as he watched Peyton with a hand on her father's shoulder. Catching the spectator, she smiled at Noah.

He didn't expect the smile to knock him back.

Turning away from the window, Noah looked out at the water, a chilly breeze was nipping at his neck. He suddenly felt like he had been punched in the gut. His phone buzzed in his pocket.

Knowing the Southport Christmas assignment was nearly wrapped up, Noah wasn't surprised to see his editor's name light up his phone.

"Congratulations, Noah. Vivian told me you saved that house you were concerned about. And on Christmas Eve. The story just writes itself," Jennimay said.

"There is a lot more to the story than just preserving the house," Noah said. "A lot more."

"Well, I look forward to reading it. I assume it will be the cover house?" Jennimay asked.

"Yes. While they are all worthy, this is the one," Noah said.

"Great! Wrap it up. I have your hotel ready for you in the Bahamas. You'll be staying at this exclusive rental house right on Great Exuma Beach. There is a glass-bottom dock that stretches from the house right into the water. The house itself will be fully stocked. All you need to do is enjoy, take photos and write about your experience. It sounds like you can use a workcation after your assignment there in Southport," Jennimay said.

"It was a… surprise. A good one, but a surprise," Noah said. "In fact, I was thinking…"

"Well, I'd love to chat more but it's Christmas Eve and I have to rush the final Christmas spread to the digital team. Sorry to press you, but I need your article and final photos as well. Good work, Noah. Jennimay ended the call before Noah could utter another word in.

Staring at his phone, he sighed.

He didn't have time to dwell on the future. He had an article to finish.

Thirty Eight

The man in the brown suit left with a folder of signed papers, making the James—Montgomery House an official historic home.

Stopping on his way out, he thanked Noah. Placing his hand on Noah's arm, he said, "You did history a great service. Not only can we now preserve a magnificent home in its original 1801 design, but we get to learn about a portion of the Revolutionary War and secret heroes. Merry Christmas!"

"Merry Christmas," Noah said as he watched the excited man amble down the steps and out the gate.

Cybil and Mabel opened the front door. In typical southern fashion, their goodbyes, which started inside and presumably some time ago, spilled out onto the front porch.

"We had such a wonderful time visiting with Henry. It is so exciting to have him back on the waterfront row," Mabel said.

"And you moving back here, I can't wait to share sunsets with my porch neighbor once again," Cybil said.

"I did miss the sunsets when I was at my cottage," Peyton admitted. "But mostly, I missed my Waterfront Row family."

Cybil gave Peyton a hug and said, "You let us know if you need anything or if there is a time you just want someone to visit with Henry."

"Thank you, I feel so much better knowing he has the support of his friends," Peyton said.

"And don't forget to talk to Noah about New Year's Eve," Mabel said. Shooting a look toward Noah, she added, "Your friend from the National Historic Register is going to come back by and we are going to dig through history on the Revolutionary War Master Spy Thomas Montgomery! I haven't been this excited since the pirate sword washed up in Bonnet's Creek after Hurricane Florence. I have so much to update in the museum archives!"

The giddy woman shook her fists in delight as she giggled and danced down the steps before being tugged along by Cybil.

"Come on, let's leave those two be. I'm sure they have a lot to talk about," Cybil said. "Bye, y'all!"

"Bye, Cybil," Noah said as Peyton joined him by the porch railing.

Turning to Peyton, he asked, "Where's Henry?"

"He's napping," Peyton said. "The past two days have been his longest in a while. They've been good days for him, but long."

"So, you are officially moving back in?" Noah asked.

"I am." Peyton nodded. "It didn't feel right before. But after everything and almost losing it, the James, I mean, the James–Montgomery House feels like my home, too, now. And Daddy will need me here even with the nurse we hired."

Peyton leaned on the rail and let her eyes sweep the Southport waterfront view. With a deep breath, she said, "I couldn't imagine living anywhere else. I'm a part of the house and it is a part of me."

Curling her arms around Noah's arm, Peyton looked up at him and said, "You are part of this house's history now, too."

Noah smiled, "I just helped dust off some of its amazing past."

Peyton grabbed Noah by the hands and looked into his eyes. "And now it can have an amazing future. Thanks to you."

Pulling her close, Noah said, "We should celebrate."

Peyton laughed, "You really *are* learning. You know what? We should. And honestly, I could stand to take a moment to just… breathe. I tell you what, I'm going to check on Daddy and then I'll whip us up some toddies for sunset."

"Sounds good. Can I help with anything?" Noah asked.

Peyton rubbed her arms. "There are some blankets in the bench by the door. I think we might need them tonight."

Noah fetched the blankets and placed them on the bench on the porch. As the seabirds started their flights toward land to roost for the night, his head lifted as he heard the familiar rumble of a pickup truck pulling up.

Ty Bates climbed out of his truck and walked up to the fence.

Noah offered him a nod.

"I was just checkin' on Peyton and Henry," Ty said.

"You can come on up. Have a hot drink? It's getting chilly," Noah said.

"Naw, I need to get Momma to Christmas Eve service. Y'all comin'? We can save you a seat," Ty said.

"Yeah, sure. That would be nice," Noah said.

"All right." Ty nodded without any emotion in his tone or expression.

Starting up the truck, he roared away as Peyton pushed her way out onto the porch with two clear mugs in hand. "What did Ty want?"

"He said he was just checking up on you and Henry. Said he and his mother would save seats for us at church," Noah said.

Peyton chewed her lip. "You want to go to church with us? I mean, you should. And I should have encouraged you any way, but… you wanna sit with Ty and his mama?"

"I, uh, didn't know what to say," Noah shrugged.

"Should've made these stronger," Peyton said, handing a warm drink to Noah. "Tom and Jerry's, my grandma's recipe."

Noah took a sip of the steaming beverage. "It's got a pretty good kick to it as it is."

"Let's sit, I'm chilly," Peyton said, nudging Noah to the bench with the blankets.

Snatching the corner of a blanket, he snapped it in the air so that it lightly fell over Peyton.

As he began to sit, Peyton lifted the blanket for Noah, "Come on, there's room for two."

Noah slid onto the bench with her and Peyton draped the blanket over them.

"Cheers!" Peyton grinned as she clinked her glass into his.

"What a Christmas!" She leaned back, cupping her mug with both hands, appreciating its warmth. Cocking her head, she asked, "You hear that?"

Noah strained his ears and listened.

"I don't hear anything," he said.

"Exactly. Peaceful. Calm. Quiet," Peyton said in nearly a whisper.

She laid her head on his shoulder. They sat in the chilly, silent night, watching the lighthouse begin to spin its beam over the water. The town tree sprang to life as did all of the porches along the waterfront.

The sun made its rapid descent to the west down the Intracoastal Waterway aided by a bank of dark clouds that were being chased by a cold wind.

Noah knew he needed to talk to Peyton about his phone call with his editor, but he didn't want to spoil the mood.

Instead, he wrapped an arm around Peyton and together, they watched the sky erupt in a magnificent display of colors against marshmallow clouds.

It didn't take long for the sun to disappear. In the lingering colors in the sky, little sparkles began to cascade down.

Peyton and Noah looked at each other.

Peyton's eyes grew wide. "You know what that is?"

Noah stood up and walked to the porch railing. "It's snowing."

"In Southport." Peyton joined him. "We haven't had a white Christmas since 1989. Some spots got nearly two feet of snow that year, if you can believe that."

Walking out into their yard, Noah and Peyton looked up as they held their hands out. Little frozen crystals fell gently into their grasp as more flakes tickled their faces.

"Snowing in Southport," Noah said. "I might need to retake my cover photo."

"Cover photo?" Peyton nudged Noah.

"Yeah. My article will headline the digital Christmas edition and be the cover of next year's *Costal Charm Magazine* holiday issue. The James–Montgomery House will be the feature," Noah said.

"You didn't tell me you heard back from your editor." Peyton smiled.

"Yeah." Noah shrugged. "We've had a lot going on and I didn't want to… I didn't want to spoil the mood this evening."

"How would that spoil the mood? It's great news!" Peyton squealed.

"Well, my editor also…" Noah started.

Cybil stepped out of her house in a thick coat covering a Christmas dress. "Ooh, it's snowing! I hope it sticks. But maybe not until I'm back from church!"

"Church!" Peyton's eyes went wide. "We need to get going!"

"You want me to save you seats?" Cybil asked.

"No, Noah arranged with Ty to sit with him and his momma," Peyton said.

"Why?" Cybil scowled.

"'Tis the season. Forgiveness. Peace on Earth, goodwill toward men." Peyton shrugged.

"I guess! I'll see you there, honey!" Cybil waved as she walked down her porch steps.

"Come on, I'll get Daddy moving. Will you warm up the car?" Peyton asked.

"Yeah." Noah nodded as he watched her jog up the steps.

The house was speckled with white flakes, which began to come down in force.

Thirty Nine

Families were bundled up as they walked up the steps to the church. They were greeted with candles and candy canes as they entered and filed toward pews draped in garland and red bows.

Noah and Peyton escorted Henry up the steps. They could barely travel a few steps without someone offering them a greeting or saying how good it was to see Henry there that evening.

Even Noah had his share of new friends that waved to him from across the sanctuary.

Ty Bates stood and gave a nod to them as his eyes located the trio that were scanning the pews.

As they walked past Cybil, she gave a quick glance at the three empty seats near her.

Peyton chuckled a thank you.

"Hi, Rebecca!" Peyton said, giving Ty's mother a hug. "Dad made it and this is our friend, Noah."

"Hello, Henry. It's so good to see you again," Rebecca Bates said. "And Noah, I've heard so much about you. Ty says you've been a real friend to the James family and the people of Southport."

"He did?" Noah smiled at Ty, who rolled his eyes and gave a shrug. "Well, the entire town, including your son, rallied as well. I suppose that's what makes Southport so special."

"I suppose so," Mrs. Bates nodded.

"Well, it's a pleasure to meet you, Mrs. Bates," Noah said. Turning to Ty, he said, "Thank you for holding our seats."

The church band began to play traditional Christmas carols as a choir sang from a platform under a large lighted cross. A trio of Christmas trees flanked the choir, giving the entire church a warm, festive atmosphere.

The music pastor came out on stage singing along with the choir and with her hands, encouraged the Christmas Eve service congregation to join in.

Noah glanced beside him at Peyton. Her eyes shimmered in the church Christmas lights. Noting Ty wrapping an arm around his mother joining in on the carols and hearing Henry singing along as well, Noah joined in, even if he kept his voice a bit soft.

The church pastor took the stage and thanked the choir and the band. Looking out at the pews, he said, "I almost hate to interrupt. I could sing Christmas carols with y'all all night and call it good. But y'all know me. I've always got a few words to share."

The church laughed.

"They aren't my words, but they are words that I am honored to share with you all." The pastor put his hands on either side of the podium. "Christmas is such a magical time. Whether it is snowflakes falling where they rarely fall. I'm overjoyed to see them at Christmas, but I'm also happy they'll be gone in a few days. I saw the weather report before I came out here. It'll be near seventy on Saturday."

The congregation murmured and chuckled along with the pastor.

"This is a season of miracles. And gifts. None more precious than the baby born in a manger in a tiny little town to a man and a woman of very modest status. But, oh, what a gift that was. There are gifts all around us. If we notice. If we accept them," the pastor continued. "They can be the gift of a loved one who had been ill feeling well enough to attend a Christmas Eve service. It could be a gift from the volunteer tree that a child who otherwise might not have received a single present this year gets to open up on Christmas Day. It could be the gift of friendship. The gift of love. The gift of finding your true purpose in life. It could be the gift of simply enjoying one more sunrise or one more sunset.

"If you look to your left, or your right. If you look down your row or to the other side of the church, there are gifts planted all around you, if you'll accept them. You see, there is a path. There is a light. There is a gift of a wonderful, purposeful, love-filled life… if you follow it. Fortunately, there were wise men and shepherds and kings that followed the path of a light on a night like this a long time ago. And we were given the greatest gift of all. Unconditional love. A king whose only command was to believe and love each other. Sounds like a pretty wonderful gift to me," the pastor said.

Smiling at the crowd, the pastor lifted his candle, "Another gift for you tonight is that I promised not to be long-winded. You all received a candle as you entered. As the flame makes its way down your aisle, please accept that light and pass it on to your neighbor. And whether you are gifted with a beautiful voice or not, please, sing along."

The band and the choir restarted their Christmas songs. The church lights dimmed as a pair of candles quickly spread their flame to other candles on either side of the church. As candles were lit, the congregation began to join in singing carols with the choir.

Ty Bates tilted his candle toward Noah's.

As Noah's wick began to glow, he moved his gently toward Peyton's. As their candles met, so did their eyes. Peyton's candle came to life. For a brief moment, the flame danced in her eyes.

Peyton smiled before swiveling to help Henry light his candle.

The entire room felt like a large, warm embrace. The only light came from the Christmas trees and the flickering candles. Noah felt an emotion sweep over him that he had never felt before. Peyton's arm snaking around his back made the feeling only the more intense.

When the song was over, the candles were extinguished.

As the band played their final song, the Christmas Eve service attendees exchanged Merry Christmases and hugs.

Ty shook Noah's hand and they began to stream out of the church.

Stepping outside, the intensity of the snowfall had picked up. Trees, streetlamps and lawns were covered in a blanket of white.

Henry looked around and smiled before catching a chill and pulling his coat tight.

"Let's get you home, Daddy," Peyton said.

"Home?" Henry looked up at his daughter, an unsure look on his face.

"Home. *Our* home, Daddy," Peyton said.

Henry's smile grew wider and he repeated, "Home."

After ensuring Henry was warm and comfortable at the James House, Peyton led Noah to the porch. For a moment, they watched the town of Southport enjoy their rare winter treat.

Children wasted no time building snowmen and entering snowball fights. Cardboard boxes and trash can lids were used as makeshift sleds, making use of even the smallest hills. Their excited laughter rang through the waterfront park.

"I'm glad they're enjoying it. I think I'll go inside and enjoy from the window. Inside the house where it is a proper temperature," Cybil called from the neighboring porch. "Southern blood ain't made for the cold. It *is* pretty, though."

"It is beautiful," Peyton said, her voice breathy as she pulled Noah close.

"What a wonderful night," Noah said.

They stood and watched. The Oak Island Lighthouse beam seemed almost surreal in the thick flakes that fell over the waterfront.

Families suddenly streamed from downtown to the waterfront. Hand in hand, they began to circle the town tree.

"Come on!" Peyton grabbed Noah's hand and tugged him down the porch steps.

"What's going on?" Noah asked.

"You'll see!" Peyton said with a grin, nearly sprinting toward the growing crowd.

Meeting friends, neighbors and a few strangers, they joined around the tree. Suddenly, a voice rose from the crowd. Other voices followed. Soon, a chorus of Christmas carols were being lifted into the air.

"Are we in a Dr. Seuss story?" Noah whispered.

Peyton elbowed Noah in the ribs. "Just sing!"

Complying, Noah chimed in with the chorus. Amidst the snowfall, his hand wrapped in Peyton's, there was nowhere else he would rather be.

Forty

The snow continued to pile up as the evening wore on. Family friends had been making routine stops at the James House to visit with Henry.

Noah and Peyton enjoyed a slow stroll along the water, their arms slung around each other.

"Mama would have loved this. A white Christmas," Peyton said.

Noah squeezed her tighter.

"She would have loved *you*, too." Peyton smiled at Noah.

"I would have liked to have met her," Noah said. Turning to face Peyton, he said, "In some ways, I feel like I have."

"She was an amazing woman. She was like the glue that held the family together. She was a big part of the town as well," Peyton said.

"I think the family, and the town, have someone else who can do that now," Noah said.

Peyton took a deep breath. "I'll be happy managing the James House and keeping Dad safe and comfortable. I'll let Cybil and Mabel handle the town for a while longer."

Noah laughed.

"You know, the town could use a male presence in keeping its charm alive," Peyton said.

"A Yankee? That's blasphemous," Noah said.

"You're an adopted son, now. Kind of like the Grinch, except your heart grew a few shades south of the Mason-Dixon line," Peyton laughed. "It's really good to have you here."

Noah kicked at the snow with his foot. "There's... there's something I need to tell you..."

An errant snowball sailed past their heads.

Turning, they found a group of children, their eyes wide and mouths agape.

Peyton glared. "Which one of you threw that?"

The kids all shared glances with each other. A little girl slowly raised her hand.

"Brittany Jacobs… you can do better than that!" Peyton scolded as she scooped up a handful of snow. Turning it into a ball, she hurled it toward the group of children. Missing Brittany, Peyton's snowball landed with a splat against a boy's chest.

Within seconds, the park was a frenzy of snowballs flying through the air.

Peyton and Noah used a park bench as a base while they fortified their frozen munitions. Snowy missiles sailed overhead.

"Ready?" Peyton asked, as Noah gave her a nod.

In unison, they popped up, firing off snowballs at children who ran from cover to cover.

A snowball whistled through the air toward Peyton. Noah reached out and caught it with his hand and sent it back toward the boy who sent it. As he did, another child fired a snowball, taking advantage of his turned attention. The snowball slammed into his shoulder, sending a spray of snow into his face.

Feigning being mortally wounded, Noah fell back onto the snow.

Peyton dropped to her knees and leaned over him. "My hero! You saved me!"

Noah reached his hand up to gently cup Peyton's face and he gasped, "If only we had more time…"

Peyton laughed. Tugging her scarf off of her neck, she waved it in the air. Rising from the park bench, she called out, "We surrender. We surrender. You win!"

The children cheered.

"Thanks for playing, Ms. James!" one of the girls said.

"Merry Christmas, kids," Peyton said.

Leaning, she stood over Noah, who was still flat on his back. Reaching out her hand to help him, she was instead pulled down on top of him.

Their candy cane tinted breath came together as they studied each other in the glow of the park's Christmas lights.

Peyton slowly lowered herself, pressing her lips into his.

Dusting themselves off, they started walking back toward the James House. Enjoying the snowfall as it recovered the tracks they had made during the neighborhood snowball fight, they were in no hurry.

Noah looked at Peyton as she leaned into him. Her eyes were so bright. Her smile was the purest joy that he could remember. The happiness of the moment was dizzying. Being in Southport, being with Peyton, felt different. It felt like he somehow belonged there, with her.

His heart churned in his chest. His mind fought to stay in the moment, to enjoy what was right in front of him. A lesson that he was starting to learn from Peyton. Yet, he knew his time in Southport was coming to an end. Christmas day was a curtain call and he was about to be shipped off to his next assignment.

Lips quivering, Noah tried to explain, "My editor…"

"Fell in love with Southport through your photographs?" Peyton blurted.

"Well, yes. And the story of the town and her people," Noah nodded.

Peyton squeezed harder and grinned. "I told you. Christmas in Southport was magical."

Noah's head spun even faster and he mumbled, "You have no idea."

Stopping, Noah held Peyton in front of him. Snowflakes collected on their shoulders. Tiny little crystals landed on Peyton's cheeks, shimmering like glitter. Their eyes moved toward each other's and locked in place.

Taking a deep breath, Noah said, "I never would have found the magic of a Southport Christmas without you."

"Aw, you would have. The town would have found a way to get into that frozen northerner heart of yours," Peyton said.

"For me, at least, you are part of the magic. You *and* Henry," Noah said.

Peyton's cheeks glowed. "You have helped make a challenging Christmas magical for us, too."

Studying Noah's eyes, she cocked her head, seeing the spark had been nearly extinguished. "What is it?"

"I, uh, my editor…" Noah struggled to get the words out. His throat tightened as he spoke. "My next assignment…"

Placing her hand on Noah's arm, Peyton asked, "Noah, what's wrong?"

"I have to…" he started.

Before he could finish, a voice called down the block at them.

Looking up, they saw a figure in a white winter coat waving at them.

Jordyn Nelmark strode up. "I'm sorry to interrupt you two."

"We were just… enjoying the snow," Peyton said.

"It's amazing, right? My photographers are having a ball even though they have the next few days off. They are sending me photos like crazy," Jordyn said. "I tried to catch you after church but got pulled away."

"It was a great Christmas Eve service," Peyton said.

"It was." Jordyn nodded. Her eyes narrowed and she asked, "Do you mind if I borrow Noah for a moment?"

Both Peyton and Noah shrugged.

"Sure," Peyton said. "I'll head in and get some cocoa going."

"That sounds great," Noah said.

"Would you like to come inside for cocoa?" Peyton asked.

Jordyn held up her hand and said, "No, thank you. I won't be long."

"Okay," Peyton said. Opening her gate, she bound up the steps to her porch and slipped into the house.

Jordyn watched Peyton disappear. Hands in her coat pockets, she swung to Noah. "You seem to really be enjoying your time in Southport."

"I am. I'm not sure how the town managed to overcome my one criticism," Noah said, holding his hands out to capture a few snowflakes.

"I'd like to say it happens every year for Christmas, but it's more like every couple of decades," Jordyn said. Shooting Noah a thoughtful look, she said, "I wanted to run something by you."

"Sure," Noah said with a nod.

"You have an eye for photo-storytelling that is very different than my reporters and photographers. I've been wanting to launch a section of the digital paper that captures the heart of Southport and the surrounding area. I want to capture the culture of the beaches, the lifestyle of the towns, and the history of the region. I couldn't quite figure out how to do that. Until I saw your work," Jordyn said.

Glancing at the James House, she continued, "I don't want to speak out of turn, but it seems like you found some reasons to stick around."

Noah looked flustered. "That's, I mean, I don't know what to say."

"I'm sure I can't match the salary *Coastal Charm Magazine* is paying you, but I was thinking you might be up for some freelance work or even a joint project with the magazine. I know I can get *Coastal Charm* exclusive access to some of the most exclusive homes on the barrier islands." Placing her hand on Noah's shoulder, she said, "Just think about it."

"I will." Noah nodded.

"Merry Christmas, Noah."

"Merry Christmas, Jordyn."

Noah watched the newspaper editor walk down the sidewalk and disappear into the night. His already dizzy head and fluttery heart were sent into a spin cycle.

Glancing up at the James-Mongomery House, he could see Peyton check on Henry as he dozed by the Christmas tree. In the corner of his eye, he could see the flash of the Oak Island Lighthouse. He felt as if those sights were now a part of him.

Forty One

Noah woke up Christmas morning with the type of excitement in his heart he hadn't felt since he was a child.

Bolting out of bed, he glanced out his hotel window. The snow had stopped falling, but the world was cast in a blanket of white.

Hurrying, he got ready. Christmas at the James House made him jittery with anticipation.

Noah still didn't know how to deliver the news to Peyton that he would be leaving the next day. He hoped the possibility of a return to Southport would dull the news. The prospect lifted his spirits after he spoke with Jordyn.

Gathering his things, he began the snowy walk to the James House.

The morning was brilliant. The sun rose from the Atlantic and cast a shimmer over the wintry land. Warming the snow just enough to make it passable without being icy, but cold enough to keep Christmas Day a wonderland of white.

The buzz of his phone nearly startled him.

Pulling it out of his pocket, he answered, "Hello?"

"Merry Christmas, Noah," Jennimay said.

"Merry Christmas."

"I don't normally make business calls on Christmas morning, I hope I'm not disrupting anything," Jennimay said.

"No. I'm enjoying a snowy walk into town," Noah said.

"Well, if it's anything like the last round of photos you sent, I imagine it is stunning," Jennimay said.

Noah's eyes cast over the landscape as he walked past Bonnet's Creek and he replied, "It really is."

"So, clearly I got your proposal. I figured it might affect your holiday and upcoming travel plans, so I thought a quick call might be warranted," Jennimay said.

"Thank you. I really appreciate it. I hope I'm not pulling you away from your family," Noah said.

"We give books as presents on Christmas Eve. That way, if anyone, especially the little ones, wake up too early or with too much enthusiasm, they have something to occupy them until we're ready to start the festivities," Jennimay said.

"That's a good idea," Noah said.

"Make a note of that for the day there are little Noahs running around," Jennimay said. Changing gears in the conversation, she said, "So, you would like to stay in Southport."

"In the area, yes. The local paper would like to run a collaboration series on the culture of the Southport and the area beaches," Noah said.

"Your article certainly makes the region seem appealing. Are you sure there's enough meat on the bones?" Jennimay asked.

"There is. The area, including Wilmington and up the coast, is rich in history. Beautiful beaches. Contemporary and historic homes. Islands, pirates, and wars that shaped American history," Noah said.

"Why would we collaborate with the local paper instead of just running it ourselves?" Jennimay asked.

"They can get us access to homes and locations that most people, including us, can't get into. They can get us into an exclusive estate on Bald Head Island, an overnight adventure at Frying Pan

Tower. They'll even make the magazine the official Marshal of the North Carolina Fourth of July Festival," Noah said.

"All right, all right. You've sold me. I'm interested," Jennimay said. Her voice changed. "I've never heard you like this. You are always ready for the next adventure. What's going on?"

Noah glanced out at the water as it lapped against the snowy shore, "I was told this place was magical, if I gave it a chance. I did and it is."

Jennimay laughed. "Now you have me worried. What happens if you fall in love with each assignment location I send you to?"

Noah was silent for a moment.

"Not every town has a Peyton," he finally said.

"Ah. The girl whose family home you saved. I thought something changed your perspective down there," Jennimay said.

"It did. She did. This town did," Noah said.

"Well, I'm happy for you. Whatever impact she and the town had on you, it must have been pretty powerful. It shows in your photos *and* in your writing," Jennimay said.

"Thank you," Noah said. "About that. The assignment in the Bahamas. Is there someone else? It's the day after Christmas…"

"Which has never stopped you before. I recall you moving a flight to Christmas Day just to avoid busy airports," Jennimay said.

"This time is different," Noah said.

"I am willing to look at a long-term assignment in North Carolina. I'd love to capture more of Southport's history. Dive into Oak Island and the Wilmington area beaches. But I need you in the Bahamas this week," Jennimay said.

"Okay," Noah said, his voice audibly falling.

Jennimay sighed. The phone went silent for nearly a minute.

Noah stood outside the James-Montgomery House gate. His ear pressed to the phone, his eyes admiring the historic home in its holiday grandeur.

"Think this Peyton can get away for a week?" Jennimay's voice came back through the Noah's speaker.

"I… I don't know," Noah said.

"I'm going to email you a packet. Why don't you slip it into her stocking?" Jennimay suggested.

"Okay…" Noah hummed curiously into the phone.

"I have to go. Merry Christmas, Noah," Jennimay said.

"Merry Christmas, Jennimay."

As he slipped his phone into his pocket, Noah heard a voice from the porch. "You gonna come in or are you just gonna stand out there in the cold talking to yourself?"

Noah looked up, Noah saw Peyton standing on the porch, her arms wrapped tightly in a shawl.

"This time, I actually had a real conversation with a real person," Noah said.

"Well, that's a relief. I was startin' to wonder about you," Peyton grinned.

Noah laughed. "Yeah, you and me both."

Noah slipped through the gate and met Peyton at the top of the porch steps.

Starting to escort her into the house, he found Peyton locked in place.

When he looked at her, Peyton's eyes pierced his. With a glance up, she led his eyes to the mistletoe they had gathered from the farm.

Noah gently lifted her chin and leaned in. Their lips were warm, in steep contrast to the cool Christmas day breeze.

When they parted, Peyton smiled and said in a whispery breath, "Merry Christmas."

"Merry Christmas, Peyton."

Forty Two

The scents of cinnamon and cardamom filled the air. A hint of pine from the Christmas tree and wood-burning fireplace added to the festive aromas.

The lights wound around the evergreen garland of the staircase and the splendor of the shimmering Christmas trees welcomed Christmas day in the James house.

Taking off his coat, Noah knelt by Henry and gave him a quick hug, "Merry Christmas."

"Merry Christmas, Noah," Henry said. He looked giddy as he cast his gaze around the house. "Christmas in my own home!"

"Yes, sir. I'm glad you're home," Noah said.

"Me, too. Me, too." Henry nodded.

Peyton pointed toward the kitchen. "I have a few things to finish up. Care for a mimosa? You can make one for Dad, just lean heavier on the juice for his."

"Sounds great," Noah said as he excused himself from Henry's side. "It smells wonderful in here. It smells like Christmas!"

"I have cardamom bread cooling on the rack and I'm just about to pull cinnamon rolls out," Peyton said as she slipped oven mitts over her hands.

Finding a bottle of champagne near a jug of orange juice, Noah popped open the bottle, catching the cork neatly in his hand as he twisted it open.

Pouring three glasses, one a deeper color orange than the others, he handed one to Peyton.

"I'll deliver this to Henry," Noah said. Pausing, he asked, "Do you have a printer here by any chance?"

Peyton frowned, "Yes. There's one in the office by the back bedroom."

Noah nodded. Handing Henry his beverage, he found the office. Locating the email Jennimay had sent as promised, he printed out what he needed.

By the time he returned to the living room, Peyton had placed a spread of breads and rolls onto a side table. While her attention was turned, he slipped the folded papers into the stocking that had her name embroidered across the white, furry cuff.

Turning, he found Peyton with her glass raised.

"To Christmas," she said.

"To newfound friends," Noah said.

Henry looked at Noah and then at his daughter, "To family. And to being home."

"Cheers," Noah said, as he took a sip.

Nearly dancing in place, Peyton raced to the Christmas tree. Kneeling , she grabbed a package and rose. Facing Noah, she held the package out and grinned. "Merry Christmas!"

Noah's brow raised slightly. "What's this?"

"It's a Christmas gift, silly," Peyton squealed.

Prying off the lid, Noah pulled open the box. Pulling away a piece of tissue paper, he revealed a neatly placed item. His eyes widened.

"Is this?" he asked.

"The cartridge pouch," Peyton nodded.

"The one the deed for the house was in." Noah admired the Revolutionary War relic.

"At first, we thought it was Benjamin Smith's since he was storing the documents. But when Mabel's team took a closer look, they found initials on the inset leather of the strap. T. M. It belonged to my great, great, great grandfather," Peyton said.

"It's amazing," Noah said.

"Now, it's yours," Peyton said.

Noah frowned. "Shouldn't this be in the museum?"

"Mabel has been having a field day linking artifacts to Thomas Montgomery. The museum already has several cartridge pouches. They said we could have it. Daddy and I both agreed, we wanted you to have it," Peyton said.

Noah looked at Henry and back at Peyton, "I couldn't. This is your family's history."

"You have given us the best gift anyone ever could. You gave us our home. You gave us our family legacy," Peyton said, while Henry nodded in agreement.

Facing Peyton, Noah said, "You have always had your family's legacy. I am looking at her."

Peyton's face flushed as she lifted on her toes and kissed him. Breathless, she pulled away and looked at him. "You have been such a gift this Christmas season."

"You have. You and Henry both. You gave me something I haven't had in a really long time. A feeling of home. A feeling of belonging. I've spent the last ten years chasing Christmas photos. But I haven't really *experienced* what the magic of the season is really all about. You have taught me so much about stepping away from the lens and living each moment," Noah said.

"So, what are you going to do it about it, son?" Henry called from his seat.

Noah gazed at Henry and smiled.

"I have a gift for Peyton, as well," Noah said. Walking over to the fireplace mantel, he gently lifted Peyton's stocking from its hook.

Walking over to Peyton, he held the stocking in front of him. A tidal wave of nerves washed over him as he handed her the stocking.

Peyton cocked her head with curiosity as she fished the papers out of the stocking. Unfolding them, she gave them a quick study.

With a frown, she asked, "What's this?"

"I have a new assignment," Noah said, looking at Peyton with a deep sigh. "The thing is, I don't want to go. Not without you."

Peyton glanced at the papers and then back at Noah, an expression of confusion etched on her face.

"The place I'm staying at is huge. We both would have our own wing. All expenses paid by my editor," Noah said. "When I'm finished, I am on assignment with Southport as my home base through the Fourth of July festival. And… maybe after that."

Shock washed over Peyton as her mind fought to comprehend what all of Noah's words actually meant.

Dropping her stocking and the packet of papers, she launched herself at Noah and wrapped her arms around him.

Through glossy eyes, she glanced at Henry.

"I'll be fine. I can barely have a moment to myself without Cybil and her troop of ladies checking in on me. You go have this adventure. Noah has done a lot for us. Let's do this for him," Henry insisted.

Through a teary gasp, Peyton nodded, her arms around Noah's neck, "Yes! Yes, I'll go with you."

Noah smiled and held Peyton tight.

Peyton's eyes went wide. "You can stay at my cottage when we're back. I'll be here with Daddy, where we belong."

"You'll be home. You'll both be home," Noah said.

After breakfast, Peyton and Henry exchanged their gifts. Sitting around the fire, they leaned back in their seats, enjoying how the glow of the flames and flickering candles played against the lights of the Christmas tree.

The excitement of the day had begun to wear on Henry. While wildly content, he flowed in and out of lucidity.

Glancing at Noah and Peyton, he frowned. "Not a pirate, huh? I always thought we had a pirate lurking around our family tree."

"Not a pirate, but a spy who helped our country be free. *That* is something truly special," Noah said.

Henry looked up at Noah and smiled. He said, "It *is* special. Pirate, spy, whatever. But we didn't need either of those to be special. We have Peyton."

"You two have a lot in common. That's what Noah said, Daddy," Peyton said, her hand clasped in his.

"He's a smart man. Stranger who came into our town," Henry said. His smile faded as his eyes glossed over. "I'm…. tired," he whispered to no one but himself as his head listed.

Peyton's heart ached as she watched his father's lucid morning slip away. She reached for a blanket and covered him up.

A smile creased Henry's lips. In between a few soft snores, he mumbled, "Merry Christmas, Bedford Falls!"

Forty Three

Southport's waterfront was surreal. A nautical Christmas card that could have been confused for a scene in New England were it not for the antebellum architecture.

Snow piled up on the bank of the seawall. Boats bobbed in the water with little icicles strung on their lines, glistening in the pink-hued evening light. The town tree was flocked with snow as its display of lights began to glow.

Peyton snuggled close to Noah, hugging his arm as they walked.

"What do you think about a Southport Christmas now?" Peyton looked up at him.

Noah smiled. "Like someone said, it's magical. I think I'm rather fond of Christmas in Southport. Just one thing?"

"What's that?" Peyton asked.

"Can it snow like this every year?" Noah asked.

Peyton stopped walking and pivoted toward Noah. Her eyes were earnest when she asked, "Would that bring you back? I might just have to wish for that."

"Oh, I think there is plenty to bring me back," Noah said.

Spinning to face Peyton, his finger gently grazed her chin, urging her lips to meet up with his.

"There's no place I'd rather be," Noah said.

Peyton wrapped her arms around Noah's neck to pull them back together.

"So, what if it doesn't snow?" Peyton asked as she leaned back. A wary eyebrow raised.

"Will you be here?" Noah asked.

"Of course. That's my home right over there." Peyton nodded toward the James—Montgomery House and let out a smile.

"Then it would be the happiest place to be for Christmas," Noah said. Grasping her hand, he continued their wintry stroll. With a grin, he turned and asked, "Just one question? What are you doing New Year's Eve?"

"Hmm. Does it have to be snowy? It sounds like I'll be spending it on a beach this year," Peyton said.

"No snow required," Noah grinned.

Stopping in front of the James—Montgomery House, his eyes swept over the snow-dusted Southern home. His hands clasped Peyton's tight, "I am so happy to have met you and your father."

Peyton's eyes danced as they studied Noah's. Letting out a breath, her voice was nearly a whisper. "I don't have words to express how grateful I am for you and everything you've done."

Noah smiled and held Peyton tight. "You don't need words."

Peyton smiled back as she pushed up on her toes and hung in Noah's embrace as they kissed in the glow of the James—Montgomery House porch lights.

About the Author

Seth Sjostrom is a serial entrepreneur, adventurer and author. His novels include the thrillers *Blood in the Snow, Blood in the Water, Blood in the Sand, Penance, Penance: Unredeemable, Penance: Absolution, Patriot X, Patriot X: Insurrection, Dark Chase and Dark Chase: Dead Run* as well as the romances *Back to Carolina, Finding Christmas, The Tree Farm, The Christmas Cafe Santa, The Nativity, Love at the Christmas Con* and *The Toy Store*. His Beach House Mysteries series includes *Trouble on Treasure Island, A Caper on Carolina Beach,* and *Peril in Palm Beach* grows with a new entry every spring. Seth partners with Hire Heroes USA and Special Operations Warrior Foundation as well as the Patriotic Pick with a portion of proceeds and volunteer hours with sales of his Patriot X series. Sales of *The Christmas Café* help to support Jen Lilley and Ale Boggiano's "Christmas is Not Cancelled" charity fundraising for foster children.

www.SethSjostrom.com
Twitter: @SethSjostrom
Facebook: @authorSethSjostrom
Instagram: @SethSjostrom

More Books by Seth

Christmas Titles
Finding Christmas
The Tree Farm
The Nativity
The Toy Store
The Christmas Café
Love at The Christmas Con

Beach House Mysteries
Trouble on Treasure Island
A Caper on Carolina Beach
Peril on Palm Beach

Other Titles
Back to Carolina
Penance
Penance: Unredeemable
Penance: Absolution
Dark Chase
Dark Chase: Dead Run
Patriot X
Patriot X: Insurrection
Blood in the Snow
Blood in the Water
Blood in the Sand

Children's Books
Letters from Santa
The Hollow
Cryptid Rangers: The Secret of the Skunk Ape
The Heart of a Reindeer
The (Too) Helpful Little Angel
Hurricane Channing and the Lost Flamingo
Hurricane Channing and the Mommy Manatee
Hurricane Channing and the Halloween Bat
Hurricane Channing and the Christmas Puppy